For our dear friends, everywhere.

DARK STORM

DRAGON'S GIFT: THE STORM BOOK 2

VERONICA DOUGLAS
LINSEY HALL

MAGIC SIDE PRESS

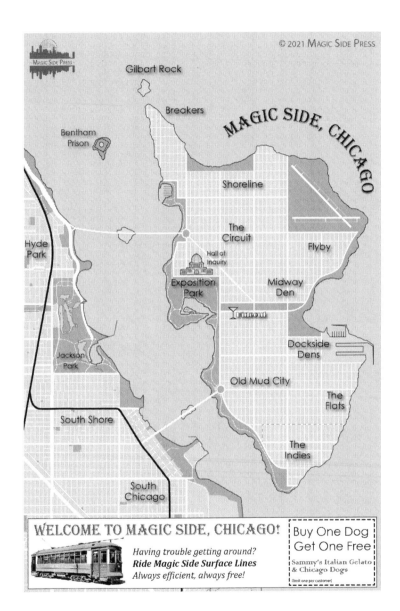

Gilbart Rock

Breakers

MAGIC SIDE, CHICAGO

© 2021 MAGIC SIDE PRESS

Bentham
Prison

Shoreline

Hyde
Park

The
Circuit

Flyby

Hall of
Inquiry

Exposition
Park

Midway
Den

Jackson
Park

Dockside
Dens

Old Mud City

The
Flats

South Shore

The
Indies

South
Chicago

Neve

"Well, here's to being promoted." My friend Rhiannon clinked her pint of Old Style against my glass and then took a big gulp.

"Thanks." I sipped my gin and tonic, savoring the sweet, bitter flavor.

Damn, it's good to be back home in Magic Side.

The Hideout, our favorite bar, was packed. Shifters. Sorcerers. Devil-kin. Even a fangless vamp in the corner. The excess noise made it hard to concentrate on Rhia's voice, but the familiar vibe was exactly what I needed. I'd had just a few too many new experiences lately and needed a bit of a rock to cling to.

Rhiannon leaned in, blond hair falling around her

face. "Come on, Neve, why do you look so gloomy? I thought you would be over the moon. You're a detective now. You've been waiting for this for how many years?"

The promotion had been a long time coming, like waiting-for-the-next-*Game-of-Thrones*-book long. I had ground myself to the bone and towed the company line for years, with nothing to show for it. Then I broke a lot of rules, almost got myself fired, and suddenly I had a promotion.

Go figure.

"Assistant detective," I corrected. "And technically, I'm still on leave for another week."

"Perfect!" Rhiannon chirped. She wasn't the glass-half-full type. She was the glass-is-overflowing-and-you-need-to-take-a-big-sip-from-the-edge-so-you-don't-spill-it type. She was exactly what you needed in a best friend. A rock. A really perky rock.

"I would kill for that kind of time off. I wouldn't leave my couch for days. I'd order pizza for breakfast and binge-watch *Parks and Rec* until my eyes melted."

"What I should be doing is figuring out how to control my magic." As a half-djinn—a type of genie—I could teleport to the Realm of Air, throw big gusts of wind, and fly, which was awesome sauce, but I needed more practice.

"You'll figure it out, Neve. We both will."

Rhia was a time traveler. She couldn't control her

magic at all and had to keep it on lockdown. Thankfully, she was also a kickass detective.

Two weeks ago, she'd been abducted by an evil djinn, but I'd rescued her from the Realm of Air.

I'd had help getting Rhia back. Damian Malek. One of the Fallen. Just the thought of him sent a jolt down my spine. His face flashed before my mind's eye. Perfect jaw. Dark penetrating eyes that foretold of danger. I could almost smell his magic signature—juniper, the sea, ancient forests. And then betrayal sunk its razor-sharp claws into my chest, tearing at my heart.

Rhia snapped her fingers in front of my face. "Hey. Space cadet. I thought I lost you there for a second."

"Nope. I'm here. Still on Earth," I muttered. My palms stung as I unclenched my fists.

Damian had betrayed me, not to mention lied and nearly got me and Rhia killed. Sure, he was out of this world gorgeous, but he was a liar and a thief, and I couldn't trust him. We hadn't spoken in a week.

"You're thinking about him again. Is that why you've been feeling melancholy all night?"

Rhiannon read my mind. She wasn't a mind-reader. She could just read *my* mind.

I shrugged. "You got me."

I took a long sip of my G&T through the tiny black straw until air bubbled amongst the ice in the bottom of the glass.

Rhiannon motioned to the bartender, our friend

Diana, for another round of drinks and then turned to me. "Listen, Neve. Damian is a deceitful, manipulative criminal who's not only dangerous but on the opposite side of the Order. Him out of your life is the best thing that could've happened."

She was right. Not only was Damian a dangerous fallen angel and treacherous crime lord, he'd also originally released the djinn that abducted Rhiannon and then lied about it.

Manipulative bastard.

I absently scratched the white tattoo on my arm.

Rhia caught the movement. "Is it acting up again?"

I hadn't had a tattoo until I'd traveled to the Realm of Air. Then suddenly, it was there. The more I used my power, the more it grew—sprouting into increasingly intricate patterns like ancient calligraphy.

"It's spread up my arm and around, um... my... part of my chest now. It stopped growing as quickly, now. I haven't been using my powers much. Just a couple of night flights."

Flying was harder here on Earth than in the Realm of Air, but worth every ounce of energy. Nothing cleared my mind like drifting over Magic Side in the dark, floating gently above the twinkling lights and lonely muggers below.

"It's cool. I want a matching one."

"I don't know what it means, Rhia. I'm worried."

The djinn had had identical tattoos across his entire

body. He'd been a murderous bastard with a ferocious temper. But I wasn't a djinn. Only a half-djinn—so what did it mean for me?

Di dropped off another G&T. I pushed the straw aside and took a big gulp.

Raucous laughter reverberated behind us, and I turned my head. A group of five guys and three girls were slamming shots. The girls were red in the face and wedged into bright tube tops. The guys were overstuffed potatoes, awkwardly stuffed into polos and button-downs, high on their own magic and money.

Not my type.

Dark, beautiful fallen angels seemed to be my type. But then, they betrayed you, so I was sort of screwed.

"Neve!" Rhiannon hissed. "Are you crazy? Don't make eye contact."

Shit. I'd been staring into space like a modern-day Venus de Milo. Nothing summoned a Chad like a girl with a vacant stare.

I could see the wheels turning in their heads. Five guys, three girls. They looked back at us—two single chicks. Thinking. Thinking. Then it clicked. They could even out the numbers.

That's the power of math, boys.

I snapped my head forward. Too late. Chairs scrapped behind us.

"Oh, gods. They're coming over. This is your fault," Rhiannon murmured.

Rhia, with gorgeous blond hair, was usually target numero uno. One of the boys leaned confidently on the granite bar top beside her, waiting for her to look over. She didn't.

He had the face of a horse, and you could just smell the stench of money on him. "Hey girl. You're sexy as hell. I just had to come meet you. I'm Lee. What's your name?"

"Amanda."

"Amanda, huh? That's a pretty name. I like your hair."

My stomach turned. *Wiff.*

Rhia spun. "Amanda, as in I need *a-man-da* get out of my face right now, before I kick him in the nuts."

That took the wind out of his sails, but his wingman swooped in beside me, hoping for a softer target. The signature of his magic smelled and tasted like beer. No, wait, that was his breath. I just couldn't smell anything else. "Hey gorgeous."

I smiled back at him. "Hey there, Spudly. I'm a mantis-shifter. I decapitate my lovers after mating."

He grinned back. "So, you're saying I have a chance?"

"No," I laughed, a little amused. I felt a bit bad for him. I was miles out of his league, but at least he wasn't a total ass, like his friend.

Lee the creeper wasn't going to take no for answer. He leaned in close to Rhia. "You guys are feisty. We like feisty. Why don't you and Mantis-Girl come join us for a drink. We can bug off later."

Rhiannon, who usually loved puns, locked her eyes forward. "We're not in the mood dude. Take a hint."

"I can put you in the moo—"

"Fates! I *wish* you guys would just *clear off*," Rhiannon said.

My right arm flared in pain, and a surge of electricity coursed through my tattoo. I yelped in surprise.

Rhia spun. "What did he do?"

Spudly jumped back. "Nothing. I swear!"

"Bullshit!" she snapped, leaping to her feet.

Magic thrummed though my body, and my tattoo burned. I twisted off the chair, staggering backward in agony. "Something's happening Rhia. My arm is on fire!"

The bar doors crashed open, and startled patrons leapt up from their tables. Then, the wind came screaming through.

A howling vortex formed in the doorway. Bar napkins flew off every table, turning the air into a cloud of rapidly shredding paper.

"Holy shit!" Spudly yelled.

The girls at the table with the other guys screamed, but it was quickly drowned out by the roaring wind.

Lee the Creeper backed away from us, eyes wide in terror. "What's going on! Are you doing something?"

My ears popped. "Ri!"

"Shiiiiiiit!" Spudly flipped into the air and landed on

his back. He tried standing, but his polo ripped off, and he fell ass over teakettle. He slid out the door on his bare stomach. "Leeeeeeeee!"

"Dude!" Lee held onto the bar top with both hands, legs kicking freely in the air. The vortex was sucking him in.

It was like *Twister*, a tornado of magic surging through me.

Rhia grabbed my hand. "Shut it off, Neve, shut it off!"

"I can't. I don't know how!" My chest heaved and my fingers tingled as dizziness washed over me. Never had I expended this much power at once. Panic flared.

One of the girls screamed, grabbed her pink pocketbook, and ran out after Spudly, apparently unaffected by the tornado.

Di darted over to us, yelling over the roar of the vortex. "Do you know what's going on?"

"No!" Rhiannon screamed, her blond hair violently whipping around her face in the wind.

The tornado zeroed in on Lee the Creeper, leaving everyone else alone. Pint glasses and cocktails crashed onto the floor as he finally lost his grip. One of his bros grabbed him by the wrist, but the vortex sucked them both out screaming into the street beyond

The wind died instantly.

Outside, the boys picked themselves up and stumbled down the street, eager to get away. Their remaining friends hurried after them, followed by a few other patrons.

I breathed deeply, my vision no longer swimming.

Silence—except for the sound of a lone pint glass rolling across the ground.

Rhia grabbed me by the shoulders, and whispered, "Holy shit, Neve. What was that?"

Her eyes reflected the terror that was roiling in my chest.

"I don't know, Rhia. It was my tattoo—it was on fire, and I don't know what it means." Tears began to creep out of the corners of my eyes, and she hugged me close.

"It's alright. We'll figure this out."

Complete and utter exhaustion overcame me, and I slumped against her.

Di looked over at us, then around at her bar. Overturned chairs and tables littered the room. The floor was covered with broken glass and tattered napkins. I closed my eyes. The chaos looked like Rhiannon's apartment after the djinn had taken her.

This was all me.

Di planted her hands on her hips. "Ok, we're closing early tonight everybody, on account of freak Chicago weather. Finish your drinks and pay up."

She passed us on the way back behind the bar. "You two, stick around."

Ah, man. What the heck happened?

I collapsed on a stool, gazing at my feet. Every part of

my body ached, and my head throbbed—like a hangover from ten too many tequila shots.

About fifteen minutes later, all the patrons had left, and most of the bills were paid.

Di leaned on the bar and smiled. "That was some windstorm, hun."

Yeah, she knew it was me.

A painful lump formed at the back of my throat. "I'm sorry Di. I don't know what happened. This is all new. It has never happened before."

She leaned back. "Shit, girl. Any chance you could teach me some of that Windy City hocus pocus? Could be useful for clearing out the riffraff."

"Really, I have no idea." I swallowed hard. "I'll cover their tabs—the folks who blew out the door, and the ones who ran off. I'll help clean up. Just please, please don't tell anyone about this."

"Me too," added Rhiannon. "Whatever it takes."

"You girls are my favorite customers—of course I've got your back. Y'all are helping me clean up though." She locked the front doors and tossed me a broom. I clutched it to my chest gratefully.

What a disaster. What was I going to do?

Not being able to control your powers was bad news. It meant freedom revoked. Because Magic Side was closed to normies, we all let our signatures show and openly used magic, but you had to control your power. Two short bridges were all that separated our little island from mainland Chicago. If you couldn't control your magic, there was no way the Order would let you travel off the island and risk alerting everyone in Chicago about our existence.

The peace between humans and Magica—people with magical powers—was fragile. As long as they didn't know about us, we were fine, but we were one bad slip-up away from being burnt at the stake, and we knew it.

Rhia grabbed a dustpan and brush and helped me clean. "So, what do you think happened? Were you thinking about blowing them away or something?"

"No! The opposite. I was thinking about how to get rid of Spudly without being too big of a jerk. Then I heard you say, 'I wish you guys would just clear off' and then my tattoo started flaring, and—"

I dropped the broom. "Oh, shit."

Rhia looked around wildly. "What?"

"Oh no, oh no, oh no."

"What, Neve?"

"You said I *wish* you guys would just clear off. I. *Wish*. You made a freaking wish Rhiannon, and I freaking lost control and blew up the bar because-holy-fates-I-am-half-a-genie-and-I-don't-know-what-that-means!"

"Oh, crap."

"Fates, is this going to happen every time someone says *wish* around me? I wish I had a fancy car—*phoom*—there it is. I wish I had a bigger butt—*pop pop*. I can't live like that. I'd have to be a hermit for the rest of my life."

She grabbed my hand. "Hey, we'll figure it out."

I nodded, terrified to my core. "Yeah maybe. Not right now though. I don't have a lick of magic left in me."

Once we finished cleaning up, Di dimmed the lights and made herself a double whiskey on the rocks. She put a cold pint of Old Style on the bar top for Ri and a G&T down for me. "On the house. It's been a heck of a night."

"You're telling me." The gin and tonic slaked my parched mouth, cool and refreshing like a breath of fresh air—not that we needed any more of that tonight.

Di leaned her back against the bar. "Not that it's any of my business, but new powers, huh?"

"Yup. Just getting used to things." I owed her a little honesty, but I wasn't telling anyone other than Rhia what actually happened. My stomach churned. I still didn't believe it.

"Hey, it's okay. You should've seen how bad it got when I first started shifting—every piece of furniture in the house was torn to shreds. Rawrrrrr." She made clawing motions.

"Thanks. I'll try to keep it on lockdown. I may need to stay away from here for a while."

"Nah. We're part of the Windy City. Gusts like this are bound to happen."

My phone rang, and I glanced at the screen. Gretchen—my boss at the Hall of Inquiry.

Dang it.

I picked up. "Hey L.T."

"Neve. Get to the Hall immediately. Grab Rhiannon if she's with you. We've got big problems."

Well crap. How much worse was this night gonna get?

2

Neve

Gretchen met us outside the Hall of Inquiry fifteen minutes later. Normally, she didn't wait outside for anyone. Something big was up.

"Thanks for getting here quickly. This is a F'd situation. Let's walk and talk," Gretchen said.

"Where are we going?" I asked.

"The Vault."

My legs stopped short, weighed down by the sudden dread that flooded my body.

After we'd trapped the djinn, we had locked it away deep in the Order's Vault. It was a magical labyrinth and supposedly impregnable. Archmage DeLoren guaranteed me that it would be safe. Given our destination and

Gretchen's obvious agitation, I had the sinking feeling he'd been wrong.

Gretchen's eyes confirmed my suspicion. "Someone broke into the Vault today. Stole the djinn from right under our noses."

My heart hammered in my chest, and my muscles went numb, but I forced my legs to move.

Rhia gaped. "How could that be?"

Gretchen plowed down the corridor in an unbroken stride, making it hard to keep up. She shrugged. "We don't know. I spoke with Archmage DeLoren right before I called you. He's baffled. We're going to meet him now."

My mind reeled.

Someone stole the djinn.

What if he gets free?

There was no question who he would come for first. *Me.* The person who had trapped him. The person who had locked him away. His face loomed in my mind, screaming in rage as he was sucked down into the little brass box.

If he were released, I'd be screwed. Done and done. And Rhiannon. And Damian. They had been at my side when I'd trapped him.

Rage bubbled over. "DeLoren swore it would be safe. What the heck happened?"

Gretchen stopped in her tracks, and I almost collided with her.

"I don't know, Neve." She bristled and her yellow eyes flashed. I half expected her to turn into a snarling wolf on the spot. Old me—two-weeks-ago me—would have assumed that she was furious at my outburst. I recognized her expression now. It meant, *no one messes with my pack.*

She locked us with her gaze. "I will do everything I can to protect you both. We don't know that he's loose—only that he's been stolen. If he's under someone else's control, he may leave you alone. If not... we'll take him down."

I nodded, torn between terror and a desire to fight the bastard, no matter how ill-equipped I was with my magic.

Gretchen stalked off down the hall, a general headed into battle. We followed, hurrying to keep up.

Rhiannon leaned over and whispered, "I'd hate to be one of her ex-boyfriends."

I laughed despite the rising panic.

He. Is. Coming. For. Me.

I swallowed hard, forcing away the whirlwind of possibilities that clouded my mind.

Maybe. Maybe not.

Stay calm.

"Can you give us any more details?" Rhia asked.

"Several false alarms went off in the north wing around two p.m., and the chest was stolen shortly after," Gretchen said, looking over her shoulder.

We stopped by a supply closet, and Gretchen tossed us each a parka. "I'm told you'll want these."

Huh?

They were the same coats the Order's security guards wore during the worst parts of Chicago's notoriously miserable winters. It was currently late summer.

I slipped one on. Even in the air-conditioned building, the parka was uncomfortably hot.

Worse, they did not fit.

"You look like the Michelin Man." Rhia winked, trying to brighten a tense situation. She was good like that.

I stuck my tongue out and zipped my jacket. "Check yourself in a mirror, Stay Puft."

Gretchen ignored our banter and headed down the hall.

I glanced up and down the corridor as we hurried along behind her. "Did the cameras catch anything?"

Gretchen shook her head. "Very little. His disguise concealed his face and signature. All I can say is that he was a tall, athletically built man. He wove some runes and popped through."

Oh no.

My heart thudded like a jackhammer in my chest.

Could it be?

I shoved my sudden suspicions down. I had to focus on facts.

Archmage DeLoren paced outside the large brass

door of the vault, accompanied by several senior-level detectives. He had bristling gray mutton chops and was built like a sea-hardened mariner.

"What happened?" I snapped, my words driven by fear and anger. "You said that the Vault was the most secure place in Magic Side. You said that I should trust your impeccable record. It's not impeccable now."

"Neve!" Gretchen barked. "Stand down."

I swallowed and fought back a glare. *Fates, Neve. What's with your temper these days?*

DeLoren was unphased. I had lit into him last time we'd spoken, and he'd maintained his composure then, too. I guess when you're an archmage, nobody else's shit bothered you too much.

"I understand your frustration, Ms. Cross. I'm furious and have no explanation for what happened." DeLoren motioned with his scarred hand. "This fool door is supposed to consume anyone who tampers with it. One mistake and you get chomped. It's a mystery how the thief broke the code."

A low, grating voice spoke behind us. "I am terribly sorry about this."

I nearly jumped out of my shoes.

A devilish faced formed on the door, the brass distorting like clay as it spoke. "This is all my fault. I wanted to devour him, but he hypnotized me with his magic. He was so incredibly charming. He knew exactly what to say to make me unlock. I failed in my duty. It would be better if I had never been forged."

"Nonsense," DeLoren snapped. "This is not your fault, or that of anyone here. I truly have no idea how the thief navigated the labyrinth once he got in. He must have been a master thief of nearly unparalleled skill and incredible magical abilities."

I braced myself against the wall as it all fell into place with certainty.

A tall, athletically built man.

A master thief.

Someone with incredible magical abilities.

Someone who was hypnotically charming.

Someone who knew where the djinn was being kept and had probably interacted with it before.

Damian. Crime lord. Thief. He'd broken in and out of the djinn's palace with ease, picking locks and breaking enchantments by weaving runes in the air. We'd broken into the djinn's magical vault, *for fates sake.*

Damian. The same person who'd been hunting the djinn from the start. The person who was furious that I handed the djinn over to the Order.

No.

Oh shit, no.

My stomach turned to bile, and my vision swam.

Rhiannon turned to me. "Neve, are you okay?"

Gretchen looked over. "You look like you've seen a ghost."

"Yeah. I'm okay." I barely forced out the lie.

With magic that sparked like lightning, DeLoren wove a spell in the air and then pressed a sequence of runes molded into the bronze door. The metal bubbled outward, surrounding us, and sucked us through the ether.

With a reverberating thrum, we emerged in a dimly lit chamber. The air hung lifeless and heavy, and sudden exhaustion overcame me. DeLoren strode over to a second brass door and pulled out an oversized and extremely complex key. "This is an anti-magic room. Great for surprising and killing intruders."

There was a hiss as gas began filling the room.

Rhia looked around wildly. "Um…"

"Don't worry. It's only poison gas." DeLoren unlocked the door. "We have several seconds to get out."

We stumbled through the door into a hilly wasteland covered by snow. Each hill had a solitary door atop it, connected to nothing, leading to nowhere.

DeLoren swept his arm out, indicating the landscape of lonely doors. "The Vault is a labyrinth comprised of hundreds of isolated rooms scattered across the world, all connected by portals. To reach the destination you want, you need to go through the portals in exactly the right sequence. If you mess it up, you die. Each room is deadly and has three exits. The thief had to navigate through twenty rooms to reach the djinn. That's roughly a billion possible pathways."

Son of a bitch.

"So how'd he do it?" I asked, my voice hoarse.

DoLoren eyed me and raised his eyebrows. "Frankly, we have no idea."

Well crap.

"Clues are minimal. Come. You're here because I want you to see this." He led us on a well-trodden path through the snow. There was a movement in the drift beside us. I recoiled as a savage-looking purple worm leapt into the air.

DeLoren absently waved his hand and a crackling bubble of magic surrounded us. The horrid worm bounced harmlessly off the forcefield and burrowed back into the snow. I shoved my clammy hands into my parka's pockets. Despite the cold, they were sweating.

We paused beside an icy path that led off over the hills. Something had melted the snow, leaving a frozen track like a bobsled run.

"This is our most intriguing clue. The intruder, whoever it was, melted a path to the first door of the labyrinth, and there were burn marks on the door. Do you have any idea what it means?"

I wracked my brain. Damian was extremely powerful, and I'd felt heat from his aura. Did he have some sort of hidden fire magic?

I bit my lip. "Not off the top of my head. I'm sorry. It's reeeeal weird."

"Same." Rhia shook her head.

"Well, it was worth a shot. Think on it."

We stood in the snow and wind, discussing the details of the burglary with Gretchen and the detectives. My mind was nearly as numb as my fingers. *Damian took the djinn. But what was his angle?*

"There is one final stop." DeLoren swept his hand in an arc and a portal materialized. Its translucent door shimmered like a mirage under the cold gusts.

One by one, we stepped through the portal and found ourselves deposited in a dark, frigid space. Light suddenly blazed, illuminating the room—a cave.

A small black box lay open in the center of the space. I strode forward and peered into the empty cavity. I held my breath, hoping to assuage the panic and rage that rippled through me.

DeLoren mindlessly stroked his muttonchops with his fingers. "After somehow finding his way to this cave, our thief managed to tear through the magic wards on this box."

Silence reigned as we all stared at the box.

"On a scale of one to ten, how difficult would you say breaking those wards would be?" Rhiannon said.

DeLoren chuckled. "An eleven. Those wards should be unbreakable. Whoever did this..." He shook his head as if trying to clear the disbelief. "Like I said earlier, whoever did this was beyond a master."

My heart thundered in my aching chest, and I released my breath in a low hiss.

Only Damian could have done this.

Skill and motive. He'd wanted that djinn so badly, and he'd found a way to get it.

We exited the cave through the portal. The wind seemed to have picked up since we'd left, chilling me to the core and violently whipping my red hair.

DeLoren placed his hand on my shoulder. "Neve, a word... in private."

I followed him a few dozen paces into the drifts, the wet snow soaking through my jeans and sneakers. He looked back, eyeing the others, and flicked his hand. A wall of ice erupted out of the snow, shielding us from view and obscuring our voices.

His hawk-like eyes immediately trained on me, and I withered a little.

"I know you are suspended. I assume that you think you are going to run off immediately and solve this crime on your own, like you did when Ms. Holloway went missing."

Yeah, basically.

He raised an eyebrow. "Hmm. I thought so. Well, you are impetuous by nature."

I crossed my arms over my chest. Could he read minds, or just expressions? "I..."

He shook his head. "I sympathize with your instincts, Ms. Cross. I do. I spent my youth being impetuous and foolish. I survived, in retrospect, due to sheer luck alone—and not due to my great talents or cleverness, as I assumed at the time."

"Okay. Message received."

Man, I'm getting cheeky these days.

He grunted. "Djinn are mercurial, impulsive, and prone to anger. It is a dangerous combination."

My temper blazed. *Who is he to lecture me?*

I flexed my fists and locked eyes with him. "Hey. I know what I'm doing better than anyone here. Are you forgetting that *I* am the one who trapped a djinn? That *you're* the one who let it get away? I know what I'm up against."

His eyes blazed. "You misunderstand me, Ms. Cross. I meant that the djinn, *as a people*, are known to be capricious, tempestuous, and easily provoked. It is a combination that is dangerous *to themselves.*"

He snapped his eyes down to the white tattoo on the back of my hand, barely peeking out from the cuff of my parka.

Oh.

He meant *me*.

So he knew, too. Did the entire planet know? I'd struggled to keep my heritage concealed for so long. My people were hunted by those craving power. How much danger was I in? More importantly, was I really a danger to myself, as DeLoren implied?

Fates be damned, what does it even mean to be half-djinn?

I was so lost. The djinn's words about my family

seared through my mind. Were my parents alive? Could they help me understand and control my power?

"I learned long ago that if you do not confront your weaknesses, you will never master your power. You will be like a great tower with rotten beams, ready to collapse in upon itself," DeLoren said.

I gulped. This day was just chewing me up, and it hadn't spat me back out yet.

I wanted to rebuke him, and also beg him for more information about what I might be, but the words wouldn't budge.

"You are part of a vast organization, Neve. We band together to counterbalance each other's weaknesses. Don't go vigilante on us again."

Before I could muster the courage to speak, he turned away and dismissed the wall of ice. He shot me one last look over his shoulder, saying, "That said, I wish you the best of luck if you do."

I stood there, agape, as he trudged back to the group.

"Let's get out of here. I hate this place, and I can't stand the cold," he groused.

One of the detectives cocked his head. "Didn't you help design it?"

"Of course. That's why I hate it. It's the stuff of nightmares. My nightmares." DeLoren ushered us out of the Vault and back into the Hall of Inquiry.

3

Neve

We left DeLoren and headed down the hall that led to the main wing of the Hall of Inquiry. My chest burned with anxiety and rage—an explosive combination.

"I am going to need lists from both of you—the names of everyone you know that was involved in trapping the djinn or that you told about the djinn," Gretchen said.

I can whittle my list down to one name—Damian Malek.

"Rhiannon. I need you here at the crack of dawn tomorrow to start interviewing all the sups you brought back from the Realm of Air."

Rhiannon nodded. "Got it, L.T."

Gretchen turned to me. "Neve, Internal Review says

you still need to stand down for a few more days. Get rest. You look like you need it. If we haven't got this bastard by the time you're off suspension, you're on the task force, too."

I nodded my head in affirmation. It was all I could manage. My legs were numb, but fury alone kept me on my feet.

I should tell her about Damian now.

The sooner the Order moved in, the less chance he would get away.

Unless...

A thought tugged at the back of my mind.

Unless he's innocent.

It was a slim chance, but it existed. And if anyone was going to bring him in, it was going to be me. I turned to Rhiannon. "Ready to go? I need some air."

Which was code for, *I need to scream.*

We dismissed ourselves, and I stalked down the hall. Emotions flooded me. Betrayal. Anger. Despair. I closed my eyes, imagining Damian's face. Perfect features. Strong jaw. Deep forest green eyes. I rubbed my chest, trying to massage away the deep ache.

Fresh air hit me as we exited the front doors. It was life itself and cleared my head. A light rain tickled my skin.

"Fates, Neve, you are in a state," Rhiannon said.

It was dark. Sodium lights bathed the building in a yellow-orange glow. We were alone, but the Order had eyes and ears everywhere. I motioned her to follow me down the stairs and across the street, not speaking until we reached the park.

"I think it was Damian," I said.

"What?"

"Think about it. He's a crime lord and breaking into highly secure places is *literally* what he does for a living." I laid it out. "Athletic male, expert thief, powerful magic, familiar with the djinn, knew where it was, and worse, he *wanted* that djinn. Motive. Capacity. Opportunity. It all fits."

Rhiannon frowned. "You do make a good point."

"I really think I do. You should have seen the look he gave me when I handed the djinn over. He was furious." I met her eyes. "I'm pretty sure he would've taken it from me if he'd had the chance."

"What do we do? Tell Gretchen?"

"I don't know—I was going to. But then I'd have to explain why I was working with him in the first place. That wouldn't go over well. And frankly, I want to confront him myself."

I collapsed on the edge of a park bench and put my head between my knees.

Is Damian guilty?

Something in my heart said innocent, but every other organ screamed *thief*.

Breathe.

I couldn't turn in my list of names until I knew for

sure. I sat back up, inhaling the cool summer night air in a slow and steady draught. I exhaled. "Okay. We have to go see Damian."

Rhiannon chewed her cheek. "I'm not sure that's a good idea."

I pulled out my phone and sent a text off to Sylvie, my friend in the records division. She usually worked late and would have access to the Order's criminal database, where she could find Damian's address. "I need to ask him myself. I need to see it in his eyes. If he's innocent, then we can warn him, and he can help us solve this. If he's guilty... I'll know."

"You're not a mind reader or seer, Neve. He could lie. He lied before."

Yup.

I shook my head. "I'll know."

Would I really?

"Okay, well I'm going with you. No way I let you go over there alone."

Several minutes later, my phone buzzed, and Sylvie's name lit up the screen above an address and phone number. "Bingo."

Time to get some answers.

I hailed a passing cab, and we climbed in. "3437 Shoreline Drive, please."

The driver pulled away from the curb. I slumped down against the old upholstery and placed my head against the window, watching the city lights pass. They refracted through the sparse raindrops running down the glass: yellow, orange, red, green. A slight chill from the wind seeped into my skin, and my chest ached.

The tall buildings of the Circuit—downtown Magic Side—gave way to residential apartments. The cab turned and headed toward the Breakers, one of the newer and more affluent districts located on the northernmost tip of Magic Side. Most of the upscale flats had lakefront property and killer views.

The minutes ticked by silently. Ten. Fifteen. Twenty.

This was probably a terrible idea.

But what other choice did I have?

Wet brakes softly squealed as the cab pulled up in front of a security gate at the far end of a cul-de-sac.

3437 Shoreline Drive.

Drawing in a long breath, I climbed out of the cab and strode over to the intercom beside the gate. Glancing at the security camera above, I pressed the silver button on the panel. Two rings echoed from the speaker, followed by a click. "Neve." There was a pause. "This is a surprise."

Damian's voice sent shivers dancing up my spine. I momentarily closed my eyes, picturing his face. Lips I once longed to kiss. Lips that had lied, time and time again. Anguish shot through me, and the vision crumbled to dust. *This man has made a habit of turning my world upside down.*

"We need to talk. Now," I said.

Silence.

Damian cleared his throat. "Sure. Come on through."

A buzz sounded, and a motor whirred as the gate slowly opened. I climbed back into the car, meeting the driver's eyes in the rearview mirror. I nodded, and he proceeded through.

Unlike the Malek Tower downtown, Damian's house wasn't colossal, but the location was incredible—a tree shrouded yard with a lakeview. Who had that? In the city? The skyline of Chicago twinkled across the dark, still water, pillars of light separating the sky from the lake.

The tires crunched on gravel as the cab rolled up the long drive, which led to a large two-story house with flat architecture and large glass windows. The interior was brightly lit, and I could discern paintings and art objects hanging on the white walls.

A set of low stone steps led up to a carved wooden doorway. I swallowed as the cab came to a halt.

We'd arrived.

No turning back now.

4

Damian

A pair of headlights swept up the driveway and glinted off the window of my study.

Neve.

I closed my eyes, calling her to mind.

Red hair whipping in the wind and a pair of haunting pale blue eyes that emanated intelligence. The scent of jasmine. Citrus. My mind's eye traced the graceful curve of her body and the intricate white tattoo that wound across her skin.

In another moment, I had almost seen where the lines of that tattoo had led.

A frustrated sigh escaped me. I rose and stared out the window. She hadn't gotten out of the cab yet.

I turned and leaned against the wall, taking a sip of my whiskey. Cold and smokey, it was a good drink for brooding.

How should I approach the damn woman? She had promised the djinn to me. We'd had a deal. I'd gone beyond the ends of the Earth, literally, to uphold my end of the bargain. She was the one who'd reneged. She had betrayed my trust, without a second's thought.

So why did *I* feel like the one in the doghouse?

Idiot.

Whiskey in hand, I strode across the hall into the parlor to refill my glass. Antique sculptures and dark batik prints offset the white walls and marble floors. "Flint, we have a visitor. Nevaeh Cross. I'll be in the sitting room."

"Very good, Mr. Malek," the butler said.

Neve had been livid when she'd discovered that I released the djinn. So what if I'd concealed the truth? The lie kept things simple. Our job was to get the djinn back. Confessing my mistake would have only complicated things, and led to perilous lines of inquiry, such as *what did you wish for?*

Besides, she hadn't been entirely honest with the Order about working with me. Everyone lies. The truth is often too complicated. Or dangerous.

A car door closed.

Maybe this was a chance to start things over. Did I want that?

Yes.

I knew the consequences of getting involved with an Order operative. They'd been on my heels for years, looking for any opportunity to seize my assets and throw me behind bars. Working with Neve was extremely risky—insane really—but that only added fuel to the fire.

The doorbell interrupted my musings. Seconds later the latch clicked, and Flint's voice echoed down the hall. "Ms. Cross, I presume. Mr. Malek is in the sitting room. Right this way."

Neve swept into the room, just as gorgeous as I remembered her. Perhaps it wasn't *just* the danger that drew me to her. Red hair, slightly damp from the rain. A long-sleeved blouse and jeans that clung to her curves. And those radiant pale eyes burning with emotion.

And her blond friend.

I glanced from one to the other, confused.

Neve's eyes were ablaze, white hot, boiling with radiant energy. "What the heck have you done!"

Well shit.

≈

Neve

. . .

Damian sat in a sleek leather chair, a glass of whiskey in hand. His aura flickered at the edge of my senses, like a blazing candle concealed behind his palm.

He looked impossibly perfect, and the memories of all we'd been through made my heart pound.

I would not let those memories cloud my mind. "Did you steal it?"

Damian leaned forward. "Steal what?"

So this was how he wanted to play. *Feigning ignorance.* I strode across the room and put my foot on the coffee table in front of him, threatening to flip it. "Did you steal the djinn?"

"What are you talking about?"

"Someone broke into the Vault and stole the djinn. Today. Was it you?" I crossed my arms, shifting my weight to one side.

Damian surged to his feet, and his eyes darkened, flashing with anger. His dark aura roared to life around him, overwhelming me with its power. The scent of ancient forests and the thunder of waves drowned my senses.

Rhiannon moved to flank me, strengthening my resolve.

"What the hell are you suggesting, Neve?" The frustration in his voice was barely restrained, like a growling mastiff at the end of a leash.

"Where were you today?"

"Work. All day. Where've you been? An asylum?" Damian slowly circled around the coffee table until he was only a foot away from me, cutting into me with burning eyes. "Tell me what's going on."

I met his gaze. "Just after two p.m. today, someone broke into the Vault and stole the djinn from the Order. Clues point to you."

"Not possible."

"It. Could. Only. Be. You."

He stepped closer, but I slammed my palm against his chest. He gazed down at it, and his fingers flexed. Suddenly taken aback by how tall and broad his shoulders seemed, I paused.

I couldn't tell if he wanted to pull me toward him or push me away.

My magic pulsed inside of me, and Damian's eyes darted to my tattoo. It radiated white light and a ball of wind formed around my hand, whipping at the placket of his shirt.

Damian leaned into my hand, as if daring me to use my power, and met my accusing gaze.

"Only a master thief could've broken into the Vault. He was a tall athletic man with a knack for charming people. He wove runes in the air to break the lock. He knew about the djinn, and exactly where it was being kept. Sound like anyone you know?" I said through clenched teeth, trying to maintain a hold on my power.

"You are accusing *me* of stealing the djinn? From the Order's Vault? The same djinn that we nearly died trying to capture a week ago? Do you think I am insane? Two weeks ago, you barged into my office and accused me of abducting your friend and being in league with the djinn. I wasn't. Where do you get off accusing me now?"

Ballsy.

"Are you *freaking* kidding me? You've lied to me the entire time we've known each other! You've been after the djinn from the start. You threw a fit when I handed it over. *Of course* I think you broke in and took it back. You're the only one who could do it. Capacity. Fore-knowledge. Motive. It all points to you."

"No," he snapped. "You're pointing at me, Neve Cross. Not the evidence."

My skin tingled from the magic coursing through my veins. Did he know that I could unleash a vortex right now in this room? "You can't weasel out of answering by feigning indignation. I want to hear you deny it. Did. You. Take. The. Djinn."

"No. Absolutely not. I did not steal the djinn or break into the Vault, nor would I ever want to."

"Liar," I hissed, pushing my palm into his chest. Tears crept into the corners of my eyes as a maelstrom of anger raged inside of me. A small voice at the back of my mind screamed, *This isn't me,* but I did not back down.

Our auras collided in chaotic waves, vibrating the air around us.

Finally, Damian slowly raised his palms and took a step back. "I know you do not trust me, but Neve, you have to believe me—I want nothing to do with that djinn."

"You wanted it the day we returned. Why *was* that?"

"You're right, I wanted it. I was going to seal it in a lead box, cast a concealment spell, and drop it in the ocean somewhere. I don't trust the Order. I never have. And given today's events, my instincts were right."

I searched his eyes for lies but found none. While I sure as heck didn't trust him, and his story didn't quite add up, he seemed to be telling the truth.

This was headed nowhere. I had to concede a little, or at least, make him *think* I'd conceded. I swallowed and let out a sigh. "Fine. I believe you. But I don't trust you."

The specter of rage departed, leaving me enervated and drained. I crossed to the couch and sat.

Damian was silent, and then he turned and left the room.

I pressed my fingers against my temples. *Fates.* The veins pulsed beneath my skin. "My head hurts."

After a minute, Damian's butler arrived with tea, placing a silver tray down on the coffee table.

"Thanks," I muttered as he silently left.

I didn't need tea, like some nineteenth century

wilting daisy. I needed a stiff gin and tonic, some fresh air, and a time machine to go back to before I'd ever met Damian Malek.

Since we were alone again, Rhiannon began rummaging in the end table drawer. "So, do we think Damian is innocent?"

I stood and ran my fingers over the books on his shelf, trying to clear my head. It was an interesting selection. Old publications. Exploration journals. Nineteenth century travelogues.

"I don't know. Damian seemed shocked. Full of righteous indignation. Then again, he's a thief and a practiced liar... so it could all be an act. We need to keep an eye on him."

Why couldn't I be a mind reader?

"I don't think I've ever seen you that mad. At anyone." Rhia looked up from the side table, where she was rifling through his mail. "We need to chat about that."

My gaze drifted to the window.

Damian stood in the rain, arms outstretched, rivulets of water running down his neck. Rain slicked his shirt across his torso, revealing the hard ridges of his muscles tense with repressed rage.

I shivered. *I'd* made him that mad. Not great.

But what I wouldn't give to read his thoughts right now.

I had gotten too familiar. The rain revealed what I

had forgotten. Damian was not a mortal man, but a fallen angel—dark and dangerous, with a perfect beauty that was terrible to behold.

He was hiding something for certain, but we were in grave danger, and I needed his help now more than ever.

5

Damian

The icy rain chilled my skin but did little to cool my blood. Fury tore at me, and my ravenous wings demanded to be released.

No.

I seized my emotions and strangled them as a low growl escaped my throat.

I needed to hit something. To fight.

After Neve had handed over the djinn to the Order, I spent three nights taking all comers in the boxing ring, trying to find some way to exhaust my anger—some way to prevent the dark angel from totally taking over.

Even that left lingering frustration. It was hard to

find someone to match my skill, but at least there were plenty willing to take a shot.

I didn't have the luxury of that brutal release now. I had to get in control.

I was the master here. Not the dark angel. Not my demons. Not the rage.

I stood glaring at the darkness until the cold rain deadened my emotions and my senses. Finally, when the worst of the darkness faded, I released my wings. With them, the last of my pent-up anger burst forth and then slowly melted away.

Clarity returned.

Warm light poured from the window into the cold night. Inside, the two women had collapsed on the couch, side by side.

Neve.

Would I ever truly think clearly when it came to that woman? Desire. Frustration. Admiration. Resentment. It made a heady cocktail.

My magic healed physical wounds, but Neve's accusations cut deep.

Did she really have so little faith in me? Did she imagine me capable of every evil in the world? Given the way we parted last time—the way I'd lied to her— perhaps she had reason to.

I swallowed.

If she only knew how much worse it really was.

I looked into the heavens and let the rain wash her from my thoughts.

I had to focus.

Someone had the djinn. Someone powerful enough to break into the Order's Vault. Gods only knew what they were doing.

This argument had wasted too much time already. We had to act. I strode back into the house and up the stairs to my chambers, leaving the slighted angel standing in the rain.

I dried off, slipped into clean clothes, and headed downstairs as the relentlessly ticking analytical side of my mind wheeled. How did someone break into the Vault?

Could I have pulled that off?

My ego wrestled momentarily with my analytical mind. It won.

Probably.

But I had no idea how.

Neve

Damian returned with a grim expression and a fresh set of clothes. "If what you say is true, then time is ticking. Tell me about the Vault. How did the thief get in?"

I glanced at Rhiannon as I considered whether we should make him privy to the details. I sighed and nodded. It wasn't like we had much information to go on anyway. If he was going to be of any help to us, we'd better give him the details.

Rhiannon brought Damian up to speed while I listened and focused on the facts. Maybe there was a clue I'd missed.

Rhia's voice drifted in. "...a billion possible pathways. The archmage said it should have been impossible."

An impossible crime.

How did someone commit an impossible crime? I scratched at my tattoo in frustration. It was itching again after our fight. Had it changed? I peeked down at the white lines spiraling up my arm.

Something clicked.

An impossible crime.

Oh fates. I staggered to my feet. "I think I know."

Rhia stopped mid-sentence. "What?"

"I know how he did it." I pointed to my arm, the arm of a djinn. "He used a wish!"

Damian crossed his arms, his brow furrowed. "How? The thief needed to get to the djinn before he could make a wish."

My adrenaline spiked, and a jolt of energy streaked through me. I was on to something. "Not if he had a second djinn. Or some other kind of genie."

"Maybe. But that seems highly improbable. Genies

are exceedingly rare and impossible to come by. I should know."

His words bounced off the Kevlar of my intuition, and I started pacing. The puzzle pieces fitting together.

The melted path.

I stopped midstride. "There was a melted path through the snow. Chambers along the way had burn marks."

"So?" Damian said.

"The thief must have used an efreet—a genie from the Realm of Fire. Their bodies are formed of flames. The thief got partway in and made a wish—*fetch me the djinn*—and boom, crime done."

"Holy shit!" Rhiannon said. "Is that possible? Are there limits to a wish? Can you do anything?"

Ignorant of my ancestral powers, I shook my head. "I don't know."

"Who would?"

Damian drummed his fingers on the doorway, brow furrowed. "Maybe Matthias, the iron mage. He enchanted the box and told us how to bind the djinn. He would know more about their powers."

"No. We should go to Archmage DeLoren. He knows I'm half djinn. Maybe he knows more about genies. We should take this to the Order right away." I grabbed my things.

"Absolutely not." Damian growled. "As soon as you take this to the Order, they'll start asking questions, and those questions are going to point to me. You two instantly assumed that I was the thief. Think of what the Order will do. They'll use this as an excuse to take me down."

"I won't let that happen."

"And how much power do you have over the investigation, Neve?"

None. I wasn't supposed to even be on the case. I shook my head. "If you're innocent, they'll let you off."

He glared. "Don't you get it? My innocence doesn't matter. All they need is a plausible warrant to bring me in and search my office, and they'll be able to find or plant evidence for a hundred *other* crimes."

"Sorry Damian, but this is bigger than either of us now. The thief probably has two genies. We don't have the resources to deal with that. The Order does."

"And yet we're the ones that captured the djinn, and they're the ones that lost it."

"And yet strangely, they're the ones I trust right now. Come on Rhiannon, let's go."

Damian grabbed my wrist as I headed for the door and locked me with a cold glare. "Should you trust them? Let me lay out another scenario. The simplest solution is that this was an inside job."

I yanked my hand out of his grasp. "That's bullshit."

"Is it? You have an unsolvable labyrinth. Yet someone solved it. The easiest explanation is that the thief already knew the answer, or someone gave them the answer. That means one of the archmages was in on the crime. They're going to need someone to blame to cover their own ass. Someone like me. Or even you. How fair do you think that investigation will be?"

Dread crept along my spine.

It was improbable. But not impossible. And that made it an extremely dangerous possibility.

This was all too much.

My powers. The stolen djinn. Another genie. Corrupt archmages.

I didn't know what to think.

Vertigo pulled at my stomach, and Damian's eyes burned into my skin. I had been so ready to believe he was the thief. The Order would lock him away and find some excuse to convict. We'd been trying to get him for years.

I shut my eyes against the world and took a deep breath. "I need to go."

"Neve."

"I'm not going to the Order. I just need to think. Or sleep. Or both."

Damian nodded. "Just don't tip them off. If it's an inside job, we could all be in danger. We can do this together. I'll help you solve this. With every resource at my disposal."

I shoved my hands in my pockets, unable to argue any longer. "Fine. Let's talk tomorrow."

He let out a deep breath. "I'll call Matthias and set

up an appointment. Maybe there's some way we can prove your efreet theory. That would suggest an arch-mage wasn't involved."

"Right." I was too drained to use much more than a couple words.

Rhia summoned a cab, and the three of us made our way to the door.

"Neve. I want to talk. Just the two of us." His voice was low and silky. Despite my overwhelming fatigue, it sent prickles down my back.

Rhiannon squeezed past, patting me on the shoulder on the way. "I'll wait outside and let you know when the cab arrives."

I closed the door behind her and leaned against it. Damian's magic flowed over me—no longer burning with rage, but calm, familiar, and soothing. Juniper. The sea. It enraptured my senses, and irrational desire flooded my body. What the heck was wrong with me? His green eyes searched mine. They were pained... and *hungry*.

I swallowed hard. "Damian. I'm too tired to talk."

He placed his hand against the door right above my shoulder, leaning in so that his face was mere inches from mine. Heat radiated between us, any sense of control melting away.

"You need to trust me if we're going to work together."

The lingering echoes of the fury and my deep-seated

mistrust rose to the surface, dampening my delusional desire. "You lied to me about your role in all this. Why should I trust you now?"

Damian pulled back, his jaw rigid. "Because I'd told you everything that matters. I'm sorry I lied. But I had my reasons."

"You're going to have to do better than that." I searched his eyes for answers but found none. "Maybe one day you'll share those reasons with me."

I turned and slipped out the door to Rhia and the waiting cab. A deep ache throbbed in my chest.

Fatigue tore at me, leaving my muscles and mind aching. But with thoughts leaping around my head like a herd of frightened gazelles, I wasn't going to be able to sleep, so I had the cabbie drop me off at the Hall of Inquiry.

Halfway there, my phone pinged with a text from Damian. *Matthias can meet. I'll pick you up at 9 a.m.*

Well, here we go.

While the Order had suspended me from officially working, it hadn't taken away my library card.

There was a mystery to solve. *Time to hit the books.*

6

Neve

The next morning, my phone pinged at nine a.m. sharp.

Damian.

I pulled back the curtain of my bedroom window. The brooding fallen angel leaned on the hood of a vintage black convertible double-parked outside my apartment.

Damn was he sharp. He looked like a model, except that dark energy vibrated the air around him, rising like heatwaves from scorching pavement.

I glanced at my reflection in the mirror. *Crap!*

I was a mess. Of course. Brushing the tangles from my hair with one hand, I texted Damian with the other —*down in 5.*

Eh. It would be *around* five. Almost certainly less than twenty. I didn't mind making him wait.

Two hours of sleep didn't help with my morning efficiency. I grimaced as I chugged down instant coffee. *Urf.* It wasn't a cappuccino and a scone, but time was ticking. We had to meet Matthias, the iron mage, and find out if he knew anything more about genies and their powers.

Luckily, thanks to my all-night research, I had a few more facts at my disposal.

I surveyed my clothes selection. What outfit said, *I'm a genius researcher who spent all night deciphering this crime,* and just a dash of, *I kick ass and take names*?

As per usual, the limited vocabulary of my wardrobe was not up to the verbose demands of my inner life. *Time to buy more clothes.*

Sighing, I settled on black skinny jeans, a white cotton shirt, and a dashing little jacket I'd found while shopping with Rhia. It wasn't everything I wanted to say, but it would have to do. Men can't read clothes anyway. At least not above a third-grade level.

I adjusted the khanjar sheath on my hip, finished my face, and darted out the door with my bag in tow. Roughly thirty seconds later, I sprinted right back in and grabbed my satchel of research notes.

Not enough sleep.

Damian stood as I sashayed down the front porch. He was a sight for tired eyes. Blue trousers, black belt, and a striped long-sleeve shirt, tucked in and sleeves rolled to his elbows. He opened the passenger door and leaned back patiently against the hood, arms folded.

"Morning, Ms. Cross."

His devilish good looks were sublime, but the dangerous aura emanating from him was nature's way of saying, *You can look, but don't touch.*

"Nice ride, Mr. Malek," I said coolly, slipping casually onto the leather seat and stretching my legs out like a content cat in the sun.

Damian's gaze lingered on me for a split second, then he shut my door. I buckled my seatbelt and saw a perfectly full cappuccino in the small cupholder. "Is this for me?"

Damian climbed into the driver's seat and secured his seatbelt. "I happened to stop by a café on the way. Figured you'd need the fuel. It was hot fifteen minutes ago."

I took a sip of the now tepid coffee. "Thanks. It's delicious and still hot. Sorry I was running late." *Lie.*

"I planned on it. We'll actually have time to spare, the meeting is at nine-forty-five, not nine-thirty."

I rolled my eyes as the car whipped away from the curb. We wove our way out of Old Mud City, heading over to the Gaslight District, where Matthias lived.

I wasn't exactly sure what Damian's connection to Matthias was. I'd tried prying into their history before, but had gotten little for my efforts. They'd been close allies once, long ago. I knew that Matthias had saved

Damian's life at some point, but they had gone their separate ways and seemed to quickly get under each other's skin.

I covered a deep yawn with the back of my palm.

Damian cocked his head toward me, scrutinizing my face. "Were you up all night?"

"Yeah. Hunting down clues. Someone is stealing genies, and ours isn't the first."

"What?" Damian's grip tightened around the steering wheel, and his jaw set. The shock in his eyes confirmed my suspicions. He didn't know. He was a liar for sure, but at this point, I was sure he wasn't the thief.

"Someone stole an efreet from Prague just over a month ago. I'm certain they used it to solve the labyrinth and get the djinn."

I brought Damian up to speed. The results of my night's work poured out in a five-minute-long, stream-of-consciousness monologue, which left me out of breath by the time it was done.

He glanced over and raised a brow. "Impressive work."

"Thanks."

He studied my face. "How much coffee have you had?"

I tallied the numbers in my head. "A handful of Nespressos last night at the Archives. Only four or five, though I think they may still be in my system. Two instant coffees for breakfast. Oh, and the wonderful but tepid cappuccino that you brought me. Why?"

"You're talking fast."

My fingers found the seat adjustment lever, and I reclined my seatback a smidgen. "Honestly, I'm just surfing that delicate wave between utter exhaustion and coffee mania."

He shot me another glance and shook his head, the traces of a faint smile forcing their way to the corner of his lip.

My phone pinged. A text from Rhia: *Questioning the sups. No real leads here. Will look into the genies and get back to you.*

I'd texted Rhiannon about my theory last night. She was going to do some digging to see if there were any other genies out there that might be potential targets.

Ten minutes later, the century-old brick apartments of Old Mud City gave way to the larger houses and tree-lined streets of the Gaslight District, and we pulled up in front of Matthias's place.

He lived in a peak-roofed nineteenth-century home, enclosed by a conspicuously tall ironwork gate. Decorated in bold reds, yellows, and browns, and surrounded by yellow and violet flowers, it stood out like a beacon amongst the other houses.

Damian came around to open my door, but I'd already climbed out. We proceeded through the automatic gate and knocked on the front door. After two breaths, the door opened a few inches, and a girl with a pair of dark-lined eyes peered out. She was probably in her early twenties at most, with midnight lipstick and an expression that said, *I'm bored already.*

"What do you want?" the girl said flatly.

Damian cleared his throat. "We're here to see Matthias."

"And you are?"

"Damian Malek. This is Nevaeh Cross. We have important business. May we come in?"

She shook her head. Her black hair was streaked with purple highlights. "Sorry. No solicitors."

Then she slammed the door.

Well, she tried to. I shot my foot out, wedging my toe in the gap before it closed completely. I craned my neck to peek inside. "Where's the normal doorman? The suit of armor?"

Last time we visited, the door had swung in on its own, and we'd been escorted inside by an empty, animated suit of armor.

She smirked. "He's getting his helmet polished."

I repressed a slight smile, but Damian was clearly peeved. "We have an appointment. Who are you, anyway?"

"Matthias's apprentice. I make his appointments." She held up an imaginary date book. "Looks like I don't have an appointment for a pair of nosy people at nine-forty-five a.m."

Her signature reminded me of Matthias, though not as powerful. It radiated with faint purple light, like steam rising from her body. The scent of hot iron, and... the taste of bitter cherries? That part was definitely different.

Were they related?

"I texted Matthias direct," Damian said.

I gave the girl my best don't-F-with-me-today stare. "Please. We need his help. We're trying to solve a crime."

The girl sighed and glanced down at my foot jammed in the doorway. "Fine. I'll tell him you're here."

"Thanks," I said.

Without letting up pressure on the door, she shrugged and shouted over her shoulder. "Matthias! Mulder and Scully are here to see you."

An annoyed voice bellowed back from deep within the interior of the house. "What are you talking about, Zara?"

"There's a pretty redhead with fancy shoes and an over-stuffed business suit here to see you."

"Damian and Neve? Show them in, for fate's sake."

The girl—Zara, apparently—sighed, and let the door swing open. "Fine. You can go in."

She was dressed in pale blue jean shorts, a black T-shirt with some kind of band logo, and bright white sneakers. Not my style, but cute—she made it work with the purple hair.

I stepped in, followed by Damian. Zara just leaned

against the wall, holding the door open. To our right, the empty suit of armor—an armor golem—stood at attention, motionless.

Zara caught my glance. "Oh no." She halfheartedly intoned. "Don't slay them, Sir Bertilak."

The armor remained still.

Matthias stepped out of his office into the hall. "Come, come, have a seat. I apologize for the confusion."

The girl shut the door behind us and patted the armor golem on its pauldron. "Excellent restraint, Sir Bertilak. I would certainly have beheaded them if I were in your shoes."

Matthias ushered us into his office. "One minute."

While Damian took his seat, Matthias stormed back down the hall. Rather than peruse his overly pretentious library while we waited, I lingered just beyond the doorway, barely able to make out their hushed conversation.

"Why are you answering the door?" Matthias snapped, in a whisper.

"I thought it was Amazon," Zara said.

"Head upstairs. I told you I do not want you anywhere near that man. He is dangerous and not to be trusted." The tiny hairs on the back of my neck stood on end. Fates. I was going to have to rethink how long I'd have to work with Damian.

"Fine. Whatever."

She clomped up the stairs, and I took my seat.

Damian was jabbing at emails on his phone, irritation showing at the corners of his eye. "Obnoxious apprentice."

I wove my fingers through my hair. *Pretty redhead*. I could live with being introduced like that. "Oh, I kind of liked her. Don't be such a stuffed suit."

He glared.

Matthias returned, flopped into his chair, and put his feet on the desk. "Right. What do you need help with this time?"

Damian, voice thrumming with annoyance, didn't waste any time on niceties. "The djinn's been stolen. We need your help to figure out what happened and get it back."

Matthias beamed, shifting his eyes from one of us to the other, gauging our expressions. "You're joking."

"Afraid not."

He carefully removed his feet from the desk and sat up. "You just captured it. Last week. Where the hell did you *idiots* leave it, your davenport?"

Damian's muscles tensed and his eyes turned dark. His magic washed through the room, and the air tingled with electricity the way it does on a hot summer night right before a lightning storm.

They glared at each other with an intensity that screamed *dysfunctional relationship*. There was definitely a rocky past here. One which Damian, of course, had neglected to mention.

I cleared my throat to clear the air. "It was stolen from the Order's Vault."

"That's impossible." Matthias sucked his teeth in irritation.

I ran Matthias through what had happened, and he gave a low whistle.

"If all this is true, you two are...," he shifted. "Let's just say, royally fucked. What a cock-up."

Great. *Thanks, Professor Douchebag.*

He leaned forward. "So, let me get this straight. You think the thief had another trapped genie—an efreet—and used a wish to solve the maze."

I nodded. I was nearly certain, but I wanted to see what he knew. "Is it possible? We don't know the limits of wishes. That's why we came to you."

"Hmm." He cleaned his glasses, which somehow made him appear more pompous than normal. "While I am not an expert in wishes, I do, of course, know a substantial amount on the subject, as I had to make the djinn binding spell for you."

"That was our thinking."

He considered the problem silently, letting us stew in our chairs, waiting.

At last, he deemed us worthy recipients of his thoughts. "Yes. It would be possible. While wishes are one of the most powerful forms of magic known, they have limits. Their area of effect is constrained, they cannot reverse time, change the past, raise the dead, or break the fundamental laws of magic. However, finding a path through a maze, even one as complex as the labyrinth, does not violate any of those clauses."

"But do you think it likely?" I uncrossed my legs and leaned forward.

"Perhaps." Matthias rose and stared out the window, a practiced expression upon his face. "It's also possible that the thief was a rogue efreet, like your rogue djinn, disguised. Genies cannot grant themselves wishes, but they do have access to other powerful forms of magic."

Damian furrowed his brow and sank backward into his chair, his body still tense.

Before he could comment, I piped up. "I'm absolutely sure it was a person in command of an efreet. I spent last night going through Magica newspapers and global crime reports. Our djinn isn't the first genie to be stolen."

"What?"

"An efreet bottle was taken from an exhibition of ancient artifacts in Prague, just over a month ago."

Matthias's jaw dropped. "Really. You think it is the same?"

"Has to be. They still haven't solved the crime, and the thief left no clues. It's too much of a coincidence to be unrelated." A surge of excitement jolted through my blood. I leaned in. "And guess what? It wasn't even the first genie that the thief attempted to acquire, either."

His eyebrows went up.

"Someone attempted to steal a genie from the Artificers in Guild City but failed."

Matthias rubbed his chin. "Really...what happened to it?"

"No idea, but I confirmed that it is safe with the Devil of Darkvale early this morning."

Matthias choked. "You just—what—called him up? The Devil? The master of Guild City?"

"Old acquaintances." I shrugged and glanced at Damian. Something flashed behind those dark eyes.

Matthias was clearly reeling and gradually sat back.

I crossed my arms. "I think someone is collecting genies."

There was a long silence as Matthias sat in shock, his mood utterly changed, and his confidence gone. Finally, he rasped. "I suppose that is possible. But why?"

I shrugged. "No idea. That's what we need to find out."

"You realize that if he—whomever the thief is—has multiple genies under his control, he will be dangerous beyond imagination."

Matthias seemed more nervous about the prospect than I anticipated. Was he worried the djinn would also come after him, the mage who crafted the spell?

"Yes. It's insanely dangerous. But we *need* to do something."

He frowned. "Like what? What can you do, really?"

Damian smacked his hand on his thigh and rose.

"We figure out where he is going next. Do you know the locations of any other trapped genies from your research?"

Shaking his head, Matthias also stood. "I'm sorry. I don't."

Hopefully, Rhia would find us a lead. I crossed my fingers.

Damian's gaze pierced Matthias, like he was gauging his thoughts. Then he continued, "I'm not aware of any others either. Thank you for your help. Please, reach out to us if anything comes to mind. About other genies, or genie powers, or any insights into who might have stolen the djinn from the Vault."

Matthias showed us to the front door, ashen. "I will."

As he was shutting the door behind us, he popped his head out. "Really, I wish you both the best of luck—but I think you don't have any idea what kind of mess you are getting into. If things go wrong...leave me out of it."

With that, he slammed the door.

"That guy," I said, rolling my eyes at Damian, but he was stoic.

We started down the path that ran between the beds of little yellow and violet flowers. My phone rang.

"Hey, Rhia." I switched on the speaker phone as Damian opened the passenger door. "Any leads?"

"Possibly. Have you seen the new display on the Arabian Nights at the Oriental Institute Museum?"

I hopped into the convertible and shook my head. "No. I haven't been to the OI since we trapped those Sumerian demons several weeks ago. And I didn't exactly have a chance to poke around."

"Well. They recently found some lost fragments in their basement collection from an Egyptian copy of the Arabian Nights. They're on exhibit now."

"Arabian Nights, like *Aladdin,* or *Ali Baba and the Forty Thieves*?" Damian interjected as he turned the car on and pulled away from Matthias's house.

"Yes. Exactly."

I rolled my eyes. *Wrong.* Technically, neither was original to a *Thousand and One Nights.* They were folktales added by Antoine Galland in the eighteenth century.

Rhia continued. "One is a ninth century fragment of a story. The other is a Mamluk-period tale about a tomb robber who hides a genie in a lamp and gives his wife a riddle to find it. Things like that are almost always simply stories, but..."

"But what?" Damian frowned.

"According to the tale, the lamp is hidden in Helwan, in Egypt. Not modern Helwan, but the ancient magical city of Helwan. Humans wouldn't know about that. That gives the story... a possibility of authenticity."

My shoulders slumped. We were grasping at straws. "Okay. Thanks for the tip. We'll check it out."

"Sure thing. I'm dying to join you, but I'm stuck here

interviewing some of the security guards. Keep me posted!" With that Rhia hung up.

I pulled up my contact at the OI and glanced at Damian. "Want to check out the text at the OI? It might give us a lead on where the thief will strike next."

Damian shrugged. "Sure. I think it's a long shot and liable to be boring, but if you actually have the hankering to do *more research*, sure, we can check it out."

Matthias had really ruffled his feathers and I wasn't sure why. I pushed it from my mind as the phone rang. This time I didn't put it on speaker. "Hey, Darlene. It's Neve. I hear you have a new Mamluk text from the Arabian Nights on display. I know you guys have restrictions, but is there any chance we could come in and check it out after hours? It's really important."

Darlene's voice wavered on the other end of the line. "Neve. I'm sorry. That's not possible. It was... stolen last night."

Oh fates. My breath started coming quickly. "One sec." I muted my phone and glanced at Damian.

"What?"

"Good news. I think Rhia's instincts were right."

"Okay... so what's the bad news?" His grip tightened on the steering wheel.

"The thief stole the text last night."

7

Neve

Seven hours later, a cab dropped me at the airport. Darlene had given me a digital copy of the stolen text, and I'd spent the day at the Oriental Institute's archives poring over it.

The clues all indicated that the thief was headed to Helwan, Egypt, to search for the lost lamp—so we were headed there too. Hopefully, we could beat him to it. Unfortunately, Magic Side didn't have a direct portal to Cairo, and I'd been banned from the Alexandrian portal, which meant a long overnight flight with Damian.

Gretchen had Rhiannon working several leads, and she couldn't get away. She was pretty salty about that. So it was just us. Together. Alone. It wouldn't be tense at all, of course.

With only two hours of sleep, I was running on fumes. It was going to be the *Night of the Walking Zombie Scholar,* for sure.

A pair of security guards escorted me out onto the tarmac to the waiting jet. Damian, black backpack slung over his shoulder, leaned against the cabin door, chatting with someone inside. His dark mood from earlier appeared to have cleared.

As soon as he spotted me, he sauntered down the steps. "Hello there, Ms. Cross. You ready?"

My heart fluttered in my chest. *Idiot.*

His hand brushed mine as he reached down to take my bag, sending pinpricks dancing up my arm. Definitely intentional. I grabbed my bag and pulled away. "I've got it. Thanks."

Thunder echoed in the distance, and Damian looked toward it, frowning. "We'd better be on our way."

"Can we fly in stormy weather?"

"Captain says it should be fine. Might be a little bumpy after takeoff." Damian stopped at the base of the steps and illuminated me with his devilish smile. "Nothing worse than what you've flown in."

Images of my turbulent flight through the raging storm clouds in the Realm of Air flashed through my mind as I mounted the stairs and ducked into the jet.

A sweet stewardess handed me a gin and tonic as soon as my bag was stowed.

Okay, things were starting to look up. I'd spent too much time waiting in airports and traveling in economy not to appreciate the small conveniences of luxury flight.

Damian slipped into a double seat on one side of a large table, and I took the spot directly across from him.

"Sláinte." I raised my glass to him and downed my G&T. Storms were fine as long as you were on the ground and sufficiently lubricated.

Damian signaled for another round. "You seem tired. Did you make any progress on the text?"

"Lucky for us, the Oriental Institute took excellent photos of the stolen fragments, so I've started working on a translation." I pulled out my notes, spreading them across the small table between us. I could have used another day of research, but we'd both agreed it best to find the genie as soon as possible. For all we knew, the thief was already in Helwan looking for it.

If we failed... the thief, whoever he was, would have three genies under their control—a djinn from the Realm of Air, an efreet from the Realm of Fire, and if my interpretation of the text was correct, a marid from the Realm of Water. With that many wishes, heck, he could probably nuke Magic Side into the ether—Guild City and Magic's Bend, too, for that matter.

Unfortunately, we hadn't a clue what he was up to. It could be a lot worse.

The captain's voice came across the loudspeaker. "Prepare for takeoff. We're expecting minor turbulence at the outset. We'll be passing through a storm, but we should be above it after a few minutes."

Wonderful. So much for a pleasant ride.

I reassessed the man in front of me. Sharp jaw. Piercing eyes. Confident smile. God-like physique.

I blinked at my own thoughts. Was I losing my mind? I *hated* this guy. I really needed to get some sleep.

Right before the plane began taxiing, the stewardess brought me another G&T, along with a platter of meat, cheese, and olives for us to share.

Damian leaned forward, scrutinizing the array of papers and letting those dark green eyes of his drift from them to me. "So, what did you find?"

"Well, the OI has two fragmentary excerpts from *A Thousand and One Nights,* also known as *Arabian Nights.* The one the thief stole is comprised of two, nearly intact pages dated to the thirteenth century. It hasn't been on display until now."

"So, this is a lost story and not part of the original text?"

I leaned back into the cushy seat. "There is no *original* text. There are dozens of versions with many unique and different tales. The stories originated from across the ancient world—with roots in Persia, India, Central Asia, North Africa, you name it."

The jet engines whirred into high gear, and the plane raced down the runway, quickly climbing skyward into the dark clouds above.

Damian took a sip of his whiskey as we lifted off the ground. "So, they're all different?"

I handed him my copy of *Arabian Nights*. "The various versions of *A Thousand and One Nights* share a similar framing story which is, frankly, really F'd up. A king discovers that his wife has been unfaithful and puts her to death. Then each night, he marries a new virgin and murders her at dawn so that she cannot be unfaithful."

"That's a grim plot device." He put the book aside without looking.

Rain began beating against the windows next to me. "Yeah. Totally F'd up. Thankfully, our heroine Scheherazade, the clever daughter of the vizier, devises a cunning plan. She reads a thousand books and poems and begs her father to let her marry the king."

I'd always loved her because she used her library card to fight evil. I popped an olive in my mouth and continued, "After their wedding night, she tells the king a fabulous story, but stops on a cliffhanger, refusing to continue. He can't kill her at dawn because he's desperate to know how it ends."

"So, he lets her live?"

"Yep. Each night, she finishes her previous tale, starts another one, and ends on a cliffhanger—that way he always has to let her live another day—it's exactly how HBO reels me in time and time again."

The jet dropped precipitously, leaving my stomach to catch up with the rest of my body. I clenched my fingers around the sides of the table.

Damian raised an eyebrow.

Great. I'd never been scared of flying. I *was* scared, however, of the sudden cessation of flight and accompanying impact with the ground.

"I hate turbulence," I said through clenched teeth.

It brought back too many memories of battling the djinn in the Realm of Air.

Damian looked at me inquisitively and then swung out of his double seat, came around the table, and dropped into the spot next to me. His body was unnaturally warm beside me, radiating heat, vibrating with power.

I hesitantly released my grip from the table and folded my hands self-consciously in my lap. I wasn't a coward, and I didn't need his reassurance. I just *hated* airplanes.

Damian took a long look at me and smiled before picking up where we left off. "So the stories that Scheherazade tells, they're like Aladdin, Ali Baba, and Sinbad?"

"Hm... kind of, but no." I nibbled on a wedge of soft

cheese to settle my nerves. "Those three stories were actually added later by European compilers. Some of the later Egyptian versions actually included a thousand tales. Our story is one of those."

"So, essentially, we're chasing a fairy tale."

I glared. "Well, so is the thief, and *that's* what matters. It seems like he's taking the story at face value and searching for a lamp in Helwan. Even if the lamp doesn't exist, we can still solve the riddle, figure out where the thief is headed, and beat him to the location. Perhaps we can ambush him, or I don't know, simply find out who he is."

"Ok. Solve the riddle. Catch the thief. Maybe find another genie, which happens to be a marid."

"Right. But first, we have to get to Helwan, a secret ancient city located in the desert just outside of Cairo." I pulled out a copy of a fifteenth century map of Egypt and pointed to the cluster of buildings marking Helwan. "It's hidden, and apparently, outsiders are forbidden to enter."

"So, like Magic Side and Guild City?"

"Yes and no. Even Magica are refused entry into Helwan."

Damian looked up from the map. "Why is it so secretive?"

"It's been that way since the mid-eighth century after a rival dynasty challenged the throne. The ruling caliphs shrouded the city with magic, and it became a bastion of their power."

Another drop in altitude left my heart in my throat. I grabbed Damian's forearm out of instinct, suppressing a yelp.

This is not minor turbulence.

Visions of flying through the maelstrom in the Realm of Air burst to mind.

"You look tense." Damian raised a perfect eyebrow.

"Of course I'm tense. I'm inside an aluminum tuna can plummeting out of the sky at 700 miles an hour."

"It's going to be fine." He pried my claws free and wrapped his hand around mine. The strength of his grip and nearness of his skin sent a wave of fire surging through me. I wanted to hate it, to pull away, but my hand was immobile.

A faint smile lit his eyes. "How are we going to get inside a magical secret city closed to all outsiders?"

The plane continued to shake around us, but the vibrations of Damian's magic drowned it out.

"*That* will be tricky." I cleared my throat, thankful for the distraction. "For one, we're gonna have to find the city. I have a general idea of its location, but it's invisible and veiled by magic."

"I see." Damian stared at the map quietly, lost in thought. "Then we'll have to sneak in."

I released his hand I'd been squeezing in a vice grip

and shuffled through the papers until I spotted one with a sketch of a man in flowing robes.

"Helwan is a trade city, known for their high-quality textiles and a special elixir they produce from dates. This is what a Helwani merchant looks like." I handed the sketch to Damian. "It's from an early 20th century travelogue. As far as I can tell, they're still actively selling their goods in Cairo. One of these guys could be our ticket in."

Damian lowered the sketch. "And how's that?"

"Helwan's main contact with the outside world is through trade, and its merchants have free passage in and out of the city. If we can track one of these merchants down, we might be able to bribe him for details on how to get in."

He considered my words and then turned, locking eyes with me. "I'm guessing you know where to track one of these guys down?"

Fates he was good looking. Those broad shoulders... I stole my eyes from his. "My friend Amal will meet us at the bazaar. We'll start with the textile merchants and see what we can find. Helwani textiles are well-known amongst the Magica, so we shouldn't have any trouble."

Thank goodness for Amal. She worked as an Order operative in Cairo. While I spoke some Arabic, I didn't know the lay of the land. Amal had lived there most of her life and would help us negotiate the teeming city.

The plane shook violently and lurched again, plummeting downwards so fast that I levitated out of my seat, held in place only by my seatbelt.

I screamed. A piercing, top-of-the lungs scream. A classic, heroine-is-grabbed-by-the monster scream.

We're all going to die trapped in this flying tuna can.

I shut my eyes, crushing Damian's hand as we hurtled downward to certain death.

Damian, on the other hand, let out a low laugh.

I cracked an eye. Everything was calm. My shriek slowed to a trickle and then petered out.

The stewardess, in a jump seat at the end of the plane, stared, her mouth agape.

My cheeks were on fire.

The captain's voice cracked through the lingering silence. "That should be the worst of it. Smooth skies from here on out."

Damian looked down at my hand. My nails were embedded deeply in the back of his hand. "I think we'll probably live."

I unclenched my talons and returned them to my lap.

Damian held up his hand and inspected it as the scratches healed.

I sank lower in my seat.

The stewardess unbuckled herself, rose, and glided down the aisle, clearly struggling to suppress a smirk. "Is there anything I can get either of you?"

I sat upright and tossed my hair, trying to regain a

modicum of composure. "I think I could use another drink."

"Of course. It was a bumpy start, ma'am."

I glanced at Damian, who suppressed a smile and said, "I'll have a whiskey, too."

Chagrined, I organized the papers on the table, which had danced about in the turbulence.

Damian took my G&T from the stewardess and passed it across. "So... once we're inside the city, how do we find this genie?"

Exhausted, annoyed, and slightly embarrassed, I slapped my translation of the *Tale of the Three Magicians* emphatically down on his lap. "We'll have to crack the riddle. Get reading. I have to take a nap—I've only had two hours of sleep."

I took a sip of my drink as I leaned my chair back and turned my face away, letting the buzz of the G&Ts mingle with the noise of the jet engines.

Almost instantly, my breathing slowed as visions filled my head. Sandstorms. Tempestuous genies. Invisible cities. And Damian at my side, striding through a vast desert of sun and sand.

8

Neve

We landed in Cairo twelve hours later. I awoke to the plane bouncing across the runway in the hazy Egyptian afternoon sun. Had I really slept through the entire flight? It sure as heck beat flying economy.

Stiff and sore, I wordlessly led Damian through the airport. He was impeccable. I was a staggering, wild-haired zombie in need of coffee. I tugged my white linen scarf over my head, hoping it would mask my unruly locks.

Damian's staff had arranged for an Egyptian driver to meet us, so we were able to avoid the morass of taxi drivers that inundated the arrivals zone. The heat outside was stifling, and I relished the air conditioning as I climbed inside.

Our driver fought his way through traffic, blaring his horn and weaving in and out between the swarm of erratic local drivers.

I fixed my eyes on the road, and I went over the plan —track down a Helwani merchant, convince him to give us information on the ancient city of Helwan and how to sneak in, crack the riddle, and find the genie. It was a tall order, and we were racing against time—the thief who'd stolen the djinn from the Order was certainly after the same prize.

It took forty nausea-inducing minutes to reach the Khan al-Khalili—the city's main bazaar and tourist trap. Relief flooded over me when the cream-colored minarets of al-Azhar mosque finally appeared, rising high into the cloudless blue sky.

Amal stood in front of the mosque waiting for us, wearing a pair of skinny cargoes and a navy blouse. Fashionably casual.

Amal was an Intelligence Officer for the Egyptian branch of the Middle Eastern Order. She tracked down the worst kind of bad guys, the kind you rarely heard about. Last year, my research helped her catch one of the region's most notorious assassins. We'd hit it off and had been good friends ever since.

Our driver screeched to a halt in front of the

mosque, eliciting a flurry of honks from the cars behind. He turned around to look at us. "I'll drop your bags at the hotel. Call me if you need anything, Mr. Malek."

The heavy heat rolled over me like a wave as I clambered out of the car. "Amal!"

Amal turned and smiled. "Neve! How are you?"

I fought my way through the busy sidewalk and gave her a hug. Her familiar magic surrounded me. Apricots and warm honey. "Nice to see you, Amal. It's been too long. Thanks so much for helping us."

"Anytime. Plus, I owe you." The sun illuminated the subtle auburn highlights in her dark hair.

She nodded to Damian as he exited the car. "And who's Mr. Dark and Handsome?"

There was no way Damian could have contrasted more with the chaos and noise of the marketplace throng. Unlike the effusive people, his dark magic and emotions were locked down, hidden from the world. He moved with silent precision and grace, and the crowd flowed around him as he crossed effortlessly to us.

My pulse quickened. Probably, it was the heat of the day. I shook my head. "He's my—colleague."

"Are you together?"

"Gods, no."

She cocked an eye and grinned. "Mmhmm. Sure."

Damian reached out a hand. "You must be Amal. I'm Damian Malek."

She took it. "My pleasure. Shall we get going?"

Damian and I followed Amal down the busy sidewalk. She moved through the dense and chaotic crowd with practiced ease before veering left down a street that was closed to vehicles.

Shops displayed their wares on either side. Shirts, jeans, lingerie. Most of the people around us were humans, but I sensed the signatures of several Magica as we moved through the throng.

"We're headed to the Tentmakers bazaar. I managed to track down a merchant there who sells Helwani textiles."

Relief released the tension in my shoulders. "Thank fates!"

"I still don't think this is a good idea, Neve." She glanced back at us with a frown pasted on her face. "Are you sure it's worth the risk? The Order can't protect you in Helwan, let alone here in Cairo."

"How much risk are we actually talking about here?" Damian raised his voice to project it above the cacophony of honking and passersby.

Amal narrowed her eyes at me. "She didn't lay it out for you?"

"I'd appreciate your assessment."

Amal stopped in front of a young man who was selling some sort of cloudy water, and they exchanged a few muffled words in Arabic. The vendor poured three plastic cups of the liquid, and Amal handed one to Damian and me. "Sugar cane juice. Refreshing and good for your health."

My stomach growled, and I took a sip. I needed a sugar boost, but the combination of the heat and the sickeningly sweet juice made my stomach turn. Damian chugged his down, so I gave him my cup along with a sincere, pleading expression. He rolled his eyes and took it. *Thank fates.*

"Helwan is hidden and off limits for a reason." As Amal took a gulp of juice, I cringed at the sugary after-taste that still coated my mouth with a gritty film. "Not just because of Helwani law, but also the Order's. The caliph who rules the city is exceedingly dangerous, and it's for everyone's safety that the city is closed."

Damian idly twisted the empty cups in his hand. "Dangerous how?"

Amal looked around and then leaned in close, speaking in a hushed tone. "He's a FireSoul. It's rumored that he is nearly four hundred years old, surviving off the magic he's stolen from all the trespassers he's executed. You don't want to cross him, trust me."

A chill skipped down my spine, and Damian's jaw clenched. A shadow of concern crept across the flawless features of his face. Something about her words had left him deeply troubled, and that lifted the hairs on the nape of my neck.

Fair enough. FireSouls were among the most

dangerous supernaturals, notorious for their hunger for power. When a FireSoul killed a Magica they could steal their victim's power, consuming it, and making it their own. The Order was always on the lookout for FireSouls and liked to keep tabs on them. They were among the rarest of the Magica, and I'd never met one before—nor did I want to.

"Second thoughts?" Amal grinned.

"I'm afraid that's not an option," I said. "So where's this Helwani merchant?"

"This way. We're not far."

Shoppers jammed the street, and I followed Amal single-file, with Damian picking up the rear.

"Is it always like this?" Damian shouted from behind.

Amal turned her head and laughed. "Yup."

Ahead, a monumental gateway spanned the street. "Bab Zuwala Gate," Amal shouted back. "It was once the city's southern gate. Under the Fatimids."

I looked up at the two minarets that flanked the opening. They were intricately carved and decorated with Arabic calligraphy.

"See those spikes?" Amal gestured to several iron bars that jutted out from the limestone walls. "Those are where the Ottoman governor mounted the heads of his enemies."

"That's definitely one way to make a statement," Damian said.

The smell of rot wafted through the air and burned my nostrils. My brows knit and I turned, looking for the origin. Before I found it, a sticky hand grabbed my wrist.

"Madam."

An uneasy quiver rippled through me, and I reached for my khanjar with my free arm.

The raspy voice continued in Arabic. "Can I interest you in a taste?"

The man offered me an amber date, displaying a toothy grin. His magic reeked of death, and his tarry eyes matched the color of his teeth. Well, the teeth that were still there.

I tugged my arm back, but his grip tightened. He brought his face near mine and breathed in deeply.

Is he smelling me?

I pushed him away, just as Damian shoved through the crowd, heat rippling off him.

The man bared his teeth and glared at Damian and then at Amal, who moved to flank me. Her hazel eyes flashed yellow—like Gretchen's did before she shifted. The man turned and vanished into the crowd.

Some of the nearby Egyptian merchants rushed up to make sure I was alright, and one chased after the vile man, cursing loudly in Arabic. I assured them I was fine and disentangled myself from the well-wishers.

"Who, or *what*, was that?" I asked, as we made our way down the street. The man had clearly been deranged. Bizarrely, his grip had left a sticky residue on my sleeve.

"Not human," Damian suggested. "Maybe some sort of fiend or demonic carrion creature?"

"He's a ghul." Amal frowned. "We try to keep tabs on them, but there's been an influx of them in the city recently. He shouldn't be here. Probably one of the caliph's spies. He may have picked up the scent of our magic."

She craned her neck to see over the crowd. "Come on, let's go. We're not far now."

Crap. The caliph of Helwan, a terrifying FireSoul, had spies and one had just sought me out and...sniffed me? Not a good start.

Damian's magic cleared my head of the ghul's rotten stink, and I realized how close he was. His eyes scanned the throng, and he placed his hand on the small of my back, motioning for me to follow Amal. I lingered for a second, breathing in his heady scent, fixating on the way his fingers felt through my shirt, and then I pulled away.

Five minutes later, we entered a covered market comprised of two-story shops. Textiles, embroidered quilts, and hangings lined the opened doors and walls of the tiny storefronts.

Amal spoke with a vendor peddling multicolored tents, while Damian kept an eye on the surroundings. He seemed on edge since we'd encountered the ghul. Or maybe it was after Amal mentioned the caliph being a FireSoul. His muscles were tense, ready to strike.

Amal waved to us. "This way."

Damian and I crossed the street and followed her into the store. A slender man with graying hair pulled aside a draped sheet of fabric and opened a concealed door in the back of the shop. We entered a large room filled with chests and stacks of neatly folded silks and tapestries. The deep aroma of cardamom filled the air.

A middle-aged man dressed in red and white robes entered from the back. His beard was thick and peppered with gray. The captivating patterns of his garments matched the descriptions I'd read of Helwani merchants.

"Assalamualaikum, ya haj." Amal greeted him with a traditional salutation, followed by, "Magic is the gift of the morning."

The merchant nodded. "Wa alaikum salam. Bountiful is the day. I am Ibrahim. How can I help you?"

He spoke in perfect English, his voice deep and heavily accented. Not a Gulfi accent, nor Egyptian, but one I hadn't heard before.

"We're interested in buying some textiles."

The merchant—Ibrahim—inspected her with a look of what appeared to be distaste, and irritation flared inside me.

"What kind are you looking for?" He idly drew his hands across a hanging sheet of fabric.

Amal shot me a questioning look.

"Silk? Cotton?" He continued, moving to another.

"Helwani," I said.

The merchant's eyes narrowed in on mine, reading my intentions. Satisfied, he turned and crossed the room to an ebony chest, unlocking it with a small brass key he drew from his pocket. He raised the lid and pulled out a bright red fabric that shimmered gold in the light. "Like this?"

His gaze fell to the scarf around my neck, and he reached down and pulled out a brilliant blue version of the red cloth in his other hand. "Or perhaps, this."

I involuntarily reached forward, compelled by the beauty of the cloth. The fabric was absolutely stunning, unlike anything I'd seen before. To have a dress fashioned of this cloth... "Yes. Those are perfect."

The merchant looked at Amal and Damian, then handed me the textiles. "Where are you from?"

I inspected the fabric. Were those gold threads?

"Chicago." I looked up and met his eyes. "Magic Side."

I had to assume he knew we were Magica, so there was no purpose in lying.

He tilted his head ever so slightly. "And why are you really here?"

Perceptive.

My eyes darted to Damian and Amal. "We need some information."

"What specifically?"

"We need to get into Helwan."

A rumble of laughter erupted from the merchant. I couldn't tell if he thought we were joking or just plain stupid. Maybe both. "Impossible. The city is off-limits to outsiders. But I suspect you already knew that."

I sensed that this was going to be a difficult negotiation. "There must be something we can offer you to make it worth your while."

I flashed Damian a look and cocked my chin, hoping he understood that it was time for a bribe. He reached into his pocket and pulled out a wad of cash.

The merchant narrowed his eyes at Damian before turning back to me.

"I'm not interested in money. But..." His hazel eyes examined me from head to toe, lingering for a moment on my sheathed khanjar. "Perhaps there is *some* other agreement we can come to."

Damian shifted and flexed his fists. Traces of what I understood to be jealousy and protectiveness flared across his face.

"Perhaps. What is it you want?" I said coolly, following his bait.

Amal motioned inconspicuously to Damian with her hand, and he seemed to relax a bit, though the muscles in his jaw still twitched.

"To continue our negotiations in private," the merchant said.

"Not a chance." Damian stepped forward, and his dark aura flickered threateningly.

The man gritted his teeth and ran his fingers through his beard, seeming to weigh his options.

"Fine. You two will come with me. But you..." His gaze shifted to Amal. "You are not welcome. I will have no business with the Order."

How did he know Amal worked for the Order? Was it really that obvious? He didn't mention anything about me, so I had to assume he didn't know *I* worked for the Order as well.

Irritation colored Amal's face, but she quickly shrugged it aside. She turned to leave but gestured for me to follow with a slight tilt of her head.

I followed her through the door to the front of the shop, and Amal took my arm, leaning in close. "He's right. I shouldn't be there. The Helwanese have a sharp distaste for the authorities. My presence will just make your negotiations with him more difficult. Plus, if the Order found out I was helping you sneak into Helwan, I'd be in a mountain of trouble. You two be careful, and don't let on... what you do for a living. Call if you need anything, though I can't promise I'll be able to help."

She squeezed my arm and disappeared onto the busy street.

I turned to join Damian and Ibrahim in the back room, but the merchant's body blocked my path. He loomed in the doorway, a sly grin stuck on his face.

"That's better. Now, let us take a respite from this busy shop."

I glanced around. Passersby filled the street outside, but the shop wasn't busy at all. Suspicion crept over me, but we had no choice.

This man was our best shot at getting into Helwan.

9

Neve

Ten minutes later, Damian and I were squeezed uncomfortably into the cab of a bright yellow Toktok—a motorized tricycle—weaving in and out of the scrambling shoppers, who darted out of the way.

The driver blasted Egyptian music and laid heavy on the horn as he raced after a second Toktok that carried the merchant, Ibrahim. When we darted out onto streets with cars, the blaring of horns grew louder.

Damian gripped the handhold on the ceiling, bracing himself as we wheeled around a corner. The cab didn't have doors and each time we rounded a bend, the shifting momentum threatened to toss us out.

"This wasn't what I'd had in mind when I agreed to

take a ride." Damian had to hunch to fit in the tiny vehicle.

We whipped around another turn, and Damian braced me with his arm. Under normal circumstances this ride would have alarmed me, but at that moment, my mind was focused entirely on Damian's leg as it pressed against mine. I was hot before, but with Damian so close, I was practically sweltering.

The pedestrian traffic cleared, and the driver slammed on the breaks. Unprepared for the sudden change in speed, I lurched forward. Damian caught my torso with his arm, stopping me from slamming my head into the driver's seat back.

Gasping, I sat back. "Thanks. I appreciate my face not being broken."

Damian's gaze drifted to my lips. "That would be a shame."

Ibrahim climbed out of the other Toktok and waved at us to join him. "This way, my friends."

Damian and I peeled ourselves out of the cab. The Toktok had parked beside a white, three-story building. Mashrabiyas—a type of projecting window enclosed by ornate wooden latticework—pierced the upper floors of its stuccoed walls.

"Please. This way." Ibrahim led us to a door decorated with carved geometric designs framed by a large wooden entrance. He swung it open, and we stepped into a dark hall that was twenty degrees cooler than the stifling air outside.

"Welcome."

I fanned the bottom of my shirt for air as we followed Ibrahim around a corner into a large reception room lit by hanging brass lamps and columns of sunlight that poured through a side window. A shallow tiled fountain bubbled in the center of the white marble floor.

"Please have a seat. I will have some refreshments brought for us." He left the room.

I joined Damian on a bench at the back of the room. Persian rugs covered the floor, and their intricate patterns reminded me of the tattoo on my arm.

Ibrahim returned from a back hall and took a seat on the bench opposite ours, carefully adjusting his robes. "So, what business do you have in Helwan?"

"We're looking for something."

Ibrahim furrowed his brows. "What kind of something?"

"That's none of your concern," Damian said.

The merchant glared at Damian, shooting daggers from his eyes. "Helwan *is* my business, dog."

The insult caught me off guard. Damian didn't budge but I felt the tension ripple through the room. This wasn't looking good, and I was pretty sure that Damian's stoic demeanor was a prelude to something more explosive.

I laid my fingers gently on his wrist beneath the table. *Calm down.*

"What he meant was, we can't say exactly what we're looking for, because the truth is, we don't really know."

It didn't come out as eloquently as I'd intended, and befuddlement clouded Ibrahim's eyes. "You have come all this way without knowing what you are looking for? I am sorry, but you look like a woman who knows *exactly* what she wants. You hide your intentions. This makes me nervous, as it is against the law for me to help you and puts my family at risk."

"You brought us here. It seems that you are considering it," Damian said. "If you do, I can make it worth your while."

I pushed down on his hand with my fingers. *Back off.*

Damian was used to bargaining with crime bosses and gangsters—negotiations in which the alpha wolf won or allegiances could be bought. But Ibrahim was a simple merchant, nervous, with a family to look out for. Money or force wouldn't necessarily work here.

"We just need some information on how to get into Helwan," I said.

An older woman draped in a black shawl emerged from a side doorway with a silver tray and three glasses of tea.

Thank fates—I needed some time to think.

She set the tray down on the table in front of us and swept back out.

The warm tea and cool air sent a refreshing trickle of energy though my veins. Ibrahim sat quietly, an inscrutable expression on his face. I waited patiently, maintaining pressure on Damian's wrist beneath the table. At last, Ibrahim opened his mouth to speak, but a doorbell buzzed from the opposite end of the house.

"Excuse me. I must get that." Ibrahim stood and left the room.

I exchanged looks with Damian. This wasn't a fortuitous start. I sighed and leaned back, resting my head on the back of the bench. The gilded wood ceiling rose to the third story and a series of mashrabiya screens provided the second floor with a view over the reception room.

"Pssst." A flash of movement behind the wooden screen above us caught my eye. A little square panel opened and a young girl popped her head out, motioning with her hand for me to come.

"Did you see that?" I whispered.

Damian nodded, and I rose. "I'll be right back."

Damian's eyes locked onto me. "Be quick. He won't be keen on you fraternizing with his household."

I ducked into the adjacent stairwell and took the steps two at a time. The door at the top was slightly ajar, and I pushed it open a few inches.

Oriental rugs, cushions, and luxurious furnishings decorated the space. Several jugs of water were placed under the window to cool the room.

A door to my left creaked open, revealing a regal woman in a bright green dress that matched her kholl-lined eyes. Her ivory skin offset a coif of jet-black hair, neatly pulled over her shoulder.

"Welcome to my house. I hear you have business in Helwan," she said smoothly.

The merchant's wife.

She smiled broadly, and I sensed warmth and hospitality. Perhaps she'd be more forthcoming with information.

I shifted a step into the room. "Thank you. Yes, we're hoping your husband will have information that will help us get into the city."

"My husband?" She raised her manicured eyebrows and chuckled. "Ibrahim is my assistant. Not my husband. He works for me and my business."

Shit. *She* was the merchant, not Ibrahim.

My cheeks burned from the deluge of embarrassment, but her lips parted in a gentle smile.

"Not to worry. But...we don't have much time. The Caliph's spies have tracked you here. Ibrahim is delaying them but won't be able to hold them off long." She indicated the mashrabiya window.

I crossed the room and peered out onto the street below. Ibrahim was speaking with two men, and he appeared flustered. My blood froze as I recognized the ghul.

Shit. We hadn't even broken into Helwan and we

were already being hunted by the caliph's minions.

The merchant handed me a slip of paper with two numbers: a bank account number and an enormous price tag. "We do not have time to negotiate, as we are all in danger now. This is the price. Will you pay it?"

I looked back toward Damian, who stood on the stairs.

"You must make the decision. There is no time."

I nodded. "We'll do it."

"Good. I will trust that you will honor your bargain." She gave me a folded sheet. "These instructions will help you find the city and get inside. You must arrive at high noon. Follow the limestone track until the ramparts appear."

I unfolded the paper and glanced at the sheet—it was full of detailed instructions and a sketch of something I didn't have time to make out.

"Thank you...?" I looked up and paused.

"Yasmina. Yasmina al-Hadidi."

I tucked the paper into my purse. "Thank you, Yasmina."

She took my elbow and towed me toward the door. "I will show you the back way out. You must hurry. If they discover you are trying to find a way to Helwan, you'll be executed."

Damian stood at the base of the stairs, veiled in shadows, concern cutting his face. "Something feels wrong."

I rushed down the steps, Yasmina on my heels. "We've got company, the caliph's spies."

Damian turned and summoned a smoking dagger from the ether.

"No!" Yasmina hissed. "You must not kill them. You would bring disaster on our house and yourselves. For now, we will tell them that you wanted to make an illegal trade for cloth, and I kicked you out."

A muscle twitched in Damian's jaw. "Understood."

Yasmina led us through a hall to the kitchen. "Not a word," she said to the woman who'd brought us the tea earlier, and then opened a back door that led onto a narrow alley.

Yasmina pressed something into my hand. "Say nothing of what we discussed. May the fates guide you on your journey."

I turned to her, but shouts exploded from the reception room.

"Go, now!" Yasmina shut the door and bolted it.

We sprinted down the back alley and hurtled down a narrow street that had been closed to vehicular traffic. Several pedestrians shot us glares as they veered out of our path.

We were attracting attention. *Bad plan.*

I whipped my head around to see if we were being pursued and nearly barreled into a couple of older men seated at a small table playing backgammon. The man closest to me jumped to his feet, knocking over his chair.

I swerved right and stumbled over a pothole. Damian caught my arm and steadied me before I crashed into the pavement. The old men hurled colorful profanities after us as we ran.

"Assifa!" I apologized in Arabic.

Two men rounded the corner at the far end of the alley and started shouting as soon as they spotted us. Adrenaline pumped through my body, and I ran as fast as I could.

The alley wound left, and the familiar blaring of horns echoed off buildings. Fifty paces ahead, the alley dumped into a wide street filled with cars. *Thank fates.*

A black-and-white taxi on the opposite side of the road slowed down as we approached, and I waved my arm frantically. *Please, please, please.* The cab's taillights flashed red, and the driver pulled up along the curb across the street.

Bingo.

I darted toward the cab, but Damian yanked my shirt and pulled me to an abrupt stop, just as a car flew by with an ear-piercing honk.

Whoops. I'd almost just lost at frogger.

The street was at least four lanes wide, though it was impossible to be certain, given the way the Cairene drivers drove. Cars whipped past us from both directions.

Chest heaving and still stunned from the shock of my near-death experience with the car, we lurched forward through the narrow openings. A battered blue sedan swerved around us, blaring its horn and sending a blast of warm air into my chest.

A gap opened between the relentlessly honking cars, and we hurled ourselves across the remainder of the street, colliding against the hood of the waiting cab. Damian opened the door, and I flew in, sliding across the faux leather seat to make room for him.

I locked eyes with the driver in the rearview mirror. He wore a white skull cap and a blue T-shirt. "The Four Seasons hotel, as fast as possible."

The driver gave a quick nod, and as soon as Damian slammed the passenger door shut, the car lurched forward and joined the stream of weaving cars.

My breath shook as my lungs still fought for oxygen. Shit, that was close. Arrested by the Helwanese authorities. Would they really have executed us? Judging from what Amal had said earlier about the Order's jurisdiction, she wouldn't have been able to help.

I turned and looked through the back window toward the street we'd just left behind, searching for our pursuers. Nothing.

Then the ghul appeared, stopping right where I'd nearly been pancaked by the car seconds earlier. His companion dashed across the crowded road, barreling over the oncoming cars, and searched the adjacent alley.

"Duck, it's the ghul!" I slid down in the seat.

Damian stared back. "I don't think they saw our cab. And we're out of sight now."

I sighed in relief, my lungs finally satiated. They hadn't seen us. We were safe, for now.

I caught the driver's gaze in the rearview mirror. As if reading my thoughts, he reached forward and switched the radio on.

Certain that he couldn't hear us over the Lebanese pop song that blared throughout the cab, I continued. "Ibrahim delayed them so we could escape."

"Did you get anything useful from the woman?"

"She was the actual merchant. I made a deal for directions. We owe her a lot of money." I held out the slip of paper. "I hope that's okay."

Damian took it and raised his brows but nodded. "Excellent work. That was our only shot."

I leaned back onto the sticky pleather seat and noticed that my fist was still clenched around the object Yasmina had given me. I uncurled my fingers, revealing a bronze circular trinket on a silver chain.

"What is that?" Damian said.

"No clue. The merchant pushed it into my hand when we left." I hung it around my neck for the moment.

"She also gave us a map and instructions." I pulled it from my purse and flipped it over. On the back, she had written a message in tight, urgent letters. *Beware—the caliph has eyes everywhere. Trust no one.*

Damian

The caliph. *FireSoul.*

I hadn't anticipated we would have to deal with a FireSoul. Bile burned the back of my throat, and shadows crept in around the edges of my heart.

This was becoming a perilous dance.

I drove the thought from my mind and tried to focus on the problem at hand. I pulled out my phone and sent Yasmina twice the amount she had asked. The merchant woman had trusted Neve with information before payment, putting her business and family at risk. I wanted to make sure she was well taken care of.

Neve was lost in thought, staring at the paper

Yasmina had given her, and we spoke little as our cab lurched through Cairo's glacial, late-afternoon traffic. By the time we checked into the hotel, Neve was pale and drained.

"You need to eat," I said as we headed to the elevator.

She shook her head. "I need to get to work on this map. And the riddle. The clock's ticking."

"Food first. You're running on tea and sugar water."

She shrugged. "I feel like I've been dining on car exhaust all day, though I could use something to go along with it."

We revitalized ourselves with a platter of grilled meats, hummus, and half-a-dozen small salads in the fifth-floor restaurant and then retired to our penthouse suite. Neve leaned her shoulder against the side of the elevator and lifted her hand to cover a yawn. Even half awake, she was alluring.

That was a problem.

I needed my wits about me, and Neve clouded my judgement. Her scent. Her lips. Her rage and accusations. They tore into my emotions, weakening the cage that kept the dark angel at bay.

We got out on the top floor and headed to our room. Unlike the cramped cabin we had shared aboard the Jewel of Tayir, the suite had separate bedrooms. I could keep my eye on Neve, but it gave us space.

Neve unwound her scarf as she swept through the

door and into the living room. She kicked off her shoes, dropped her purse on a chair, and flopped onto the couch.

"Food coma," She sighed as she leaned her head back on the cushion and closed her eyes. The way she spread across the couch sent a rivulet of desire running down my spine.

I pushed it away. Focus on the problem at hand.

"What did you learn from the map," I asked with a slight roughness to my voice.

She draped her arm to the side. "If you want any information out of me, I'm going to need a strong Turkish coffee."

I raised an eyebrow. "At this time of night?"

"At any time, day or night. I'm half-djinn. The other half is espresso. You better make it a double." Neve grinned and peeked one eye open.

I turned my back to hide a flicker of a smile, headed to the kitchen, and filled a long-handled copper pot with bottled water. I mulled over the women in my past while I mindlessly prepared the coffee. There'd been many. None of them could remotely compare to the chemistry I had with Neve.

I stole a glance at her. She could infuriate me beyond words. And yet, something drew me to her. Was it those unearthly blue eyes, or the fire behind them? Her beauty or her growing power?

I let the coffee slurry nearly bubble over three times and shut off the stove, pouring the steaming black liquid into two short glass cups.

"That smells divine." Neve lengthened her body in a feline stretch and the bottom of her shirt pulled up, revealing a smooth patch of ivory skin.

"One double jet fuel." I handed her the steaming cup. "It's hot."

She cradled the cup between her hands, breathing in the steam. Her lips parted, and she pressed them to the glass's rim.

Desire flared.

For just a second, I let her magic wash over me— jasmine with a hint of citrus. Like a cool summer's eve. I breathed in a single taste and then locked myself down. I could not let these reckless desires distract me. I had gotten too close to her in the Realm of Air. I had let her bait me at my house.

I needed to stay sharp. I needed to stay in control, but the dark angel within pushed back against the bonds of logic.

I snapped my gaze from her lips and cleared my throat. "So. To business. What does Yasmina say about getting into Helwan?"

Neve

I stretched my arm out and pulled Yasmina's folded letter from my purse on the chair. "Let's see."

Damian's gaze traced my movements, sending a soft shiver down my spine. He'd been watching me all evening.

I liked that.

Not that I liked him. He was a criminal and a liar. I hated how the shadows consumed him when he was angry and the way his dark magic could stop the heart of his opponents. He was ruthless and complicated, and I wanted nothing of it.

But some part of me liked the way he snapped his eyes away when I caught him looking.

He shouldn't be looking at me in the first place, not after all the lies he'd told.

I unfolded the paper. The writing was in Arabic, so I translated as I read aloud. "Depart from Helwan on the Nile—by which she must mean modern Helwan which is situated along the river—and head due east into the desert. Follow the limestone track on your right. You will see the horns of the gazelle in the cliffs ahead. Continue until the rhino appears in the south, then head toward it."

"I take it those are local landmarks?" Damian sat down at the far end of the couch.

"Yes." I flipped the paper over, revealing two sketches of an escarpment. One had a deep v-groove and the other had three curving points.

I traced the paper with my finger. "The V represents the horns of the gazelle. But this other sketch is odd. I don't see any resemblance to a rhino."

"Maybe not from the side. But at an angle..." Damian pulled up a photo of a rhino on his phone. With its two curving horns and upright ears, it matched the sketch almost perfectly.

"Well, there you go."

"So far, that's not a lot to go on." Damian leaned closer, looking at the sketches on the paper.

His magic brushed again mine, it's power intoxicating. Even though he had it locked down tight, it leaked through—vibrating like a rattlesnake poised to strike.

There was a sensation there, amongst the waves and trees and salt breeze that I couldn't quite put my finger on—a signature driven down beneath all the others. Was it part of his fallen angel magic or something else?

The mystery of it pulled at me. It was like a forgotten word at the tip of my tongue. I could almost taste it.

His magic was so restrained. I would have to get closer to get any true sense of it.

"There's more." I flipped the paper over and slid next to him under the pretext of showing him the text, though I knew he couldn't read it. "At high noon, the ancient city of Helwan will show herself."

I glanced up at him. His pupils were dilated, and he remained absolutely motionless as if my proximity was a threat.

Interesting.

I stretched my leg out.

His gaze followed and then snapped back to the paper. "That sounds like what happens with the fae realms—except the fae realms open at dusk and dawn, not noon."

I leaned in as I read, my shoulder brushing his. "Do not approach the city from the front gate. Find the smaller passageway along the northern rampart and enter there."

I had been close to Damian many times, but never focusing like this. His magic pulsed like a relentless heartbeat. I opened my mind, searching for that elusive signature.

Still too far.

I reached out and slowly slid the paper from his hand, letting my finger brush against his. Damian's entire body tensed as our magic intertwined, raising goosebumps along my skin.

His gaze drifted up my arm, across my chest, and to my eyes. "Is that everything?"

His voice was strained.

I gently brushed a strand of hair from my face and smiled. "Other than her warning on the back, yes."

His head shifted forward a fraction of an inch and

then darkness flickered in his eyes, and he stood. His aura blazed for a moment before he reined it in. The fire did not leave his eyes.

Damian tore his gaze from mine, crossed to the balcony doors, and opened them wide, letting in the sound of the late evening traffic and the warm night air.

Very interesting.

His composure turned cold, and the traces of emotion on his face fell away.

I had gotten so close. Far too close.

Who knew anything about this man and what he might want?

I hadn't learned anything more. Damian was hiding something. His emotions, certainly, but also something more.

Fates. What else could a fallen angel have to hide?

I couldn't trust him. I couldn't let myself be drawn in by my curiosity or the power of his magic.

Damian cleared his throat and stepped out onto the balcony. "You should get some rest. We've got a long day tomorrow."

I stretched and rose from the couch. "You as well."

He didn't seem to hear. I collected the belongings that I'd strewn across the floor and headed toward one of the bedrooms. I tossed my shoes and scarf onto the blue sofa in the corner and turned to close the door.

"Thanks for the coffee."

He nodded absently as he gazed out on the lights

below. I flicked off the living room light, leaving Damian illuminated by a single lamp.

Dark shadows moved around him. His silhouette was tense, and his hands gripped the iron railing as he stood motionless, watching over the city.

Was he looking for something? Or just hiding from himself?

11

Damian

Cairo greeted the sunrise with blaring car horns, waking me early. Neve, on the other hand, had slept through the relentless noise, and we'd wound up behind schedule.

Cairo traffic was bad this morning. Our driver slowed to a crawl as he searched for a path through the morass of cars. Nine-thirty a.m. Sleep deprivation and the ceaseless honking made it difficult to keep a cool head.

My thoughts echoed in my head, as chaotic and distracting as the car horns.

What was I to make of Neve?

I knew she didn't trust me and that she was still angry at me. But her emotions changed like the wind.

Three days ago, she had been so enraged that she was ready to send a bolt of wind through my chest.

But her mood had changed. She was on the hunt for the hidden genie and had seemingly forgotten all else. She had been the same way in the Realm of Air. Focused on her task, living in the moment, trepidation cast aside.

And last night, she had seemed... almost flirtatious?

Maybe I was misreading her. Either way, it was dangerous. I needed to be thinking about how to protect her. Not about her. Helwan would be perilous.

I glanced down at the Garmin GPS in my hand. The little emblem that represented us stood at a standstill. I sighed and raked my hand through my hair, putting the device in my bag.

Helwan was concealed with magic, and I wasn't certain I'd be able to sense its signature. So I'd spent much of the night reviewing satellite imagery of the outskirts of modern Helwan and plotting the positions of what appeared to be the limestone track that Yasmina had mentioned in her instructions.

"Look! It's the Step Pyramid." Neve pointed through her window. She was cheerful this morning and hadn't mentioned a word about yesterday.

I leaned toward her and peered out her window, catching sight of the upper platforms of the blocky pyramid. "It looks rather small from here. I thought it would be larger."

"Well, it's actually quite impressive when you're standing in front of it. Maybe we can stop there on our way back." She glanced at the driver and then whispered, "After we've secured our package."

"That's an idea. Perhaps there's some lost treasure still hidden within? Somehow missed by the light-fingered archaeologists?"

Neve glared at me.

Of course, I didn't mean it. I knew there was no buried treasure in the pyramid, but I liked to rustle Neve's feathers. The way she pursed her lips when her temper flared was sinful as all hell.

"No, there certainly is not. And archaeologists don't have light fingers. I mean, they do when it comes to excavating. But no, not in the way you mean. They aren't thieves. Plus, treasure hunting is beyond thievery, its heritage destruction." Her voice was sharp, and she drew her lips together, just as I'd imagined.

I leaned back, enjoying the moment.

We broke through the traffic and our car cruised over the Nile. I mindlessly watched a sleek boat drifting down the current with its triangular sail unfurled. Ahead, the yellow desert sands juxtaposed the verdant green on either side of the river. A stark contrast between life and death.

"Are you sure this is where you want to go, Mr. Malek?" The driver tapped on the GPS mounted on his dashboard. "There is not much here."

I had given him an address near a stable on the outskirts of modern Helwan. The city appeared to have expanded recently, and new developments stretched into the desert. The stable looked over the barren sands and was close to the limestone track.

"Yes. That's the spot."

Neve

The car sped down a highway that skirted the edge of the city. The pavement was black and unpitted, suggesting the roadway had been constructed recently. After a few minutes, we exited onto a gravel street sided by several buildings under construction.

The driver slowed next to a pair of white-washed structures stained brown from the desert sand. "Here we are."

Across the street, the desert disappeared into a cloudy haze. It wasn't a sandstorm, though the season was well upon us. This was more like city pollution and trash fires.

Damian pulled two white linen scarves from his backpack. He handed me one and wrapped the other around his head, leaving a flap that could be tucked in to cover his nose and mouth.

"Lawrence of Arabia?" I teased. There was a slight resemblance, though Damian's looks were several notches above Lawrence.

He shrugged and collected the bag of snacks and water that the driver had picked up for us. I took the linen scarf and wrapped it loosely over my head and around my shoulders, so that my hair was mostly covered, save for a strand or two.

We exited the car and thanked the driver. He looked confused and slightly uncomfortable with leaving us in such an odd place. I didn't blame him. Backwoods villages weren't exactly part of the typical tourist venture.

The driver pulled away, and Damian glanced down at my fanny pack with a confused expression on his face.

"What?" I looked down at my waist bag.

Was there something wrong?

He didn't answer, just shook his head, and headed toward the white—well, mostly brown—stables just ahead.

I wasn't sure I liked our plan.

"Are you sure we should go on horseback?" I asked —as if Damian would suddenly change his mind.

"Would you prefer to walk into the desert?"

"Can't we just fly?" I whispered, subtly mimicking wings with my hands.

"You know that's not an option. Too high a risk of being seen by locals."

"A jeep?"

"Too noisy and easy to spot. Who knows what kind of spies the caliph has lurking in the desert. I actually considered putting us on donkeys, but I wanted to see you on a horse." The corner of his mouth twitched in a rare hint of a smile, and I scowled.

I glanced at my phone. Nearly ten a.m. Time was growing short. Yasmine's instructions said *at high noon the ancient city of Helwan will show herself*.

How long would the city be visible, and how short was our window? Neither my notes, nor Yasmine's message provided any indication. We could always try again if we missed it, but we were racing against time and a *thief* who was also after the same genie. For all we knew, he was ahead of us.

I sighed and tamped down the anxiety that flitted in my chest. There was no point in dwelling on things out of our control.

Damian disappeared into the stables, and I ducked in behind him. Inside were several stalls with hay strewn across the ground. The smell of manure and grain drifted on the air. In the back, Damian spoke to a middle-aged man who wore a traditional gray robe. The man held the reins of two horses—one jet black and the other pure white.

They were majestic creatures. That didn't make them any less disconcerting. I'd never ridden a horse before. Didn't you need lessons for that?

The man, who I assumed was the stablemaster, walked the white horse forward and handed me the reins. I awkwardly reached my hand out to pet the creature's nose. It jerked its head up, and I flinched.

Not too keen on me either, are you, beastie?

Damian rested his hand on the horse's forehead, slowly stroking it. The creature lifted its head a few times, appearing to enjoy the scratch.

The stablemaster returned with a wooden set of three stairs. He gave me a sharp look as he placed them beside the horse. I took the stairs slowly, begrudgingly taking Damian's hand for extra balance. "What's her name?"

"Nour," the man said as he placed my left foot in the stirrup.

"Light." That's what the name meant in Arabic. "Fitting."

I stroked the horse's ivory mane.

The stablemaster looked up at me, seeming slightly annoyed, and he tapped on my right shin. "Now the other leg."

I stared blankly. *And do what with it?*

Damian gave a low laugh. "Shift your weight into your left foot and swing your right leg over the saddle."

I did as I was told, slightly less gracefully than I would've liked. Somehow, I ended up in the saddle.

The man adjusted the stirrups, and Damian handed me the reins. "Hold them loosely. If you want to go left, gently tug left. Right, give a tug on the right. If you need to stop, pull back. But gently. She's well-trained and will know with just the slightest twitch of the hand."

"That's it?"

"Yes. Pretty much."

A wave of excitement washed over me. I was riding a horse, and it wasn't so bad!

The stablemaster brought the pitch-black horse next to mine—the contrast was startling.

"Layla," the man said, looking up at me.

"Beautiful." And also fitting since Layla meant night.

Damian loaded our supplies into the saddlebag, then patted the black horse and slid his hand to the knobby thing on the top of the saddle. I was sure there was a name for it, but it escaped me. He raised his foot to the stirrup, and in a flash was up in the saddle.

Holy moly. I was such an amateur.

He turned to me. "Ready to ride?"

"Do I have a choice?"

The stablemaster eyed me dubiously and handed Damian a business card. "If you have problems, call me. If you get lost, just turn back toward the city and give the horses their head. They'll find their way home—the horses know what they're doing."

The implication being that I didn't.

Fair enough.

Damian shifted forward ever so slightly, and Layla trotted out of the stable.

I sat and waited, but Nour didn't budge. I glanced down at the stablemaster who stared back at me blankly. He lifted his arm and gently slapped the horse's rump. She took off after Layla, and I lurched backward, terror streaking through me.

I was *so* not comfortable with this.

Leaning forward, I clutched the horse's neck, trying to steady myself. Every step rocked me. I was bouncing off the creature's back like a bounce-back paddle ball. Up ahead, Damian had stopped Layla. Once we caught up, he resumed trotting alongside us.

"You can't ride her like that. Sit up," he said.

"I can't. You don't understa—nd." Each stride jolted my spine, yet Damian rode so fluidly beside me.

"It's all about the legs. Sit up and use your legs to cushion the bouncing. Trust me."

Fat chance.

I couldn't imagine letting go of the horse and trying to sit up. Every bounce threatened to throw me off. But if I didn't buck up now, we'd miss our chance at Helwan.

I mustered my courage and raised my back ever so slowly. Once upright, my body still bounced in the saddle. I felt bad for Nour—this couldn't have been comfortable for her—it sure as heck wasn't comfortable for me.

"That's it. Now use your legs," Damian said.

I pushed my feet into the stirrups and braced myself.

Slowly, the bouncing softened, and my movements seemed to fall in sync with Nour's.

Damian nodded. "There you go. You're a natural."

He was lying, as usual, but I did feel like I was getting the hang of things.

Damian and Layla took the lead and headed along the gravel road into the desert. "So, have you cracked our riddle yet?"

"Cracked? No. But I think I'm headed in the right direction."

"Tell me."

"So in our story, the *Tale of the Three Magicians and the Water Carrier*, a tomb robber finds a magic lamp and hides it in Helwan. That's what makes me believe the genie is hidden in the city."

"Makes sense."

"The tomb robber tells his wife a tale to lead her to the lamp's location. His story is like a riddle, where each part provides a clue."

Damian nodded. "So what are the clues?"

"The riddle is about three magicians crossing the desert. One is six hundred years old, the second is four hundred years old, and the third is three hundred years old. Those numbers are specific and have to be important for some reason."

"What do they mean?"

"Not sure yet. Anyway, after a windstorm, the caravan's water carrier—a young boy—finds a lamp with a genie. The genie says it will grant them two wishes. Since there are three magicians and two wishes, they start fighting. Amid the tussle, the water carrier grabs the lamp and makes a wish."

Damian danced Layla in a circle back to my side and grunted. "I like this kid. Opportunist. What did he wish for?"

"That no one in the city of Helwan would ever go thirsty again. As a result, a bunch of springs popped up and a branch of the Nile forked off by the city."

Layla gave a snort, and Damian raised an eyebrow. "Not very exciting. Was that all?"

I pursed my lips, and Damian's gaze followed. "The water carrier was heroic because he wished for something for the people of his city. In his limited worldview, the most valuable thing he could conceive of was water."

He stole his eyes from my lips. "Sounds like he accidently wished himself out of a job."

I narrowed my eyes, annoyance flickering at the back of my mind. *How well did you use your wishes, Damian?*

I looked straight ahead as we continued down the path, doing my best to ignore his comments. "The story continues. The water carrier runs off with the lamp, abandoning the three magicians in the desert. They use their spells to see where the water carrier hides the lamp, and each has a different vision. One sees a hill like the back of a crocodile, one sees a formation like the head of a jackal, and one sees a hill like the hump of a camel. They can't agree on which way to go, and all die searching in the desert."

GPS in one hand, Damian pulled ahead. He gently tugged the reins left and maneuvered Nour off the gravel road and proceeded along a narrow dirt path down an earthen hill. "Those sound like some of the same landmarks mentioned in Yasmina's directions to the city. Maybe the lamp isn't in the city. We could just follow the landmarks to its location."

"I thought so at first too, but the text explicitly states that the lamp was hidden *within* the city. The fact that the magicians died searching the desert for it is another clue that it's actually in Helwan, not the desert. All we have to do is figure out what clue the magicians represent."

I dug my heels into Nour's side as a matter of emphasis, hoping she might be convinced to catch up to Layla, who kept inching ahead. Instead, she broke into a full gallop.

I screamed as we darted past Damian.

He cursed and kicked Layla into high gear in our wake.

Nour thundered into the desert. My breath caught in my throat and, as I gripped the reins in panic, her stride proved easier to match. My legs and hips followed her movement, and after a few hundred yards, my trepidation melted away and elation flooded my senses. The wind tugged my scarf off my head, and I felt *alive*. It was almost like flying.

I grinned as we galloped through the desert. Layla began to close the distance between us but Nour must have sensed her approach, because she lunged forward even faster.

The race was on.

12

Damian

Nour surged ahead as Layla and I closed the distance. Neve's white linen scarf trailed behind, whipping in the wind with her wild hair. She gripped the horse with her thighs, hips rocking as they galloped through the sand. The rhythmic movement transfixed my eyes like some kind of fae glamor, and my hands tightened on the reins.

Layla and I caught up, and I tore my gaze from Neve, scanning the escarpment that rose out of the dusty air ahead. We had traveled only a mile, and already the haze had completely enveloped the stable and buildings behind us.

We followed the limestone track that peeked out of the sand on our left, a geologic formation that ran perpendicular to the rocky hills which extended north to south. I squinted in the bright sun, trying to discern the outline of the escarpment and any sign of the gazelle's horns.

There.

It was subtle, but as we neared a V-shaped cut in the ridge appeared. It looked exactly like the sketch on Yasmina's instructions.

I gently pulled back on the reins, and Layla slowed. She didn't seem winded, but I wanted to give her a rest. Nour followed suit.

I brought Layla up alongside Nour and Neve. "Not bad."

Neve beamed with joy and patted Nour's neck. "That was amazing."

"The gazelle's horns." I pointed at the notch in the escarpment, somehow more visible.

The sun was almost directly overhead. Neve shielded her eyes from the glare and scanned the horizon. "Just as Yasmina said." She pivoted to the south. "The rhino must be in those hills over there, but I don't see it yet."

"We'll keep following the escarpment north and hope the formation reveals itself soon." I glanced at my watch—we had just over an hour until noon.

A slight breeze picked up and a dust devil danced across the sand.

The hairs on the back of my neck stood on end, and

my muscles tensed. Something was wrong. An unfamiliar presence. Something—or *someone*—was here. I
craned my neck around, checking the desert behind us.
Nothing but the tracks of the horses.

"Do you feel that?" Neve stared at me with wide eyes.

"Like we're being watched?"

"Exactly."

Layla raised her head and whinnied. She sensed it,
too. I nudged her with my heels, and she started into a
trot. "Not sure what it is, but I don't like it."

"The caliph's spies? Maybe they followed us."

"If they did, they're masters at concealment." I
scoured the rolling sands. There was nothing but wide-
open desert, nowhere to hide.

"Could it be Helwan's signature?"

"Maybe." That was certainly possible. Helwan was
concealed by magic. In such a barren landscape, its
signature would be hard to miss. But this didn't feel like
a signature. More like we were being watched.

Stalked.

Something moved in my peripheral vision. A spot in
the sand just beyond the limestone track shifted, and a
hole opened in the desert. As sand poured down into
the pit, adrenaline flooded my veins.

There was a rumble as sand exploded from the hole
—and something else—a glistening black monstrosity
that charged Neve and Nour.

As I fought to control Layla's panic, Nour brayed and

reared up, kicking her front legs toward the heavens. Neve screamed and tumbled backwards out of the saddle, her foot nearly catching in the stirrup. She landed on her back but managed to roll to the side before being trampled by hooves.

I leapt from Layla and landed lightly on my feet. The horse whinnied and took off down the path we had just traveled, with Nour following close behind.

The massive creature loomed over Neve. Black armored plates covered its body. The monster bared its two large pincers and arched its long, segmented tail over its back.

A giant scorpion.

It lashed its barbed tail forward with blinding speed. Neve shot back on a jet of air just in time, tumbling to the ground only twenty paces away. She scrambled to her feet as the monster charged, pincers snapping.

I pulled a black, smoking spear from the ether and threw it, but the scorpion reared up and the weapon grazed off its exoskeleton. Neve dove to the side and shot a burst of wind that pushed the creature back ten feet.

I charged forward and summoned my dark blade, a sinister weapon that I had forged in ages past. I had infused both the sword and my spear with my fallen angel magic. They fueled my rage when drawn. I channeled that fury as I deflected the scorpion's powerful claw and drove the blade between the plates of its armor.

The scorpion spun, whipping its tail back and forth, drops of venom hanging from its eager stinger.

I leapt sideways, and the stinger crashed into the sand. My sword glinted as I raised it high, gripping the hilt with both hands. The air thrummed with magic as I brought the sword down in a swift strike. It lodged deeply into the exoskeleton but did not pull free.

"Watch out!" Neve cried.

Pain wracked my body as the scorpion slammed its pincer into my chest, sending me tumbling across the sand and rock.

I gasped for air as I stood and turned to face my opponent. My chest ached where the wound healed— one of the few abilities that wasn't stripped away when I fell.

This is the fight I've been needing.

I called on my dark magic and held out my hand, feeling its heartbeat.

The monster shuddered.

Then it shook off my magic and charged.

Neve

The scorpion skittered forward as Damian stood his ground, hand outstretched, pouring his dark magic into the horrible creature.

No time for that.

I slammed a burst of wind into its side, sending the creature skidding backward. I tried to pin it down with a spinning dust storm, but the scorpion staggered forward one leg at a time.

It wasn't enough. I needed to be able to do more than knock it around.

I snatched a sharp rock from the escarpment and fired it like a bullet with a blast of wind. The rock cracked into the beast but didn't break through the carapace. It ignored my attack and lashed its tail at Damian.

I grabbed the largest slab of rock I could raise and catapulted it at the scorpion. It hammered into the beast with a loud crunch. The scorpion staggered back, dragging a broken leg and suddenly very aware of my presence, and very mad.

I'm gonna need a bigger rock.

I raced toward a large chunk of limestone as the scorpion charged after me. I called the wind and levitated the massive rock thirty feet into the sky, then slammed it down on the scorpion's back with a sickening crunch. The rock rolled to the side, and a sticky substance began leaking from the creature's wound.

With a screech, the monster staggered to its feet, unsteady and pissed off.

Uh oh.

As it lurched forward, Damian's spear shot past my head and sunk deep into one of monster's eyes. It hissed and reared back. He flew forward, dodged its flailing claws and tail, and drove his sword deep through the other eye.

The scorpion's legs and pincers spasmed and then fell still.

My heartbeat thundered in my ears, and my temples throbbed.

Damian braced his leg on the scorpion's carapace and pulled his sword from its eye. A yellow, sticky substance dripped from the long black weapon.

I slowed my ragged breathing. "Impressive."

"Thanks." Damian climbed off the scorpion and cleaned the blade in the sand.

"I meant the scorpion. Impressive size. I've never seen anything like it. But you, too. You did great." Damian shot me a piercing look, and I grinned. "What about the horses? Do you think they'll be okay?"

"They'll be fine. They're probably already back at the stable eating alfalfa. Unfortunately, they also took most of our supplies. The saddlebag had food and water. I have a little in my pack, and we should be able to buy provisions in the city, but we don't want to spend another day out here."

Well, shit.

Despite the bad news, I smiled at the thought of

Nour having a munch—even if I wasn't going to get one anytime soon. I had really enjoyed our ride.

Though I sure as heck hadn't enjoyed the fall.

My entire body ached. I took a few short breaths, trying to figure out if I had broken any ribs. Breathing was okay, but damn I was sore.

I probably didn't have a concussion.

Damian pulled out his spear from one of the scorpion's other eyes and tapped it on the limestone boulder. "Quick thinking with the rocks."

"I think I have a future in shotput. Let's make sure there's lots of stones around next time we have a battle."

I took a deep breath as the euphoria of battle evaporated. What *time* was it? Our mode of transportation had just galloped off, and I had no idea how far we were from the city or how much time we had left.

I reached into my fanny pack for my phone, but all I felt was a wad of cash and my lip balm. I scanned the sand but saw nothing. It must have fallen out during the ride.

Double shit. So much for calling in the cavalry.

Not that there was any reception out here...or anyone could find us.

Looking up, I shielded my eyes which teared up from the bright sky. *Damn it.* The sun was well overhead, which meant we didn't have much time.

Damian checked his watch. "Let's get a move on. We have forty-five minutes until noon."

That was something at least.

The sun's heat bore down as we trudged down the limestone track. Damian's legs were longer than mine, and I had to speed walk over the uneven ground to keep up. My skull throbbed, and beads of sweat rolled off my brow, stinging my eyes. Why did it have to be so hot? I readjusted the linen scarf so it shaded my head.

After nearly half an hour of misery, Damian tilted his head toward the hills in the south. "There it is. The rhino."

Three curved ridges rose from the broken line of hills. "Thank fates."

"Now we head toward it, right?" Damian pulled a water bottle from his bag and tossed it to me.

I fumbled the bottle but caught it before it hit the sand. "That's what the instructions said."

I gulped down a few sips of mercifully cool—well, mercifully tepid—water, and we headed south toward the hill with the rhino profile. Marching through the sand made my calf muscles burn. Damian didn't seem bothered by the trek and stopped every few minutes to let me catch up. He kept glancing at his watch.

I'm going as fast as I can.

"How about we fly?" I gasped.

"Maybe if we were in the hills, but it's still pretty flat here. We'd be easy to spot." He tapped the watch face. "Anyway, we're close. It's eleven-fifty-five. Any minute now."

"Where is it?" I scanned the desert, but it was empty save for the hills and sand. I picked up the pace and shuffled ahead of Damian but worry rolled over me like a thundercloud as no sign of the city appeared.

The dull throbbing that had begun behind my right eye had spread across my forehead. My pants clung to my clammy skin, and I was beginning to feel nauseous.

"Stupid heat," I muttered.

Damian grabbed my arm. "Wait a second. Hold on."

I glanced ahead, but nothing had changed. Empty desert. No magical city. I sighed audibly. "What do you see?"

"There. At nine o'clock."

My eyes found nine o'clock, but there was nothing but sand. "Are you sure you aren't imagining things? Heat stroke is a real thing, you know. It can make you hallucinate."

He looked at me with concern. "Speaking of which. You're looking pretty flushed."

He raised the back of his hand to my forehead, gently touching it. I drew in a sharp breath as his magic brushed against me. Although it was usually warm, this time it was like diving into ocean waves on a scorching day. A shiver ran down my spine.

Damian's brow furrowed. "You're burning up."

I unscrewed the lid off the half-full bottle and chugged the rest of it. "What I need is a cocktail and about a dozen Advil."

"Well, you're in luck." He reached around into his backpack.

My heart leapt. "You mean you brought booze?"

He cocked an eyebrow and handed me three red pills. "Only drugs, I'm afraid."

"Fine by me." I tossed the pills in my mouth and swallowed them. "You owe me a drink once we find this damned city and get inside, though. For saving your life back there with the scorpion."

"Deal." Damian squinted into the distance, then pointed to the same spot as before. "There it is again."

I squinted, ignoring the sledgehammer pounding against my skull. I didn't see jack. Was the city really out there, or was he going insane?

"There's nothi—" I gasped. The air danced like a mirage, and a silver flash appeared a quarter mile out. "Wait a sec. I saw something!"

With a cascade of light, the outlines of a city coalesced in the shimmering air, and golden ramparts materialized. The shockwave of the city's magical signature hit like a wave of hot, electrified air, leaving a residual scent of spice and tangerines.

"Holy fates!" I stumbled backward, my skin tingling from the blast of energy.

We dashed, helter-skelter, across the sand, unsure how long the mirage would remain.

Within a minute, the whole city had taken shape, surrounded by a massive wall. A large double-doored gate pierced the western rampart, and the outline of a smaller doorway appeared along the north wall—the door Yasmina had indicated we take. The upper floors of dozens of narrow buildings peaked over the city walls, reminiscent of apartment buildings.

"I suppose there's no chance we can just fly in?" I said, my feet sinking through the sand, which poured into my shoes.

"Don't get your hopes up. I think it's covered with a magical dome, just like the djinn's palace."

The air above the city gyrated, and the faint outlines of a translucent arched dome glinted in the sunlight. I wondered if birds ever flew into it. Not that there were any birds out here in the desert. Just giant scorpions.

The desert was eerily quiet for having a city smack dab in the middle of it. I couldn't complain—the less people out and about meant the less chance we'd be noticed and questioned. Though, I couldn't quite shake the unnerving feeling that we were being watched. Was it really Helwan's magical signature? Or had the caliph's spies followed us somehow?

I couldn't see any watchers on the wall. *That* was suspicious. Someone had to be up there, scanning the desert. Unfortunately, our approach would be completely exposed.

"We should run for the base of the wall. Get out of sight as fast as possible." Damian read my mind.

My head throbbed as we raced forward through the

shifting sand, and my lungs were burning by the time we stumbled to a halt beside the door.

"Holy fates, we made it." I collapsed, with my back against the wall, calves cramping and knees aching. "I thought it was going to fade away before we got here."

Damian scrutinized the iron door—it was about five feet tall and had no doorknob. "We're not in yet."

Magic seeped off the city, and the low vibrations of it tickled my skin. I frowned and heaved myself off the wall, massaging my calf muscles. "How do we get in?"

Unfortunately, Yasmina's instructions hadn't mentioned that detail.

"Good question." Damian felt around the seams of the door and gave a push, but it didn't budge. "Must be sealed with magic."

"Can you unlock it?" I'd seen Damian break the locks on several magically sealed doors in Cappadocia and the djinn's palace in the Realm of Air. Heck, I'd even accused him of breaking into the Order's Vault.

"Maybe." His fingers traced a series of emblazoned runes in the air, as if he were carving them from magic. The air distorted and crackled with energy. Before he'd finished, a *whoosh* of air blew into my face, and Damian disappeared through the threshold.

"Damian?"

He was gone.

"Aw, come on! Are you serious?"

13

Neve

I did *not* need this crap today.

I pushed on the door where Damian had just disappeared, hoping it would suck me through, but nothing happened. Freaking door.

This was the only entrance on this side of the city's wall—the one Yasmina had indicated we should enter—and I couldn't just slip through the front gate without being seen.

Think, think, think.

I traced my hands along the seam of the door, searching for a secret symbol or any indication of how it opened. Nothing. My irritation morphed into anger as the minutes ticked by, heating my blood. How long until the city vanished back into the desert? I had no idea.

I examined the threshold again. I'd seen Damian weave runes to break locks a few times. Strangely, once I thought about it, it seemed like he hadn't yet finished his spell when he disappeared. *Maybe* he'd done something that triggered the door.

"What the heck. It's not like I have any better options," I murmured, positioning myself in front of the door just as Damian had before he'd vanished. Recreating his movements, I waved my hand through the air, waiting for something to happen.

Only nothing did.

Rage welled up in my chest, threatening to spill over. It vibrated through me, too intense to be normal. It was an odd sensation, and one I wasn't familiar with.

I rapped the solid iron door. "Let me in, damn it all!"

Pain shot through my wrist—and then a surge of energy erupted out of my palm, blasting into the barrier. A detonation of energy bounced right back at me, and the electric surge enveloped my body, snapping me forward with such intensity I nearly blacked out.

Seconds later, the force dissipated, and I crashed onto a hard-packed surface. Pain exploded in my knees, and my palms stung.

Blinking twice, I sat up and dusted the dirt from my hands, inspecting my surroundings. A fat gray rat rifled through a heap of trash down an alley ahead. I knelt on a dirt-paved street that ran along the inside of the city's wall, the iron door at my back. White-washed buildings towered over me—oddly like the historic tower houses in Yemen.

Damian slipped out from behind the corner of a building and lifted me to my feet. "Time to go."

I grabbed a fistful of his shirt. "What's going on? You left me out there!"

"A guard spotted me as soon as I came through. I knocked him out and hid the body. But we should go before more circle around. Anyway, I knew you would figure it out."

We ducked into a nearby alley and took off at a jog.

"I didn't figure it out. I just got sucked through."

"The portal is triggered by magic—so only Magica can enter. You must have used your magic on it to get through."

"Right." I guess I *had* unleashed my magic when I banged on the door. But I hadn't called on the wind, so what power did I use? An uneasy feeling knotted my stomach as I recalled the rage I'd felt back there. Strangely, the overwhelming anger and irritation were completely gone now—like they'd erupted from my body right before I was sucked through the door. *Freaky.*

A shout from behind cleared my mind, and I spun around. Two guards rounded the corner, and one pointed at us with a gloved hand. I did a double take. The guards wore long, leather-armor coats that reached their knees and white scarves draped over their heads. Sheathed swords hung from their waists, and they gripped long halberds.

Seriously medieval.

"Like I said, time to go." Damian grabbed my hand and towed me forward.

We wheeled around a corner as the trailing shouts grew louder. I glanced up. Clotheslines with wet laundry stretched between the buildings. There was no way Damian could fly through those with his wings.

I tried a wooden door on my left leading into a boarded-up apartment building that rose at least seven stories. It was locked. Damian slammed his shoulder into the door, and it opened with a crack. We bolted in, and I paused at the door. Our pursuers hadn't appeared around the corner yet.

Damian grabbed my shoulder with a tug. "What are you doing?"

"Leading them off our path." Raising my palm, I shot a surge of wind at the door of the building across the way. It burst open, knocking over a wooden crate that had been stacked beside the entrance.

"Clever thinking." Damian closed our door and sealed it with magic.

"It worked in the Realm of Air, so hey, why not try it

again?" I bolted toward the stairwell behind us, taking the stairs two at a time.

Shouts echoed from the street, and I cursed under my breath. We'd only just arrived and were already being pursued by the city's guards—and probably the caliph's spies as well. How were we going to scour the city for the genie with them on our heels?

I reached the final landing and slowed. *Eight floors.* The stairs continued up to a door. "The roof?"

"Let's find out." Damian unlocked it with a burst of magic and shoved it open.

I followed him out onto the roof. Like most of the surrounding buildings, it was covered in antennae and satellite dishes. The protective magical barrier that covered the city flickered in the sky overhead.

Crouching down, I peered over the three-foot wall that enclosed the roof top, scanning the street below. One of the guards stood outside the doorway that I'd blasted opened as a decoy.

"It worked!" I whispered to Damian.

The wind carried their heated voices from below. From what I could discern, the other guard was knocking on the apartment doors inside the building, causing somewhat of a commotion.

I leaned my back against the concrete. "So now what?"

Damian had crossed to the opposite side of the building, apparently calculating our next step. He had a natural talent for evading the authorities. "We put some space between us and them. Find some new clothes in the process."

"New clothes?" I looked down at my dusty knees and sweaty shirt. "Ah, right. To fit in." It was like a cosplay event here, and we were definitely out of character.

Damian came over. I clasped his outstretched hand, and he pulled me to my feet. "It looks like there's a market street a few blocks down. Once we're safely disguised, we can begin our search for the genie."

"Good plan. And find a bite to eat. I am starving."

A smile ghosted the corners of his mouth, and he dug into his back pocket. My ears pricked up at the crinkle of a wrapper. "This can tide you over."

He pulled out a Snickers bar, and my heart jumped. "Sweet fates. You are a god, Damian Malek."

I took the Snickers and peeled back the wrapper, sinking my teeth into the gooey crunchy delight. My mouth full, I raised the bar toward him, offering him a bite. "You're not you when you're hungry."

I considered my earlier outburst at the door. Did I have magical hangry powers? That'd be something.

He shook his head. "No, thanks. I already ate mine while I was waiting for you to get through the portal."

"Wait a second," I said between mouthfuls. "I thought you were being chased by guards."

"Multitasking." He turned and walked to the other side of the rooftop.

Shoving the final bite of the Snickers into my mouth, I jammed the wrapper in my pocket and followed. "Where did you get candy bars?"

Surely, he hadn't had them in his pocket this whole time?

"Magic." He stepped onto the concrete roof edge and looked down at me with a half-smile and an outstretched hand. "Ready to jump?"

I wiped my sticky hand on my pants and took his, pulling myself up onto the narrow ledge. This side of the building was clear of clotheslines, and the ground beckoned from far below. I stepped out into the air and summoned my magic, dropping a foot before my energy spread around me and slowed my descent.

Damian's magnificent wings unfurled, and he stepped off the ledge, descending gracefully. Boots on the ground, his wings tucked behind him before disappearing. I'd never get used to that.

We followed the faint murmur of the hustle and bustle of the marketplace that echoed down the street. The tall residential towers were replaced by short, squat structures. Canvas awnings of all colors sheltered the open storefronts, and Magica of all kinds filled the street. A woman with snake eyes pushed past me, and a man who smelled like a shifter offered me a raisin to taste.

I shook my head. We were drawing too much attention as it was.

We paused at a shop with several dresses hanging from a rack. *Bingo.*

An attractive young woman with light brown eyes and a dark braid emerged and greeted us, switching quickly from an unfamiliar dialect of Arabic to English. She wore a light gray fitted dress with a red scarf draped over her shoulders.

Her gaze fell to my fanny pack and then my shirt, and I caught a flicker of disdain before her eyes met mine with the broadest Pan-Am smile I'd ever seen.

"Welcome! Are you looking for a new...dress?" she said, her voice smooth and seductive.

I ignored her slight of the eye and beamed back at her. "Yes."

"Please, come in." She gestured with her arm and then inspected Damian with noted interest.

I rolled my eyes. "He's with me."

Her gaze flicked to mine and darted down to my clothes again. I knew immediately what she was implying—*you're* with *him?*

Fair enough.

"Hmm," she said with shocked emphasis.

This woman rubbed me in all the wrong ways. I wanted to ditch the place, but we were on the clock, and I needed some new clothes fast. Plus, I didn't hate the selection.

Damian scanned the array of women's clothing and underwear, seemingly unphased by the woman's attentions. "You go ahead. I'll find some clothes for myself. I'll be back in ten."

"Okay. See you shortly."

The woman watched Damian's back as he left. Was she biting her lower lip?

I crossed my arms. "Are you going to help me find a dress or not? Trust me. He's not *that* interesting."

Lie.

My words shattered her daydream. She whipped her head around, and a shocked expression cut her perfect little face.

Good.

Like a chameleon, she painted her expression with another fake smile. "Of course. I have just the number."

Ten minutes later, I stepped out of the tiny dressing room wearing a deep blue dress that cinched my waist and fell to my feet. The fabric appeared to be loosely woven Helwani cloth. Light and flowy, it was much more comfortable and airier than my pants. I inspected myself in the mirror on the wall and forced back a smile. The deep V-front plunged toward my belly button and was trimmed with a shear lace inset that matched the cuffs on the sleeves.

I'd expected conservative clothing in the ancient city, but the dress was more revealing than I'd anticipated.

The woman appeared behind me holding a long blue headscarf cut from the same fabric. She arranged it over my head, allowing the front portion of my hair to peak out, and draping the bottom half over my shoulder. She examined me in the mirror.

"Beautiful." She broke into a smile—genuine this time—and I couldn't help but feel a bit contrite for my sharp thoughts earlier.

Realization crossed her face, and her delicate eyebrows shot upward. "I almost forgot." She disappeared into a back room and returned carrying a sheer black rectangle of fabric with satin loops at the corners.

Draping the fabric over my face so that it covered my nose and chin, she secured the satin loops over my ears and stepped back. "Now, you are perfect."

I looked like Jasmine from Aladdin—but hotter. It would do perfectly.

The woman crossed her arms and cocked her head with a slight grin. "Your man is waiting for you."

Damian. Shit. Time had slipped away.

I grabbed my fanny pack and hurried to the front, my gaze falling to the street and Damian...

He wore a leather breastplate that molded to his chest over a tan tunic that fell to his hips. His dark pants were tucked into a pair of leather boots that covered his shins. The black cloak that hung over his shoulders completed the look—a medieval assassin. A *hot* medieval assassin.

Is this why people were so into cosplay?

I realized that I was staring and smiled. In all fairness, he was staring too, so I didn't feel too silly.

"Okay, love birds. Time to pay up and get a room." The lady leaned on the door of her shop with a bored expression.

Love birds? Embarrassment washed over me, and I broke my gaze from Damian. "Right. How much do I owe you for all of this?"

She raised her lips in a sly grin. "Six and a half gold dinars, or considering that you are not... local, one ounce."

Gold dinars? Were those even still in use today? I turned and shot a questioning look at Damian and did a few mental calculations. *Holy shit.* That was like two thousand bucks. For a dress. My heart broke. *My beautiful dress.*

Damian pulled out a small leather purse and tossed it to the shopkeeper. "That should cover it, plus some. For your time *and* your discretion."

He must've had time to visit a money changer while I was swooning over this dress. The woman caught the purse and peered inside. Surprise flashed in her eyes, and she looked up. "Of course. Your secret is safe with me."

Her gaze fell on me, and she nodded ever so slightly before turning and disappearing into the shop.

I glided down the steps and met Damian on the street.

"You look—" His voice came out rough, and he cleared his throat.

"Like a porn princess?"

Fates. Did I really just blurt that out? What the freaking heck had come over me?

His face froze in shock. "Well, that wasn't what immediately came to mind. But now that you say it—" he tilted his head and looked me up and down. "Yeah, I can picture it."

I liked the way his eyes lingered on my hips.

A light tug on my fanny pack derailed my train of thought. Whipping my head around, I caught sight of an urchin darting through the crowd. My hand slipped into my bag where I'd stashed my money—it was *gone.*

"Hey! Stop!" I raced after the little beastie. He took one look at me and turned into a blur, darting forward at incredible speed. He ducked beneath legs, dove under a cart of produce, and ran straight up the wall above a merchant.

Damian flashed by me. Fates, he was just as fast as the kid. Faster.

With a flying leap, the urchin cannonballed into an alley. Unable to catch up, I shot a precise bolt of wind at his back. The boy cartwheeled through the air and landed in a pile of trash.

Damian was on him in a second, and he grabbed the boy by the scruff of his shirt.

Terror shot through me as I recalled what had happened to the last thief who'd stolen from me on Tayir—the dark magic that flowed through Damian as he squeezed the life out of the cutpurse who had robbed me.

"Stop!" I flew forward.

Still holding the young boy aloft by his shirt, Damian turned his head to me. Wait—was he smiling?

He set the boy down and dusted off the stinking brown cabbage that coated the urchin's clothes. He said something to the boy that I only caught the last half of.

"—is not how you do it. There will always be someone faster or stronger. You have to cause a distraction first, and then you go in for the prize. You must be quick and cunning. The lady must not suspect anything."

I stopped in front of them, hands planted on my hips. "Wait. Are you giving this little cutpurse advice on how to thieve?"

The young boy stared up at me with watery brown eyes, and a flare of guilt tugged at my heart. He was no more than twelve years old, and his clothes were dirty and tattered. Poor thing.

Damian clapped the urchin on the back and pulled something flashy out of his pocket—a couple gold coins. The boy's eyes widened and focused on the money. "This is yours." Damian dropped it in the boy's grimy hand. "There's more if you can help us."

The boy inspected the coin, and a wide smile spread across his face. "Anything you need, mister. I am at your service." He turned to me and bowed. "And yours, madame."

Impressive. The cutpurse spoke English *and* was polite. With the proper incentive, this might work nicely. I sure as heck wasn't going to let my bag out of my sight.

Damian patted the boy on his back. "Come on. Let's go then. We need some food and a safe place to sleep."

14

Damian

The sun crept toward the horizon, and the heat of the day had finally abated. Khalil, the boy, led us to a sheltered rooftop where we could rest out of the way of prying eyes. He was exceptionally useful and knew the city well. I had sent him out for supplies to replace some of the equipment we had lost.

With time ticking away, I would have liked to press on through the night, but we were both drained after the desert trek, and would stand out in the city once the crowds thinned. We needed rest, a proper meal, and a solid plan for searching Helwan.

Thankfully, Khalil brought us koshari for dinner, an

aromatic dish of rice, lentils, and chickpeas covered in fried onions and tomato sauce.

He'd also managed to wrangle a bottle of arak—a cloudy liquor made from grape and aniseed. I'd given him an extra coin for securing that.

I leaned back and took a sip of the arak—a little liquid morphine. It had been a good day. The fight with the scorpion had revitalized me in a way that food and drink could not. I gave a contented sigh, relishing the quickly fading aches and pains of battle.

Neve scooped a spoonful of koshari into her mouth, and her eyes met mine. Her lips rose in a half smile, dislodging something in my chest, and I sucked in a sharp breath.

This woman. She got under my skin. Her magic. Her scent. Her eyes. I had never let that happen before. I shifted my gaze out over the darkening cityscape. The sinking sun silhouetted the high buildings and mosque minarets.

"It's not the worst place to be stuck for a night. Nice view. Good company. And the drink I promised." I handed Neve the arak, and she smiled.

"True on all accounts." Neve took a swig of arak and scrunched her face into a ball. "Whoa. That's strong!"

"Delicious, right?" Khalil grinned up at Neve and took the bottle. "Made right here in the city. Helwan's finest."

I found that hard to believe but nodded anyway. This kid was learning all the tricks fast.

Neve grabbed for the booze bottle. "You're too young to be drinking that."

The boy chuckled and puffed out his chest. "The boys in Helwan are weened early. By three months of age, we are already drinking arak—milk of the star." Khalil raised his bicep, pushing back his dirty sleeve. "It's what makes us strong and virulent."

Neve stared at Khalil in shock, then suppressed a laugh. "I think you mean virile. But yes, I see. Perhaps that is where you also get your crafty skills."

She reached into her purse and pulled out her transcription of the tale from the *Arabian Nights*. "We'd better get to solving this riddle, before the virulence of the arak takes hold."

She shot me a wicked grin that sent fire along my skin. Perhaps the arak had already taken hold. I grabbed the bottle and took another swig, doubling down. "Okay. Let's have at it."

Neve read her transcription of the story aloud, while Khalil leaned back on the roof, his feet crossed and his hands under his head. When she finished, he said, "That is an interesting story. I've never heard it before, but I know those places."

"What do you mean?" Neve said, lowering the transcript so she could see him. "Where are they?"

Khalil sat up and leapt to his feet, pointing east.

"That is the camel. You can see it rising behind the minaret." Neve crouched down beside Khalil, her face close to his, following his finger toward the soaring spire. I followed their gaze.

The mountains of the eastern desert rose and then dipped, creating the silhouette of a camel's hump.

"That's it!" Neve murmured.

I rose and joined them. "Where are the others?"

He pointed south. "You can see the ears of the jackal."

They were the horns of the rhinoceros we had used as a landmark earlier. From Helwan, it looked like the head of a jackal.

"And the crocodile?" I asked.

He pointed north. "That ridge there, behind the mosque."

"Holy mother of fates." Neve turned to Khalil, her face pale from either shock or the arak. She grabbed him and kissed him on the cheek. "You are a genius, Khalil!"

"I am?" He realized that Neve was serious, and his eyes gleamed. "I am!"

She stood and let her gaze sweep the city. "Khalil. Can you tell me anything about those large mosques?"

"Of course, I know everything about the city!" He pointed to three buildings. "There in the north is the Mosque of Marwan, built by the founder of Helwan in the first century after the Prophet, peace be upon him.

The second is the Golden Mosque, built when the Tulunids ruled Egypt. The third is the Green Mosque, built by Caliph Nasiri Din to rival al-Azhar in Cairo."

Neve grabbed my arm. "Holy fates. I understand the riddle."

Neve

Damian read the transcribed text for a third time while I traced the outlines of his sharp features—mentally taking note of the sweep of his cheekbones.

I needed to stop.

He was hiding something I couldn't put my finger on. The dark shadows that had swept over him last night in the hotel flashed in my mind, sending shivers skittering up my spine. Truth be told, Damian was dangerous, and I didn't know much of anything about him. I sighed and stretched my legs.

Khalil had left to scrounge up some bedding for the night—apparently, we were sleeping on the roof.

The setting sun cast a brilliant orange hue over the city as it descended into the desert. I breathed in Damian's heady scent, catching the fresh notes of juniper and the sea...and that infuriating sensation that I couldn't quite make out. It was almost as if he was masking it. But why?

I'd only known a few people who kept their magical signatures under such a tight lock. It was a requirement for Magica who lived in places like Guild City, which was hidden smack dab in the middle of human London. Luckily, Magic Side didn't require its inhabitants to mask their signatures, which made it even more odd that Damian would be hiding one of his.

He turned to me. "What do you think this all means?"

He was referring to the Arabian tale in his hand, of course.

Excitement sparked beneath my skin as the thrill of the hunt overtook me. "I am certain that each of the magicians in the story represents one of the mosques. By the thirteenth century, when our story was written, the Mosque of Marwan would have been roughly six hundred years old, the Golden Mosque would have been four hundred years old, and the Green mosque three hundred years. The dates aren't exact, but I'm certain that's what the numbers in the story mean."

"Do you think the genie is hidden in one of the mosques?"

"No. All the magicians died without finding the lamp. But we should visit one of the mosques first thing tomorrow. Maybe getting a view from high up on the minarets will give us another clue."

Damian rose to his feet and stretched. "Brilliant work."

Color rushed to my face as the light faded from the sky, though anxiety consumed my joy just as quickly.

The thief might be here in the city at this exact moment. He probably wasn't watching the sunset and drinking arak. Guilt simmered beneath waves of exhaustion. What if he'd already cracked the riddle?

Stop jumping to conclusions.

Impatience clawed at me. I wanted to check out the mosques now, but at this hour we might draw attention, and we couldn't risk that. Tomorrow would have to be good enough.

I took a deep breath and let my shoulders relax a little. Fates, I was tired.

Damian took a seat beside me and passed the arak. "Well, here's to finding the genie tomorrow."

"Fingers crossed." I took a sip of the bitter anise liquor. Either it was growing on me, or I was getting tipsy, because it didn't taste so bad anymore.

I studied the man. Maybe he didn't seem so bad anymore.

Strong, powerful, and perhaps more relaxed than I had ever seen him. More alive. This was a man who loved danger and adventure—who had somehow become trapped in a world of steel and glass buildings.

Maybe there was an opening in his armor.

I passed the bottle back and started fishing, trying to

sound only half-interested. "So where did you find the djinn in the first place? It must have been one heck of a journey."

He turned his head to look toward the far horizon, but not before I caught a hint of a smile.

Bingo.

He stretched his shoulders and sighed. "It was quite the adventure. I'd heard faint whispers of its location somewhere along the ancient Silk Road, but I didn't know the lamp contained a djinn until I found it."

"In China?"

"Kazakhstan, actually. In a burial mound." He must have read the shock on my face because he continued, "There was no destruction involved. I left the mound undisturbed."

I doubt that.

"But you were looking for a genie? Not a djinn, specifically."

"Yes."

Time to press my luck. "Why?"

He stiffened.

I let the question quietly linger, desperate to know the answer. The silence stretched out between us, until he finally dropped his gaze from the horizon to the dusty rooftop around us. "You're fishing, Neve."

"I am. I need to know."

He shrugged. "I needed to fix something that I couldn't do on my own."

"You're evading. What did you wish for?"

He studied my expression and looked away. "For the Cubs to win the world series. I knew it wasn't going to be possible without some form of divine intervention."

His words hung in the air as shock rolled over me. Finally, the arak drove an incredulous laugh from my chest. "You did not."

He peeked out of the corner of his eye and let a disarming smile creep to the corner of his lips. "No. I didn't. The Cubs won it on their own. Though I don't know how they did it. I'm not ruling out magic."

His jokes were dry. And so rare. It sent a warm shiver of joy down my spine.

Unfortunately, he was intentionally stalling. Not wanting to reward him for lies—even amusing ones—I sent a disapproving stare his direction. "Come on. Tell me the truth."

After a long moment, he looked over and measured me with a piercing gaze, reading my expression, searching for reasons to trust.

The irony.

Finally, he sighed. "Alright, woman. You really want to know? I wished for freedom."

"For the djinn," I stated flatly.

He shook his head. "First for myself."

"I don't understand what you mean."

He gave a low growl that shocked me, as if even talking about this hurt him. "I spent my life compelled by a lust for power. I built an empire. Mastered magic. Took everything I could get my hands on. It didn't matter who I hurt. It consumed me. A drug. An addiction. I had no control."

Damian's dark energy burned around him, and rage flickered like fire in his eyes. Resentment coated every word that rolled off his tongue.

"I knew I had to put things right, but it was beyond my capacity alone. So, I tracked down a genie and wished to change the things that I'd done." The muscles in Damian's jaw tightened, and a grim smile ghosted his face. "But wishes can't change the past."

I sat speechless. The truth seemed to hurt more than any wound I'd seen him take.

"You'd think I would have thought of some backup wishes in case the first didn't work. But no. I hadn't even considered it. I just wanted to put an end to the guilt. But there was no end." He paused for a moment and stared down at his hands. Dark shadows masked his face. "So I wished to be free of my craving for power, hoping at least I could change my future."

"And did it work?" I whispered.

He turned to me, and I saw the weight of guilt on his shoulders. "Not quite how I'd imagined it. But it never is, is it?"

"So, what happened?" I felt like I was pulling teeth with each question. But I needed to know.

"Every wish takes as well as gives. I no longer feel the

same need for power, but I also lost a part of myself that day." He looked off into the distance. "Though I suppose it's good to be free of my compulsion, no matter the cost."

"And then you used your third wish to set the djinn free?"

His silence was an answer in and of itself.

Fates. I'd assumed Damian had tracked down the djinn for some nefarious purpose. Instead, he was just trying to change the horrors of his past and shake free of his demons. I couldn't blame him for that.

If only he'd told me this from the beginning.

But of course, that was not the kind of thing you could just admit to anyone.

Guilt pulled down his shoulders, and his eyes were filled with dark flames. But judging from the pain in his voice, it was clear he'd erected an unbreachable defensive barrier.

And I was just scratching the surface.

Damian

I took a sip of arak, focusing on the burn as it went down. Anything to get my mind off my past and the old demons that always lurked at the corners of my thoughts.

I'd never told anyone these things.

Was I mad? Sharing a part of my past with this woman who worked for the organization I'd spent decades trying to undermine. *Fool.* Telling the truth had burnt me last time.

Yet there was something about being open with Neve that was intoxicating, like the irresistible urge to lean out over a precipice.

Neve tugged at the cloth of her dress, unsure of what to say.

Could I blame her?

I had revealed I was a monster consumed by power. What could you say to that?

I hadn't even told her the worst. The things I could never reveal.

So we sat in silence as the sun dipped below the hills in the distance, and the call to prayer echoed off the buildings around us.

Finally, she stirred and cleared her throat. "I don't know what it feels like to crave power so badly you would wish it away. But I do know what it is like to feel powerless in the face of your own power and to hate the thing you are becoming."

The strength of her words caught me off guard. "Powerless? You're mastering your power well and quickly. Every battle, you discover something new. You're a natural."

"Not all of it. And I'm getting worried."

Setting my bottle down, I waited in silence.

She took a breath and continued, "Remember two nights ago when we found out the djinn was stolen, and Rhiannon and I came over to your house?"

How could I forget? That night she barged into my house, face flushed and as beautiful as ever, radiating fury and shooting off accusations. She hadn't backed down. Which I liked, even though it was a pain in the ass at the time.

I nodded and kept my mouth shut.

"Before we heard that the djinn was stolen, Rhia and I were at the Hideout having a drink. Several guys were there giving us a hard time. They wouldn't let up. And *believe* me, we tried hard to turn them off."

Anger streaked through me, and I tightened my fist reflexively. That was an occasion I was sorry to have missed.

"Rhia wished that the guys would clear off. And that sorta...unleashed my power."

"Unleashed how?"

"My emotions and power went haywire. I've never felt anything like it before. It was Kansas in there. Except I wasn't Dorothy. *I* was the tornado. Napkins, chairs—people—flying everywhere. The two guys who'd been bothering us were sucked out the front door in a whirlwind. Like it came just for them. It was horrible. I mean, they totally deserved it, but...I had no control."

My mind burned. Could Neve grant wishes? Was she transitioning to a full djinn? Was that even possible?

I locked eyes with her. "So, to be clear, you're telling me that your friend wished them away? And you granted it?"

She shook her head. "Yes—no. I didn't grant anything! I had no control. It was the worst feeling I have ever experienced. It was like the magic was wrenched from me, stolen, without my say, without my permission!"

I had no idea how to calm the fear I saw in her eyes. "It's bad, isn't it?" she asked. "Shit. I knew it was bad. I am so screwed."

"Not necessarily." I reached out to reassure her but stopped. I'd already gotten too close to her. Considering her powers and my past, I was playing with fire. "The wish must have triggered some innate part of you. You might not have known how to control it, but it's still your power."

"Do you think I'll become a monster like the djinn? The more I use my powers, the more my tattoo grows. It looks just like his. And my anger. Am I doomed to be like him?"

Possibly.

I shook my head. "No, Neve. You are not a monster, and you'll never be like him."

She leaned forward and ran her hands through her hair. "Hopefully."

I didn't know for sure, but genies—and djinn in particular—were divisive and vengeful beings. And power hungry. I fought back the thought of Neve having to face my own demons.

"You can't run from this, Neve. You must face it head on. In Cappadocia, you told me that you wanted more powers. Well, here you go. Wish granted. I can help you learn to control your power. I've had to learn new ones in my time. It's possible."

"When?"

The question hit me like a bullet, and I bit my tongue. *Idiot. This is what comes from talking.*

Her eyes pierced into my heart, waiting for the lie. I'd have to settle for a half-truth and hope that she didn't dig deeper.

I met her gaze. "When I fell."

Neve

Damian's words dropped like lead.

What powers had he been forced to learn after he fell?

I watched him closely, waiting for an answer. There was no fire or pain in his eyes. Just a look of finality, and I knew I wouldn't be getting any more information from him on *that* subject.

Fine. He could have his secrets, for a time. I had gotten more from him tonight than I dared hope. Even a sliver of hope itself. Telling Damian about my whirlwind in the Hideout had lifted a boulder off my shoulders.

"Do you really think you can help me master this?"

"Absolutely." Confidence shone in his eyes, and I shuddered in relief. That is what I needed to hear, whether it was a lie or not.

He shrugged. "We can even start tonight. I could try to wi—"

"No! Absolutely not. Never say *that* word around me. Never without my permission." My words shot out with fire before I even had a chance to think.

Damian's eyes widened. He set his jaw. "Understood."

"I didn't mean to snap. It's just that wishing is a big deal. I could be forced to do what you say."

"I understand. I apologize." His words were genuine, and I appreciated them.

The creaking of a metal door behind us startled me. I turned and caught sight of Khalil carrying a mountain of blankets and a couple of flower-print sleeping pads.

"Sorry. I didn't mean to interrupt you." His eyes darted between us, and a sheepish grin streaked across his face.

"It's about time." Damian rose and took the bundle from Khalil. "Thanks," he said softly as he patted the boy on the shoulder.

I rose to my feet, realizing suddenly how sore my muscles were. Thank fates we hadn't gone exploring the mosques today.

Khalil took a sleeping pad and blanket and arranged them in the far corner of the roof.

"Will this work?" Damian glanced at me.

"It's perfect. I could sleep just about anywhere right now." I yawned.

Damian took the remaining pads and blankets and laid them next to each other, a few feet apart. Close, but not too close.

I kicked off my shoes and laid down on the pad, using my large headscarf as a pillow. There was no moon, and the stars twinkled in the tarry black night. I'd never seen such a clear sky. You would have never known we were just on the outskirts of Cairo.

Damian laid down on the other pad, folding an arm behind his head as he looked up at the heavens.

The stars faded out as sleep overtook me, and I dreamt that I was a genie, relentlessly hunted by three magicians through the whirling desert sands. The water carrier took my hand and pulled me down into a dark cleft in the rock. His embrace made me feel safe as the footsteps drew near.

How much longer could we hide?

Neve

I woke to an eerie melody that filled the air. The morning call to prayer. The muezzin who recited the words did so masterfully, like a poet or artist, drawing out each word. The beautiful call echoed above the rooftops.

I cracked an eye open. The sky had turned a fiery orangey pink. Sunrise.

A heavy arm slipped around my torso and pulled me close. Both my eyes flew open. *Damian.*

He was still asleep, his movements unconscious. His magic was different—not just hot, but flickering, like the embers of a dying campfire.

Warmth trickled through me. I drew in a shuddery breath and closed my eyes. Unable to help myself, I leaned into him, wanting to feel more. He made a low noise and pulled me tighter. His warm breath on my neck sent shivers across my skin.

When had he come over?

Not that I was complaining.

A yawn sounded from behind us, a bucket of cold water on my desire. Damian's hand retreated and, reluctantly, I sat up. Embarrassment swept over me as I craned my neck toward Khalil.

The boy still had sleep in his eyes and appeared to have noticed nothing. *Thank fates.*

My eyes fell to the mass of blankets around me, and my cheeks blazed red hot. Sweet heavens. Sometime in the night, I must have rolled over to Damian's pad.

Creeper.

The clanging of cups sounded near Khalil. "You guys like coffee?"

Thankful for the distraction, I jumped to my feet. "Make it a double, Khalil."

Damian stirred. Face flushed, I hid the evidence of my migration.

Khalil fetched some piping hot falafel from a vender on the street below, and we quickly prepared for the day as we gobbled down breakfast.

Damian didn't mention anything. Had he noticed?

By the time the sun broke over the city walls, we were already on our way, following Khalil toward the Mosque of Marwan, our first stop.

We wound through the increasingly crowded city streets until we reached a square-based minaret constructed of finely carved limestone that rose above the adjacent buildings. A gallery of open windows was visible about three-quarters of the way up.

"The minaret of Umm Asim," Khalil said, briefly looking back at us. "Named after one of the caliph's wives."

"Can we go up to get a view of the city?" Damian said.

Khalil shrugged. "Should be no problem."

We climbed the front steps of the mosque and entered a colonnaded hall that surrounded an open courtyard. Opposite the entrance was the prayer hall, and I spotted the mosaicked mihrab-niche that indicated the direction of Mecca.

A man wearing a long white robe greeted us, and Khalil spoke with him in Arabic before dropping a coin into his palm. Though he had masked his signature, I sensed the faint traces of myrrh and apricots. The man gestured for us to go through a door at the end of the hall. Inside, a metal spiral staircase spanned the interior of the hollow minaret.

"Go ahead. I will wait here for you," Khalil said.

Damian and I started up the rickety stairs that creaked and shifted under our weight.

I gripped the metal railing. "I understand why Khalil didn't want to come."

We neared the gallery of windows where light beamed in. The stairs narrowed and continued up, but I turned to the window.

A light breeze blew through my hair as I looked out over the rooftops. Jumbled buildings filled every inch between us and the city's walls. The minarets of the two other mosques that Khalil had identified last night rose in the distance.

Damian scanned the cityscape. "What exactly are we looking for?"

I pulled out my translation of the tale. "According to the riddle, each of the magicians received a vision of where the water carrier hid the lamp. I think there must be a connection between the mosques, and what they saw."

"Makes sense."

"The Mosque of Marwan represents the six-hundred-year-old magician who saw a vision of a mountain that looked like the hump of a camel." I pointed southeast. "There. The camel's hump."

I pursed my lips as my gaze drifted down from the mountain, across the city. I paused when I noticed the domed structure of highly embellished limestone rising from the city center. The hair on the back of my neck stood on end. It reminded me of something, but I couldn't put my finger on it.

Realization struck. I leaned over the stairwell. "Khalil! Can you please come up?"

An exasperated sigh sounded from below and then the creaking of steps. Khalil appeared a minute later, out of breath and with a bead of sweat on his brow. I pulled him beside me and pointed to the structure I'd spotted moments ago. "What is that domed building in the center of the city?"

"It's the grand sabil. For drinking water. The cisterns that store the city's water are located below."

"That's it!" My heart raced. "The riddle says the water carrier disappeared with the lamp. The *cistern* is the water carrier! The story is an allegory, just like the mosques. The water carrier was never a person at all."

Damian rapped his knuckles on the stone. "Brilliant."

"The sabil lies on a line running directly from this mosque to the tip of that mountain. I bet if we go to each of the other mosques, the sight lines will point to the cistern too. It's triangulation."

Voices sounded from the base of the stairwell.

Damian grabbed my arm, breaking my thoughts off. "No time for that. We've got company."

The ghul from the marketplace stood in the street below, staring up at me. My skin crawled. "Damn it! It's the caliph's spy. How did he find us so fast?"

Damian climbed onto the windowsill and extended his arm toward me. "Doesn't matter now, it's time to fly."

16

Damian

I grabbed Neve's hand, pulled her onto the minaret's windowsill, and pointed west. "Head that direction, and I'll follow with Khalil."

"But the sabil is the other direction!"

"Right. We'll be easy to track in the air. We need to throw them off the scent. We'll double back on the ground."

"Okay." Neve leapt off the building and soared west.

I hoisted Kahlil up and tucked him under my arm. "Okay, kid. Flying lessons."

I leapt into the air. Khalil squirmed in my arms as the rooftops raced by. I looked at the crowd below. People were watching.

"Fates, put me down! I don't want to die!" The boy screamed, his bravado having apparently not come along for the ride.

"Neve!" I shouted. "Touch down here."

Neve swung around the neighboring building as my feet slammed to the roof. I released the boy, who was unnaturally pale.

"You look like you need a shot of arak, kid." I slapped Khalil on the shoulder and tossed him a pouch of coins. "Things are going to get rough. Run. We'll lead them off."

Khalil scrambled down a drainpipe and jumped onto the awning of a shop that hadn't yet opened. He shot down the alley in a superhuman blur as Neve cried, "Thanks for everything, Khalil!"

I flexed my wings. "Okay, we keep heading west to draw them away from the kid, and then we double back to the sabil on foot."

Neve nodded, and we took off.

Several blocks later, we dropped down into a deserted alley. The streets were still fairly empty in this part of the city, leaving little room for cover. No sign of the ghul yet, but that didn't mean he wasn't close on our heels. Hopefully, we had flown faster than he could run. I was willing to bet that we'd already been spotted by more of the caliph's spies.

I pulled the hood of my cloak over my head. "Cover

your hair with your scarf. You stand out like a fire at night."

Neve wrapped her head with a scarf. "Can you track the fountain with your seeker magic?"

"Not a problem." Closing my eyes, I focused on the fountain. As its form materialized in my mind, I felt the familiar magnetic tug in my chest. "This way."

We veered left down a narrow alley between several apartment buildings, much like the one we'd taken refuge in yesterday. Above, a woman with reptilian scales for skin wrung out laundry and hung it on a clothing line strung over her balcony.

We ran until we reached a more populated portion of town, then lost ourselves in the crowds of Helwanese Magica. The traffic became mercifully dense, slowing our pace but providing ample cover.

After fifteen minutes, we reached the large fountain. It sat in the middle of a busy intersection with foot traffic flowing in all directions. The structure was carved from white marble and decorated with floral designs and ornamental pilasters, with a pool of water in the center.

I stepped forward, but needles raked my skin.

"There it is again. That freaky feeling." Neve looked around, searching for the threat.

A presence had been following us since our trek through the desert. We'd assumed it was the caliph's spies. Now, I was certain it was something else. Subtle vibrations of magic thrummed in the air, and a memory surfaced.

"Wind demons," I murmured.

This heist was going bad fast.

Trepidation flashed across Neve's face. "How? The djinn had sent those. Do you think he's been released and is after us?"

"Let's stay focused. We need to get the genie. Then we'll deal with the wind demons."

Neve nodded.

Across the way, a Helwanese merchant started shouting furiously at a man in a wheeled cart loaded with bundles of textiles. That was probably as good a distraction as we were going to get, so I slipped into the throng and navigated toward the fountain, Neve close behind.

As we neared, a woman reached down toward the pool of water with a cup attached to a thin chain secured to the fountain's wall. She dipped it into the water, then raised it to her lips and drank. Her skin glowed and flickered in the sunlight.

Neve tugged on my sleeve and pulled me to a set of marble stairs behind the fountain. They extended below into darkness, but a locked metal gate blocked the entrance.

"That must lead to the cisterns," she said, "Thank fates it's still locked. The thief must not have gotten here yet."

Small miracles.

The padlock was too far gone to pick. I gripped the rusty bars and pulled. The lock snapped. I looked around, but nobody was interested in our business. We slipped through, and I closed the gate behind us.

I cast a locking spell on it, as well as an alarm that would ring in my mind if our pursuers forced their way through.

I pulled out the pair of cheap flashlights Khalil had acquired, handing one to Neve.

Neve flicked it on and descended the dusty steps. The air grew cooler and damper, and I raised my flashlight. The low ceiling above the stairs gave way to a larger room, and we stood at eye level with the tops of several stone arches that supported the roof.

Neve shone her light down to the base of the stairs, revealing a small quay and a placid pool of water. As we neared the quay, I counted at least three rows of columns extending from the pool, all carrying the arches overhead. The shadows of dozens more columns indicated the room extended back for a distance. Magic hummed across the water—the genie was *definitely* down here.

"Okay. We're in the water carrier. Where is this genie?" Neve said.

I scanned the space. Apart from the stone quay we stood on, the room was flooded. A small, wooden dinghy bobbed gently along the edge of the quay—probably used by the maintenance crew.

I shifted my beam to the dinghy. "Let's see what's back there."

The darkness and silence heightened my senses, and the magic pouring off the genie guided me like a homing beacon.

Neve eyed the dark pool of water suspiciously. "Can't wait."

I couldn't fault her lack of enthusiasm. The last time we had waded through a sunken passageway hadn't ended well.

I knelt and untied the rope from a wooden stake that was shoved into a crack between two of the quay's stones, then climbed into the boat and picked up the oars.

Neve stepped in, and the boat rocked violently as she took a seat on the bench across from me. I gave a push off the quay and began rowing. It was quiet, apart from the dipping of the oars.

Neve sat with her back to the bow, facing me. She tucked her arms and legs tight together, away from the sides. "This might be the city's water supply, but I've never heard of a creepy underground waterway that didn't have monsters in it."

"Crocodiles." I could sense their magic down below. "A lot of them. Big ones."

She shuddered and inched toward the edge of the

boat, shining her beam down into the water. The light illuminated the bottom, about ten feet below. At least it wasn't black water. It'd be easier to spot them.

I kept rowing, and she inspected the room with her light. We passed through the rows of columns that rose from the water. The magic from the genie was stronger, but as we drew near, it seemed to be magnified everywhere, and I couldn't pinpoint its precise location.

Where the hell was it?

Neve

I did not like this.

I'd seen too many nature episodes that showed crocodiles bringing down water buffalo to think we were safe in our little dingy. Plenty of factoids leapt into my head, unbidden. Crocs were high-precision-killing machines with a bite force of three-thousand-seven-hundred pounds per square inch. The scaley monstrosities had managed to outlive the dinosaurs and survived physically unchanged for hundreds of millions of years.

How could Damian be so calm?

He actually seemed to be enjoying himself. He was the kind of man who preferred danger to the mundane. Essentially, a lunatic.

Not that I was much better.

The faster we found the genie, the sooner we could get the hell out of Dodge.

A splash sounded ahead. Not a big one, maybe the whooshing of a tail.

Here we go.

I directed my beam of light toward the origin of the splash but saw nothing. Just a slight ripple.

A faint noise of dripping echoed through the chamber. We rounded a column, and my flashlight crossed something swinging back and forth in the air.

"What the—" My beam followed the rope that dangled from the ceiling down to a bucket dripping with water. The rope dropped through a square opening in the ceiling. The bucket rose as someone pulled it up to surface level.

"People who live above must be able to access the cistern," I noted.

The water carrier had wished that no person or beast in the city would ever go thirsty. I loved it when fairy tales turned out to be more literal than they seemed at first glance.

The beam of my flashlight bounced off a wall on my right. There were no ledges or platforms anywhere, just water and columns. Frustration welled in my chest. "Where the heck is this thing?"

Damian directed the boat toward the left. "I think

I've pinpointed the genie's magical signature. Up ahead."

"Are you sure it's not the crocodiles?" Excitement flitted through my stomach, but I didn't want to get my hopes up too high. Could it really be this easy?

Damian frowned. "Of course, I'm sure. Well, ninety-five percent."

I raised my eyebrow. "Where's the other five percent?"

"Nine-five percent sure it's the genie, or some other extremely powerful creature. Five percent it's a crocodile."

"Okay. I'll take those odds."

Damian rowed for another five minutes and then slowed his pace. A light vibration hummed in my ear, like the wings of a hummingbird. Only softer and higher pitched.

Damian stared at me. "Do you sense its signature, too?"

"I think so. It's like a slight vibration."

Damian nodded and started rowing again. "Exactly. And it tastes metallic and electric. It's close."

The humming grew stronger, and it buzzed through my body. I shone my flashlight around the space and up toward the ceiling, then down into the water. The beam hit the stone floor of the cistern fifteen feet down, scattering light across the bottom and illuminating several pieces of stone and mortar rubble.

"There!" Damian said.

My heart leapt, and I turned to see what he was pointing at. There, on the empty bottom, was an ivory colored bottle resting on its side.

Not a lamp, *but hey*, we were going off a fairy tale.

"That's it." It *had* to be the genie. It looked old, and the magical signature had grown extremely strong.

Damian clicked off his flashlight and set it down in the boat, then raised his arms and pulled off his shirt, revealing his strong form. He tossed the shirt onto the bench next to him.

"You're going for a swim?" An image of an African crocodile from the Discovery Channel popped into my head.

"You watch for crocs. And keep your light aimed at the bottle." Damian turned toward the stern, and my eyes followed the curves of his back. His muscles flexed and he dove in, disappearing over the edge of the boat with a splash. The boat rocked front to back, and the beam of the flashlight danced across the water.

I leaned forward, shining my light on the bottle as Damian swam down to the bottom. I tapped my foot on the hull, holding my breath—a bad habit.

Come on, come on.

A slight movement in the water on my left caused the boat to rock ever so slightly. Keeping my light on Damian so he could see the bottle, I rotated my head, feeling the beginnings of a rising lump in my throat.

Dizziness skewed my vision, and I released the air from my lungs as I forced myself to breathe normally.

The water was calm. The sound of my heartbeat had replaced the humming in my ears. I scanned the placid darkness behind us.

A gentle ripple formed on the water.

Then a shield of horny scales broke the surface. Horror gripped me. The crocodile floated, still as a rock. It must have seen—heck, *smelled*—Damian, but it wasn't moving. Just floating.

It was gigantic. An absolute monstrosity. Twenty-five feet long at least. What the heck did it even eat down here?

Not Damian. Not on my watch.

I turned slowly, careful not to make any sudden movements. I needed to alert him. But how?

He'd just retrieved the bottle.

Gripping the flashlight with a clenched fist, I clicked the light off and then on three times with my other hand. Damian stopped and looked up, using his arm to shield the light from his eyes.

The crocodile surged forward and slammed into the side of the boat with a wood-splintering crunch.

Everything was dark.

The flashlight was gone.

I slid off the bench and dropped to my knees, holding the sides of the boat with my hands, trying to steady the rocking.

Light flickered from below—my flashlight sitting on the bottom of the pool. Then it went out. Shit!

Where was Damian?

Remembering that he'd set his flashlight down near the stern, I frantically felt around in the bilge water. *Nothing.*

"Shit! I need light!"

I peered into the dark water, heart thundering.

A soft glow appeared overhead, illuminating a dark shape in the cistern below.

The shape lunged upward and crashed into the hull. Wood splintered, and I plunged into the cold water.

I thanked fates for the mysterious light above but could still barely see. Debris filtered down through the water around me, and the remnants of the dingy sank to the bottom.

I spun.

The crocodile thrashed forward, its giant maw lined with curved teeth. I jetted backward on a column of air as its jaws snapped down.

Unbelievable agony shot through my lower leg and foot. I screamed and a bubble of air formed around my mouth. I gasped, suddenly able to breath underwater.

Well, this will keep me alive another thirty seconds.

Blood clouded around me. My calf was clamped tight in the croc's mouth. It started to roll over, and a new wave of pain shot through me.

Then Damian slammed his dark spear into the side

of the croc's head. My leg came free as the monster opened its jaws and snapped at him. Darkness crept in at the corner of my vision.

No way.

I forced my eyes open. I could barely see because of all the blood in the water.

Damian gripped the beast's tail and towed it backward a few feet. He must have been using his magic, otherwise there was no way that'd be possible.

I surged forward with a jet of air, trying to find a way to help. I had to grab Damian, get us out of here.

The monster flipped over, and Damian lost his grip. It slammed its tail into him, and his body surged back through the water.

The croc turned back on me with unbelievable speed, spreading its jaws, coming in for the kill.

This is it.

I unleashed all the magic in my body, firing a bolt of air into the monster's open mouth.

The water column filled with a torrent of blood and bubbles, obscuring my vision.

Where was it? Where was Damian?

A hand grazed my side, and I screamed into my bubble of air.

Damian. He pointed up.

The croc thrashed on the surface of the water.

What the heck was it doing?

It couldn't swim down. I'd inflated it with my burst

of air, and it was bobbing on the surface like a murderous balloon animal.

Screw you, Tick-Tock.

Darkness crept over me, followed by the most amazing sensation I had ever felt.

Warmth surged through my body as Damian's arms wrapped around me. His magic poured through me like an uncontrolled river. My bones snapped back into place, but even that pain was euphoric in the torrent of his power. Relief like I had never felt filled me, and pleasure.

Gods. What was this ecstasy? Each time Damian healed me, it was more intense.

And then the ecstasy stopped. My fingers clawed uncontrollably at Damian's back as our heads broke the surface. His magic was like a drug, and I needed more.

"Fly!"

What? My head was still spinning from the healing magic he'd poured into me.

"Either fly or climb the gods-damned column before anything else tries to eat us!"

Shit. Good point. Calling my magic, I surged into the air. I looked down, but Damian was gone.

He'd dove back down to the bottom. He must have dropped the bottle during our fight with the croc.

I crossed my fingers. *Please don't let there be any more crocodiles down there.*

A violent belch echoed through the cistern, causing

my heart to ricochet against my ribs. I spun.

The crocodile I'd inflated thrashed on its back like a balloon with tiny useless legs. It was kind of cute, even though it'd nearly killed us. Luckily, it would live to see another day once it deflated.

Speaking of which…"You can deflate somewhere else."

I blasted the beastie with a jet of air that set it skimming across the surface of the water away from us.

Man, I hope that's not the direction we're supposed to go in.

I looked around, totally lost. A little glowing light bobbed nearby, illuminating the space. At least I could see, which was a miracle. I reached out toward the light, and it drifted close.

Damian's head broke the surface, and the glowing light zipped up to the ceiling.

"Take this." Damian thrust his hand up, the ivory bottle clenched in his fist. "I guess we know why it was just lying on the bottom."

I hated to think how many people had solved the riddle but failed the crocodile exam.

My hand tingled as I wrapped my fingers around the smooth, cold neck of the bottle.

Triumph welled in my chest.

Sweet and holy fates. We have it!

I grinned at Damian. "Nice job. Now let's get the heck out of here."

17

Damian

That was damn close.

I held onto the pillar, pulling my thoughts together, struggling to gain control over the rage of battle.

Neve was alive. That was what mattered.

She'd almost bled out, yet somehow had had the wits to disable the crocodile in one swift blow. That stirred something in me I couldn't explain.

We also had the genie bottle.

The high-pitched ringing and electric currents of its signature were hard to ignore. Its power called out to me and, despite my resolve, I felt the all too familiar flames of desire rising deep within.

Hopefully, we could be rid of it soon. Neve would have to keep it for now.

She levitated a safe distance above the water. I was certain there were more crocs in here and didn't want her too close to the surface.

"Where's the light coming from? Your magic?" I asked.

"Not mine. I think it's the glowing light that helped us on the airship and in the djinn's dungeon."

Interesting. Perhaps she already had more powers than she suspected. Its arrival was fortuitous. Fighting the croc in the dark would have been difficult.

The soft, glowing light descended from the darkness, floating toward us. It swirled by and continued, weaving through the columns.

"I think we should follow it," Neve said.

"That's going to be a problem for me. The columns are too narrow for my wings. I'll need to swim."

"I'll levitate you...that's how I used to do it before I learned to fly the right way."

I looked up at the low ceiling. "Remember how you launched the rocks at the scorpion?"

"Yes?"

"Don't do that to me."

She gave me a quizzical look and a half-bemused smile.

I could joke. I didn't often. But something about Neve drove the shadows away. She was liberating.

Neve twirled her hand in the air, and a little whirlwind formed just above the water. I raised an eyebrow.

"Jump on."

This was a ridiculous plan, but I trusted her, so I jumped.

Air and mist roared around me, whipping at my pants and bare skin. Arms outstretched for balance, I tilted back and forth on the unstable cushion of air. "I can see how this was difficult to learn."

"Here we go." She waved her hand, and we shot forward low over the water, Neve flying right beside me. It was like skydiving without ever landing.

The columns raced past as we zipped across the water. The light guided our way through the network of chambers, shooting forward and waiting for us to catch up.

"I can see the quay. We're almost there!" Neve said.

Blessed fates. Not that I cared much for them.

I landed on the stone quay, glad for the solid surface beneath my feet. It was exhilarating to fly wrapped in Neve's magic, but I preferred being in control.

Neve dropped to the quay beside me. Her red hair draped across her shoulders. Her dress was soaked and torn, revealing the length of her leg, and the scars where the croc had sunk its teeth in.

I knelt beside her. "Let me look at how those are healing."

In the water, I hadn't had time to precisely apply my

magic. I had blasted it into her, hoping it would seal off the worst of the wounds.

Neve's skin trembled when I placed my hand on her calf, and I felt the deep vibrations of her magic entwining with mine. She gasped as I traced my finger across her skin, letting my magic work over the scars.

She gripped my shoulder and, after a short hesitation, released it and quickly pulled her leg back. Her voice broke. "We should go."

I let my breath return to normal and stood. "Agreed."

Neve grinned. "I think your lack of shirt is going to be a problem."

My pants were also tattered and bloody from the crocodile's claws. I was going to draw a lot of attention. "We'll need to find a merchant or fly very fast. I doubt you can planes-walk us out because of the magic dome. We'll probably have to get away from the city before your magic will work."

"How far away do you think the gateway out of the city is?"

I focused on the gateway we'd used to enter Helwan and felt a familiar tug pulling me toward it. "Farther than I would like. The city is probably crawling with the caliph's spies."

As we started up the stairs, the mysterious glowing light turned and headed back into the dark cistern, fading before disappearing.

That would require looking into once we were home.

Neve stopped at the top of the steps and leaned against the wall to make room for me to pass. The street was even more crowded now. No sign of the ghul, but he could be lurking somewhere nearby. I didn't expect him to give up easily.

With a quick movement, I unlocked the enchantment spell I had placed on the gate.

"We'll head right, down this street." I gestured toward the main thoroughfare that passed in front of us. The gate creaked as I pushed it open a foot. "Let's move fast. I have the sneaking suspicion the spy is near."

"I need to get you a shirt first, Conan. Or at least a cloak. We should try to be inconspicuous as long as we can."

"There might be an ambush." I scanned the street.

She pulled a handful of coins from her sodden hip pack. "Probably. But then, they picked the wrong day to mess with Neve Cross, crocodile hunter."

I ground my teeth. "Fine. But at the first sign of danger, fly."

Neve slipped out the gate, and I pushed it closed behind us. She crossed the street to a clothing merchant and gestured to some shirts hanging high in the rafters.

While I grabbed a shirt, a pushcart filled with ring-shaped bread trundled by, and I lost sight of her for a second.

She shrieked, and I catapulted around the cart, immediately locking eyes with the ghul.

He held Neve in a choke hold.

Neve

Freaking ghul!

His arm squeezed my throat and my airway closed.

Survival instinct kicked in. I raised my elbow and shoved it into his side, hitting his hip bone. The ghul grunted and flinched, and I brought my heel down on his foot, feeling a crunch. His grip loosened on my neck, and he snarled in pain, giving me an opening to twist and slam my opposite elbow into his face. Another crunch and I ripped myself free from his arm, spinning around to face him.

Damian flashed in front of me in a blur, grabbing the ghul and slamming him into the concrete building. The ghul reached out and sliced Damian's bare bicep with—*claws?*

Where the heck did those come from? His fingertips had grown several inches and were as sharp as daggers.

Damian darted back, barely avoiding the ghul's raking claws, and drew a smoking sword from the ether.

People started screaming around us, and the crowded street descended into chaos.

So much for low profile. An arm grabbed my shoulder and spun me around. A medieval looking guard raised a scimitar to my throat. "You're coming with us."

The forms of the silat came instantaneously to mind. I slammed his arm up and away with my free hand and spun from his grasp. I wrenched my khanjar from it sheath, kicked him in the knee to turn him around, and slammed the blade into his back.

The man gasped, and I blasted him away from me with a bolt of wind. I spun.

A second guard lay dead at Damian's feet, but he was still engaged with the ghul. The monster lashed out with blinding speed, undeterred by the cuts from Damian's sword.

Summoning the wind, I released a gust at the death demon. His eyes shifted toward mine, and he craned his head upward, opening his mouth.

What the f—

A burning sensation gathered in my chest and then spread down my arms into my fingers. My magic weakened...almost as if it were being sucked right out of me.

The ghul's throat flexed as he gulped down air. Terror gripped me as realization sunk in. He wasn't gulping air, but my *magic*.

Damian had paused, blade drawn and muscles

tense. Apparently sensing what was unfolding, he opened the palm of his freehand, sending a wave of magic at the ghul. The demon slammed into the building, his arms pinned at his sides. Pain wracked the creature's face, but he grinned, baring those tarry, reeking teeth. Then he breathed in.

Fates.

"Damian, watch out, he'll drain you dry!"

Damian took no heed of my warning but strode toward the ghul like he was taunting him. Shadows danced around Damian's shoulders, then trailed through the air into the ghul's mouth as the demon's chest heaved with each gulp of power.

Yet the fallen angel appeared nearly unfazed. Damian stopped inches in front of the ghul and brought his dagger up between the demon's ribs. The ghul gasped and slumped to the ground.

"Holy crap." I crossed to Damian. "A magic drinker. Have you ever seen anything like that?"

"Yes," Damian said, his voice rough. I turned to him. His eyes had grown dark, and his shoulders tensed.

A chill scurried down my spine, and I shivered.

The ghul lay on his side, staring blankly across the pavement, black blood pooling around his body. A trail of white, translucent smoke snaked from his blue lips, drifting upward between the buildings.

"Let's fly," he said. "I bet there are more of these. We should get out as fast as possible."

We leapt into the air and soared over the city. My magic felt drained after the encounter with the ghul.

"Take it all in," Damian said. "This will likely be your last look at the wonderous city of Helwan."

Damian was right. I'd likely never be able to come back here again. There was so much to explore here. Regret tugged at my chest, and I breathed out a sigh.

We soared straight to the gateway. Our ticket out of here.

We'd be drinking champagne tonight. Dining over the Nile.

Of course, we'd have to get through the gateway first, which was surrounded by armor-plated guards with long halberds.

"I've got this! Just get ready to head through. I'll planes-walk us to Tayir as soon as we get out of the dome's magic field."

Irritation tore through me. I wanted to get the heck out of this city already. I dropped to the street in front of the door and unleashed a seismic blast of wind, fueled by my sudden anger. The guards hurtled backward into the wall, collapsing to the ground.

"Now! Before they get up!" I grabbed Damian's hand, and the flames of his signature raced up my skin.

We released our magic into the door to open it. My vision went dark, and a force sucked us through the gateway.

I shot out of the ether, landing on my knees. The city was gone. Only burning sand remained.

Sitting up on my bruised knees, I dusted myself off and looked toward Damian, who was crouched several feet from me. His face contorted—a combination of confusion and rage—and every muscle in his body tensed.

A choked gasp escaped my throat, and fear froze my joints.

Matthias dropped down from the sky on leather wings, flanked by two genies.

One was the djinn. His white tattoos danced across the blue canvas of his skin. He glared at me and let out a chilling laugh, causing my blood to curdle in my veins. The other genie—an efreet—glowed and radiated heat. Red, blue, and green flared from the cracks of his charred flesh.

Nausea swept over me, and I realized I was holding my breath. I released it in a whisper.

The air rippled around the genies, like heat waves over hot pavement. Their power washed over me like a tsunami. A mixture of incense and brimstone flooded my senses. I had never felt anything like it.

Matthias's voice cut through the air. "Thank you for recovering my genie. Now hand it over."

Confusion momentarily clouded my mind. What the heck was going on?

And then it hit me like a truck.

Matthias is the thief. He'd stolen the djinn from the Vault. And the efreet from Prague.

"Matthias, you bastard," Damian spat as he drew his blade from the ether.

"Damian. Old friend. No need for violence. I'm impressed. Leave it to you to hunt down two genies." His eyes flicked to me. "Three, I should say. Your magic is growing, Neve. I can *feel* it. No wonder Damian is so interested in you."

My mind reeled. He knew about my magic? What did he mean it was growing? What did he mean about Damian?

I gritted my teeth and shook my head, trying to get a hold of the situation.

Damian growled, his voice choked with rage. "You're dead, Matthias."

A deadly fire erupted in Matthias eyes, as horns grew from his head. "No, Damian. But you and your little genie will be dead, if you don't give me what I want."

I surreptitiously reached down for the lamp. If I could summon—

Matthias shot forward and grabbed my hand. The djinn spun, and a blast of sand blew Damian off his feet.

"No." I yanked my arm free and kicked him in the chest. "You can't have it."

Damian roared and unleashed a sickening green storm of electricity. Deadly magic I'd never seen him use. His signature pulsed stronger than ever, and the familiar heady scent poured over me—this time tinged with a woody, smokey note unlike anything I'd breathed before. "Go, Neve!"

No. I couldn't leave him.

"Now! Use the lamp! Fix this!" Damian leapt forward and threw a streak of sand at Matthias and the genies. Enhanced with magic, it hit them like a sandblaster.

Tears in my eyes, I summoned my magic and rocketed skyward as I pulled the lamp from my pouch.

How do I even use this thing?

An icy force wrapped around my waist and yanked me downward.

I slammed into the sand and pain rocked my body, exploding through my chest. Stars filled my vision, and I struggled for breath. My lungs completely deflated, failing to work. I clawed forward through the sand, but a stabbing pain shot into my side, and I flipped through the air, landing on my chest. Wheezing, my vision faded in and out as I tried to lift myself to my elbows.

To my side, Damian had pinned Matthias, whose face had turned sheet white, but the efreet had approached from behind, gripping Damian's neck with a burning hand.

A blunt force sunk into my side, flipping me onto my back. The bottle flew from my hand into the sand beyond. The djinn towered over me. His eyes blazed, and his teeth flashed in an evil grin. He reached down and squeezed my jaw with a cold grip. "Now, where did we leave off, half-breed? I believe I was breaking your bones and tearing off your limbs?"

I clenched my teeth, fighting off the pain as his nails dug into my cheeks. Blood trickled down my lips, tasting of iron.

This is not how I am gonna die.

"No! She comes with me. That was the deal." The booming voice of the efreet rocked the ground, and an orange flame licked around the djinn's back.

The djinn released his grip, and I fell onto my elbows. The djinn's face twisted in rage and fury, and he shot up, turning his back to me.

My eyes searched the space for Damian. But he was nowhere. *Gone.* How could that be?

The djinn launched an icy blast at the efreet who blocked it with a fire-tinged blade. They were fighting. Distracted.

I rolled over and pulled myself to my feet, my ribs protesting and my legs heavy as iron. I stumbled forward, whispering the name of the wind, and—

Darkness.

18

Damian

Matthias.

You son of a bitch.

I was bound, imprisoned in the Realm of Fire, kneeling in the middle of the efreet's cavernous throne room.

Massive shards of obsidian rose from the floor, supporting the cavernous ceiling like pillars. Channels of lava flowed along the outskirts of the chamber, flooding the air with sweltering heat and toxic gases.

"Where is she?" I choked on my rage and the foul air. I struggled to stand but was forced back down to one knee.

A guard grasped my hair and shoved my head down. "Submit."

I forced away my last vision of Neve—lying bloody in the desert sand. I had been too far away. Matthias's magic and that of the genies had bound me to the ground. I had failed her.

"Grovel before your new master." The guard's breath reeked of carrion and bile. Instead of armor, he had a dense network of metal studs implanted directly into his blistered skin.

I spat. Matthias had used us to find the genie, and then offered me up as slave to the efreet. I would not be bound. I had to find Neve. I had to undo the disaster I had created. Again.

The guard's nails dug into my scalp, and he forced my head lower. I would have ripped his arms off, but both my magic and my hands were beyond my control. My wrist and ankles were bound with anti-magic shackles, clipped to a long iron rod wielded by a human guard. I was a marionette.

Fury consumed me. "I have never bowed before any being, living or dead, and I will never do so."

"You do so now, fallen," my captor hissed.

"I kneel, awaiting death. Yours or mine." I jerked against my bonds.

"Let the angel gaze upon me, so that he may see my glory." The voice shook the chamber, roaring like an inferno.

The guard yanked my head back, slipping an obsidian blade against my throat. "Shall I quench the flames of your wrath with his blood, great master?"

The efreet sat upon a throne of red-hot iron, radiating as if it had just been pulled from the forges. His flesh glowed like embers, and flames licked up the sides of his body. They flickered through the spectrum of light: red, yellow, green, blue.

I was staring into the sun.

"You have been defeated, dark angel. You are fallen once again and are now my chattel. Bow before me and serve me."

I jerked my head from the guard's clutches, pain searing my scalp. "Release me from my bonds, coward, and I'll set my blade against your flame."

A pencil-thin lance of fire shot forth from the efreet's finger and gouged my cheek, my skin searing away. I ground my teeth against the pain. The shackles bound my magic, and the wound remained.

The efreet's voice shook the hall, and the rivers of lava surged and churned with each word. "Although my powers know no bounds, I am also merciful. In exchange for your life, you will forge magical weapons for my warriors."

I tried to shake my head, but the guard had renewed his grip. "I do not know the craft."

"Above all things, you are a *liar*. I know your past.

Matthias has revealed everything to me, ancient smith. You will forge me blades like the one you bear, like the one you made for him. Weapons of blackened steel, poisoned with wicked magic and burning with eternal flame."

The pounding of iron rang through my memory – standing at the forge, beating red-hot iron upon a cold black anvil. Matthias at my side, his hands enchanting the weapons we would bear in the war against my kin. The weapons I bore to this day.

Matthias, you bastard.

How many years had we worked together? It seemed countless. Time had eroded the bonds of our friendship. My insatiable lust for power, his relentless drive for control—our weaknesses had driven us apart. But after a century, how could it end in this? Betrayal.

Rage colored my vision, and my past crumbled around my feet.

What madness had he brought down upon me? Upon *us*.

Visions of Neve filled my mind. Her flowing blood matching her crimson hair. Fury tore at me, clouding my reason. I slammed forward, fighting the rods and chains.

"Your life for the blades," the efreet demanded.

"The only blade I have for you is the one I'll plunge through your heart."

The efreet chuckled softly, like the crackling of a

dying campfire, and an inferno poured over me, agony ripping through my skin.

The floor quaked as he rose from his throne and strode forward, approaching me step by thundering step. "You are defeated, dark angel. Fallen, again. If you disobey, I will destroy that which is precious to you."

The efreet reached his ember hand toward my face and opened his palm. A dancing blue flame erupted and took the shape of a woman with blazing red fire for hair.

Neve.

Choking guilt flooded me, and somewhere deep in the recesses of my mind, a weak voice called for restraint. I had to find her. Get her out of this hell.

"What have you done with her?" I growled.

The efreet took a step closer and stared down at me, ignoring my question. "If you defy me, I shall slowly burn the flesh from her body. If you try to escape, I will mount her on the obsidian spikes of my tower, a living feast for the beasts of the sky."

I would rather have burned alive than submit to this monster. But I could never give Neve over to this fate.

The words were bile in my mouth, but I forced them out. "I will forge your weapons, as long as you do not harm her."

"Of course you will." He snorted, cinders erupting from his body and floating into the air. "Because you are a frail thing of flesh and blood, bound to petty sentiment."

The truth of his words stung.

"So are you." I lifted my head, a bitter smile twisting my lips. "You grovel before Matthias, doing his bidding, not your own. Bound to a frail thing of flesh and blood."

His face contorted, and he spun to the guards. "Take him to the forges. Set him to work. First, the manacles that will bind my new half-breed pet. And then the blades."

My body jerked to life as my captors yanked the rods controlling my wrists and neck and brought me to my feet. Sweat ran down their bare skin as they shuffled forward, dragging me along.

We descended into the dark chambers of the obsidian citadel. Visions of Neve in the desert struggling against the efreet haunted me. I would save her.

Then, I would have vengeance.

Fury like no other pulsed through my veins. And something else. Something I had fought so long to repress.

Fire awoke, scouring my soul. My body quaked, and the darkness within me took life, a savage dragon ripping forth.

I vowed to grind the efreet's heart to ash.

To rip the magic from his body.

To make his fire my own.

19

Neve

Pain.

Every vein in my head throbbed, and my ribs and spine ached.

And then, something cool. Wet.

My eyes fluttered open. Blurry shapes moved above me. A firm sleeping pad cradled my aching body, and a damp sheet clung to skin. It was hot, like lying in the midday sun. Had I fallen asleep on the rooftop in Helwan?

A purple shape moved beside me.

"Damian?"

"No, I'm sorry. I don't know who that is." A woman's voice. Velvety and sweet like crème brûlée.

She dabbed a wet cloth against my head, and I flinched.

"Hold still now. You look like you lost an argument with a truck."

"I lost my friend. Where is he?" I tried to sit up, but she gently pushed me down.

"I don't know. I'm sorry."

Panic spiked beneath my skin. Where was I?

My vision began clearing, but not fast enough. Lights. Colors.

We'd been sleeping on the rooftop. In Helwan. *Helwan.* Was this the woman from the dress shop?

Long dark hair. Olive skin. My skewed vision obscured her face, but no, she was different. I sensed her magic. It felt like cool ocean water trickling over my skin but tasted of butter and sweet cream. And something more, a feeling of familiarity? Comfort. Like being wrapped in heavy silk blankets.

"Who are you?" My voice cracked, and I licked my dry lips.

"I'm Amira. A friend."

She jabbed me with that icy cloth again, and I jerked back. "Ow. What are you doing?"

"Touch-ups. You have a few cuts that didn't quite make it through your skull. I thought I would widen them up for you."

A joke?

No time.

"Amira, I'm Neve. I've lost my friend. I need to find him. Now."

I tried lifting myself up, but a jolt of pain shot through my side. This time she helped me to sit, and my vision finally cleared.

"Your name must mean stubborn. I like it." She smiled.

Then vertigo came, and my stomach went prancing away on holiday as wooziness took up residence.

"Careful now," she said. "You've had a pretty hard blow to your head."

A blow to my head. Falling. Colliding into the desert sand.

I steadied myself as it all came rushing back. The efreet. Matthias. The djinn. We'd been betrayed. And worse, we'd essentially handed over the genie to the thief. To Matthias, who'd been working us all along. He had three genies now. Practically limitless power.

But where was Damian?

I leaned forward and cradled my face in my hands, nearly gagging from the nausea.

"Here. Drink this." She handed me a warm porcelain cup.

Hot tea. I breathed in. The aroma calmed my stomach.

We'd been fighting. Not fighting. Demolished. What had we been thinking?

Get the genie before them—balance the odds, that's what.

"I need to go."

"Honey, I admire your spunk. But you aren't going anywhere anytime soon."

The woman—Amira—seemed about my age. Her dark hair framed a heart-shaped face. She wore a purple sash and top that left most of her midriff exposed, as well as flowing pants of some airy fabric.

Why was it so gods damn hot in here? I needed answers.

The urge to charge off raged inside me, battling with the urge to hurl. The rest of the room slowly came into focus along with my thoughts.

My heartbeat surged, but I battened down the rising panic. "Where am I?"

"You and I are both prisoners in the Searing Citadel. More like the *Boring* Citadel if you ask me." Amira faked a yawn.

My heart sank to my feet. "Searing Citadel?"

"You're in the Realm of Fire at the behest of a cruel efreet. The accommodations aren't too bad, considering we're trapped in a tower in the middle of a volcano. There's no escape, by the way." She raised a perfectly plucked eyebrow at me. "I can tell you're a runner."

The efreet. We were his captives like Rhiannon had been in the Realm of Air. A new ache crept through my chest. Would I ever see her again?

"I can get us out. I'm a planes-walker." I slid my legs over the side of the bed, but the unexpected weight of them dragged me off. My bare feet hit the warm stone floor, and I fell to my knees with a metallic crash.

"Take it easy." Amira crouched beside me and put a hand on my shoulder. "You're wearing the latest fashion in anti-magic cuffs. So if you were thinking of just planes-walking away, think again."

I gazed down at the shiny brass cuffs on my ankles. My skin tingled under the metal. *Magicuffs*—we used them at the Order to prevent criminals from using their magic. At least they were small, and someone had taken the time to craft rounded edges, so they didn't cut into my skin.

Amira touched one with a finger, and I pulled my foot back. "Yours are much nicer than mine. I'm very jealous, and I would steal them if I could get them off you. They were just made this morning specifically for you, it seems."

I looked down at her ankles. Her magicuffs were much larger and looked uncomfortable.

I sighed. "Great. Personalized shackles. Is the torture personalized, too?"

"No torture here. Unless you count the *unending* boredom. In that case, it definitely feels personalized."

Well, that was a blessing, at least.

Amira helped me to my feet, and I scanned the hexagonal room. Burning lamps hung from the ceiling, illuminating colorful curtains draped from the wall, and brightly woven rugs were strewn across the warm stone floor. Several beds lined the wall. Most importantly, it was not a jail cell. There were two open doorways, a split cloth hanging in front of them.

"Amira, do you know what happened to me?"

"Not the details. They just dropped you off. By the looks of it, you made the efreet pretty angry."

"I need to find my friend and a way out of here. Can you help me?"

"First, love, you need a bath. I can help you with that. The rest, maybe later." Amira pulled aside the curtain hanging over one of the doorways, revealing a small lamplit bathing room.

"I don't have time."

"Unfortunately, time's one thing you've got. There's going to be a lot for you to take in, so take things step by step. First, you need to clean your wounds. Your clothes are shredded, and I can see your hiney. I'll bring you some fresh ones."

I started to protest but caught my reflection in the boudoir mirror above a small washbasin.

Case in point.

She turned on a spigot over a shiny brass tub and tipped a little vial of oil into the water. "Good news. Being in the Realm of Fire means the hot water never runs out. Hope you don't like cold showers or iced tea, though." She stood and headed toward the door. "I'll be outside. Take your time."

I gazed into the mirror again, almost not recognizing

the person staring back. Red hair matted in red blood on a red face. At least I had a theme going.

My stomach growled as I gingerly stripped my sweat-soaked clothes off, depositing their remains in a pile. I adjusted the two necklaces that hung from my neck, rubbing the opal Rhiannon had given me. My hand instinctively reached to my side. My khanjar was gone.

No surprise. Here I was a prisoner—not to be trusted with daggers.

The spigot creaked as I shut off the water. One foot after the other, I sank into the piping hot water. A thousand tiny cuts screamed, and then abated as the heat began to soothe my aches. It did not soothe my mind.

Betrayed by the freaking bastard, Matthias. Had we set this in motion by going to him to help us trap the djinn? Or had he been planning this a long time?

My blood would have boiled over if the tub hadn't been doing it for me. He *used* us, *ambushed* us, and locked us away in here to rot. At least I hoped it was us. And not just me.

I hung my head down over the water and drank in the aroma of the steam. What had Amira added—lavender? Herbs?

I wished it had been juniper. And sea salt. And pine. Like Damian.

I squeezed my eyes shut, sank down beneath the water, and held my breath until my thoughts cleared.

Neve

Eventually, my mind cleared. I rinsed the suds from my flushed and tender skin and dried off with the coarse towel that Amira had laid out. The bath had restored my spirits, and I was ready to storm the citadel.

The mirror revealed that I wasn't too bad off. The caked-on blood had made my wounds look worse than they were. Now that it was gone, nothing seemed too serious.

I poked my shabby pile of clothes. I'd lost my beautiful headscarf somewhere in Helwan, and everything else was shredded. My closet wept a little for the loss. "Amira? Did you say that you had fresh clothes?"

"Absolutely, try these on." She shoved a fistful of blue cloth through the curtain. "It should match your eyes."

The clothes fit reasonably well, but they sure didn't leave much to the imagination. A dark blue chest wrap and bottoms with a light blue translucent split skirt—that was it. Blue islands amidst a sea of skin.

The outfit felt light and airy, which a mercy considering the heat in the room. I slipped out of the bathroom, and Amira beamed and handed me a pair of slippers. "You look fantastic considering the state you were in."

"Thanks for the clothes. The bath. For everything."

"Of course, we're bunkmates now."

Not for long, I hoped.

The air felt warm and stuffy, practically tomblike. I brushed damp beads of sweat from my forehead, suddenly thankful for the airy clothing. "Is it always this hot?"

"Yes. I mean, honey, we're in the Realm of Fire in the middle of a volcano. We are literally in a living hell. Today's not too bad. It gets worse. Some days I just melt into water and slosh around the citadel."

Great. This year's vacation—*Sweat City in the Realm of Suck.*

I explored the room, peeking behind curtains at the little beds. Sweat and spatters of blood soaked my mattress, a grim reminder that I'd gotten away lucky. "So, we're really not locked in here?"

Amira pulled open the doorway, revealing a dark hall. "Nope. You're a servant now. But you can come and go as you like. We have free access to the upper floors of the citadel."

That would make scouting easier. "What's on the lower levels?"

"The forges. The armory. The dungeons. All off limits."

Bingo.

"The dungeons. That's where I need to go to look for my friend."

Amira crossed her arms. "It's well guarded. No way we're getting in there."

"I have to."

"Neve, what you have to do now is figure out what the hell you're supposed to do in service of the efreet. If you are slow in your service or disobey, he will literally burn the skin from your body." She turned and gestured to a blistered scar on the small of her back. "I do everything perfectly. That was just a reminder to keep behaving."

Needles pricked the back of my neck, cascading down to my feet. *Freaking sick bastard.* I would destroy this efreet.

Amira pivoted back. "Whatever notions you have running in your head right now, stop them. Just keep your head down and stay alive."

I unballed my fists and massaged some blood back into my fingers. "Okay. How about a tour? Let's start with that. I need to get the lay of the land."

She curtseyed and swept her arm to the door. "Welcome to hell. It sucks."

20

Neve

Amira took me on a whirlwind tour of the Citadel, weaving through a maze of dimly lit halls constructed from strangely shaped blocks of black mineral and basalt. She swept down the corridors gracefully, almost as if she were gliding across the black stone floor, like droplets of rain running along a window.

I traced our path in my mind, trying to hold onto the information for later. Some doors led to barracks and state rooms, while others opened into closets and store-rooms. The corridors and doorways were endless—like a labyrinth.

I despised labyrinths, and the snaking hallways

made my head pound. "This place is more like a fortress than a palace. Why are there so many rooms?"

"I think the efreet is raising an army. I don't know why."

Possibilities spun through my head. Invading another plane. Magic Side. The human world. In every case, the consequences would be dire.

What would an efreet, master of cosmic powers, even want? Freedom? Dominion? Revenge? I couldn't fathom.

Perhaps the army was actually Matthias's plan.

I barely focused on Amira's words as she explained my duties. It involved a lot of tea, cleaning, and random auxiliary services. I was to be half maid and half entertainment—I didn't really pay attention to the details. I wouldn't be there long, and I had to focus on memorizing the layout. The myriad of hypnotic pathways steadily syphoned my ability to think.

Amira grabbed my arm pulling me close as we walked. "Really. I am *so* excited you're here. I've been bored out of my mind."

"How long have you been here?"

She shrugged. "Oh, several weeks at least. Seems like years. You have no idea how wretched it is here. No TV. No books or magazines—they'd probably just burn up, I guess. No beauty products. It's uncivilized."

She was obviously making light of an unbearable situation.

I cocked my head. Amira's cheeks glowed with a soft rouge highlight, her eyes offset with delicate black mascara and a sparkling dark-purple eye shadow. "Uh, Amira, you are definitely wearing makeup."

"Of course I am. I *refuse* to be a barbarian. I just have to make it myself."

"You make your own makeup?"

"Of course. I make it at home, too, but there I can just order ingredients off the internet. It's much easier than grinding the mica and mineral pigments I get from the guards here."

"That seems like a lot of unnecessary work, but awesome."

"Speaking of makeup. Where did you get that?" Amira pointed to my chest.

"Get what?"

She reached forward and lifted the circular bronze trinket around my neck that the merchant, Yasmina had given me. "That's a pretty one. Where did you find it?"

I pulled the necklace over my head to inspect it better. I hadn't really had a chance to look at it since Cairo. "It was a gift. But I really have no idea what it is. Do you?"

"Of course. It's a kohl container. You know, for lining your eyes." She took it and unscrewed the lid, pulling out the narrow applicator that was attached. She examined the white powdery substance that covered it and frowned. "Except, this isn't khol."

"What is it then?" And why had Yasmina given it to me?

Amira sniffed the container, and a ripple of disgust crossed her face. "Come with me. I think I know what this is."

She took my hand and towed me down a stairwell. We stopped before a swinging door that appeared to lead inside the kitchen, judging by the wonderful aromas that drifted out. My stomach grumbled.

Amira popped her head into the door. "Jax! Why is there a sack of sugar sitting in the hall? You know if the grand chamberlain sees this, he will have your head."

I looked down the empty hall. What was she brewing?

Amira closed the door, leaned her back against the wall, and winked at me. Seconds later, a slender man with light orange hair and a weaselly face stormed out the kitchen door. He turned his head side to side, eyes scanning the empty floor, and then scowled as he turned to face Amira.

"Amira! What the hell are you—"

She held the kohl applicator to her lips and, as the man turned, she exhaled deeply. The fine dust spread through the air with a puff, coating his face.

The man's eyes froze wide open, and he collapsed to the ground.

"Ha! I knew it." Amira beamed in triumph.

"What did you do? Is he dead?" I crouched next to

the crumpled man whose eyes stared back at me blankly.

"Toadstool dust. Jax isn't dead, just paralyzed. Every muscle transfixed. He can still see and hear me." She leaned down and patted his head. "Next time, you will give me what I ask. No skimping on the baking soda. *Right*, Jax?"

"How long do the effects last?"

"Mmm...thirty minutes to an hour if you're lucky." She gave me the necklace back, and I put it on. "Come on, help me move him inside the kitchen. He's really bothersome and very stingy with his baking supplies, but I wouldn't want the grand chamberlain to take his head."

Amira grabbed Jax's shoulders, and I took his legs, and we carried his rigid form through the door into a long pantry. We deposited Jax beside a pile of flour sacks.

I looked at Amira. "Somehow, I don't think this experience is going to make him any more charitable with his baking supplies."

"You're probably right." Amira grimaced, then shrugged. "Follow me."

We entered an extended chamber with low, vaulted ceilings. Brick ovens lined the walls, and long stone tables occupied the center of the room. Several cooks scurried about butchering slabs of meat and pouring ingredients into vast black cauldrons.

My stomach rumbled as a deluge of warm toasty aromas overwhelmed me.

Scones?

I was instantly on high alert, functioning like a trained predator tracking its favored prey. I grabbed Amira's arm. "Fates. Is someone baking?"

"Oh my goodness, I completely forgot to feed you. I am a horrible friend. What do you like? I work here in the mornings, so I can nick whatever we want."

"Anything baked will do. Muffins. A cracker. Anything."

"I made biscuits this morning. Even cold, they're going to be better than anything else here. I am an *amazing* baker."

She found me a seat and rushed off to reheat some biscuits in the oven. The kitchen staff bustled about, completely ignoring my presence. I watched them, trying to learn as much as I could. If Damian was a prisoner, then someone would have to bring his meals, right? Maybe I could find that person and then find him.

A few minutes later, Amira returned with a plate piled high with yellow bready goodness and a pot of tea.

"Oh-my-gods-I-am-so-hungry-thank-you." I shoved a biscuit in my mouth. It was pillowy and tender, with brown toasty edges from the brick oven. The rich lemony flavor mingled with the crunchy demerara sugar on top. "I thought I had died and gone to hell, but clearly I'm in heaven."

Amira grinned. "I told you, I *am* an amazing baker. Not that the food is any good here, normally."

Something clicked. "In general, the food here is bad?"

"It's fine if you like meat stew seven days a week. I'm a vegetarian, so it sucks."

I leaned in close. "Do you think if we bribed the guards with your biscuits, we could get into the dungeons?"

"Neve, that's crazy. You've got to stop fixating on your friend. We'll get word to him through backchannels. There are a lot of servants, and some of the soldiers like me, which is not surprising. I *am* beautiful." She grinned. Her cockiness was good natured and mostly tongue-in-cheek, as well as infectiously charming.

"Amira, I need to know that he's okay. Please, help me with this. It's important."

She sat in silence, head down. Finally, she sighed. "Okay. We can try. Sometimes I bring soldiers gifts in exchange for favors. We can see how far we get."

I hugged her twice. Once for saying yes. A second time for the biscuits—manna from heaven. I radiated with energy. We had a plan.

She mounded the remaining biscuits into a basket and supplemented it with a few other baked goods. "Even if this doesn't work today, we can try again, as long as we don't draw undue attention."

"Thanks, Amira. You're the best."

With our devious biscuit-bribery basket in hand, we spiraled down into the depths of the keep.

After several turns, a guard stepped out of a niche, blocking our progress down the passage. He brandished a short, double-ended spear and wore only sandals and a chainmail tunic. Sweat glistened on his skin, and the torchlight cast deep shadows that outlined the contours of his muscles.

He gestured with his spear. "Servants are not allowed past this point."

Amira cocked her head and spoke in a silky voice. "But we have such an important delivery."

She touched my arm lightly as she stepped forward and whispered, "Stay back here and look alluring."

I did my best *Pretty Woman* impression and leaned against the wall. Searing pain scalded my shoulder where the skin touched the stone, and I jumped forward with a yelp.

Amira shot a piercing glance back at me, and I shrugged, casually adjusting my top.

I didn't know the walls were freaking hot.

Amira swayed up to the human guard, basket on her hip. She leaned in slowly, tilted her chin, and whispered in his ear. His eyes darted across her and then to me, but he shook his head. My pulse quickened.

Amira slowly pulled back the cloth from the top of the basket, revealing her warm, golden biscuits inside. She let her fingers creep in, emerging with one of the toasty sugar-coated delicacies. She raised it to her lips and gently pulled away a flake of crust with her teeth, then offered the remainder to the guard.

I had never seen such a sensual biscuit in all my life. Neither had my stomach, apparently. It rumbled, although I'd eaten an inappropriate number of biscuits not twenty minutes before.

The guard was salivating, whether at the woman or biscuit, I couldn't tell. Amira whispered into his ear again and put three more precious biscuits into his hands. He took them and disappeared back into the niche.

The exchange seemed well received, and she returned. "Okay, I think that worked—though I have to visit again with more to keep him quiet. He'll turn a blind eye to us, if we don't cause trouble. Apparently, the dungeons are quite a ways ahead. We have to go through the forges to get there."

"You are amazing, Amira."

"The power of food porn. It's why I had to get off Instagram. Let's hope the other guards are just as malleable. Being caught and tortured is *not* on my to-do list."

We crept along until approaching footsteps halted our progress. Amira pulled me into a storeroom, and we cowered, waiting for the footsteps to pass. I couldn't resist the rising aroma of baked goods and slipped a biscuit out of the basket.

I peeked through the cracked door and nearly gagged in disgust. A monstrous man lumbered by—or what was left of a man. His engorged muscles were so enormous they threated to rip themselves from his bones. He wore no armor save for an iron codpiece and a chainmail hood. He wielded a cruel falchion in one hand and a coiled whip in the other.

I doubt he'll be interested in biscuits.

After the monstrosity had passed, we waited a minute and then continued down the passage. Though we had to bribe another sentry, Amira's biscuits proved quite convincing.

As we continued down the dark corridor, the heat intensified to sweltering levels, and ringing hammers echoed off the stone walls.

A large archway led to a room that radiated noise and shadowy amber light. The beating hammers were deafening, and my lungs burned from the acrid and smokey air.

I crept ahead and peeked in.

The hazy air shimmered with heat and reverberated with the clang of hammers on steel. Molten vats of lava illuminated the room with a deep red-orange glow. Steel weapons rested in racks along the walls. At the far end of the room, prisoners poured cauldrons of molten metal into crude molds. Chained teams of smiths worked at anvils, their syncopated hammers reverberating with each blow. A guard barked curses at the captives.

And Damian.

Alive.

He stood before a black iron anvil, his chest stripped bare. A ring of magical runes glowed on the ground around him—some sort of binding spell. Heavy chains stretched from the floor to a collar around his neck. In his left hand, he held a glowing orange blade. In his right, a heavy black hammer.

Shoulders tensing, he raised the hammer high and slammed it down upon the hot steel blade. The glowing metal rang as sparks erupted into the air and across his bare skin. His heavy chains rattled with each blow and sweat rolled down his chest.

He was *magnificent.*

He worked his weapon in a steady pounding beat, then used short, quick strokes as he deftly tilted and turned the blade, bringing it to a keen edge. *The way he worked...* it was not that of a muscled brute, but of a master craftsman.

Where had he learned to do that?

Perspiration trickled down my skin as I crouched, watching him. My legs ached, but I couldn't pry my eyes away. There was something different about him.

Damian shoved the sword deep into the hot sparking coals and drew another forth. He held it aloft, inspecting it for imperfections. It glowed the color of new straw. Twisting it in his hand, he stood with every muscle tensed, the pinnacle of human physique—a statue of a god wrapped in chains. The moisture drained from my mouth as he thrust the blade into the steaming trough beside him, quenching the steel with a hiss.

Strange desire surged within me.

He lowered the weapon and began to cast a spell, tracing glowing runes into the blade with his bare fingertip. I closed my eyes and imagined his magic washing over me, a cold ocean in the heat of the forge. Moisture cascaded through me, and I tasted salt in the air.

"Someone's coming!" Amira's voice shattered my hypnosis, and she pulled me into the chamber and behind a cluster of barrels.

"What's going on?" The guards would spot us in here for sure.

"Shh, someone was stomping up the corridor behind me."

Thank fates she had my back.

One of the burly guards thundered into the forge and began yelling at a bare-chested warrior.

"We need to go, now." Amira grabbed my hand and pulled, but I slipped.

My foot shot out, colliding with a rack of spears. My breath caught as one of the cruel-looking bladed pikes tilted and slid sideways. It hooked its neighbor, and soon the entire arsenal cascaded off the rack.

Oh gods.

The rattle of falling weapons echoed through the chamber. The smiths stopped their work, and the hammers quieted.

One of the lizard-skinned guards snapped his whip and hissed, "Find out what is happening! Take no chances with the prisoners!"

He waved his hands, and a ring of blazing runes flared to life around Damian. The chains restraining his neck and ankles lit with a blinding yellow light, and he collapsed to his knees, gritting his teeth. Nearby, overseers leapt into action, beating down the prisoners with iron batons. Two warriors in leather armor drew their blades. One pointed to our position and turned to alert the others.

The moment he looked away, I darted from behind the barrels, pulling Amira into the corridor.

We ran.

21

Neve

We arrived back by the kitchens, and Amira flopped against the wall, panting. "Holy heavens, I think we're safe."

"How do you know?" I gasped, trying to catch my breath. We'd just barely escaped from the forges without being caught.

"I don't think they saw us. Just heard us. It was close. What a totally insane idea. We should start walking normally. Try not to look suspicious."

I followed her down the hall while my mind reeled.

Damian was *alive*. Chained and under guard, but alive. He was making weapons for the efreet, but not, it seemed, of his own volition.

I needed a plan to get him out of the forges. Get the magicuffs off us. *Escape.* "Amira, how do we get out of here?"

"I've told you. There's no way out. It's impossible."

"I don't believe that."

Amira took me by the arm, almost baring her teeth. "You are going to get us burned alive. That little adventure nearly cost us."

"I'm sorry. Thank you for taking that risk. But I must get us out of here. *All* of us."

She shook her head. "You don't get it. I need you to see what we're up against."

She led me to a door and up a narrow spiral staircase. Every few spirals, there was a door. Amira explained that some led to balconies, while others led to additional floors.

My chest heaved and sweat trickled down my chest. "How far up does this go?"

She stopped and put her hand on the wall. "Far. I've never counted all the steps," she said between breaths.

"Are you okay? Do you need a break?"

"I'm fine," she snapped between huffs.

I started climbing, leading the way.

After a few silent flights, Amira piped up behind me, still panting. "I'm sorry for snapping. It's just that this place is *literally* sucking the life out of me since it's my opposite plane. Even climbing these stairs makes me asthmatic."

I turned to her as I rounded a bend. "What do you mean, opposite plane?"

"As you probably noticed, I am from the Realm of Water... this is my opposite plane, which means it's slowly draining me of my strength. Moreover, even without these stupid shackles, my magic wouldn't work well for me here. It would be very weak."

My slippers skidded to a halt. "You're from the Realm of Water?"

She winked. "Well, technically, I'm from Houston. I visit home from time to time, but the Realm of Water doesn't have cable TV, so Houston it is."

"Are you a planes-walker?"

"That and more. I'm a halfer. Like you."

The stairwell reeled, and I braced myself against the wall.

Amira frowned. "You didn't notice? We're almost cousins. That's why I adore you already! We're going to be best friends."

Steady on, water woman.

I didn't typically make friends easily. I had...well, trust issues, and I already had a best friend—Rhiannon —whom I missed more than my own soul. But Amira was kind and had already put herself in the way of danger for me. Moreover, she might be able to clue me in on what the whole half-genie gig implied.

Also, she *was* an amazing baker.

"All right. Friends, it is." I continued up the steps. "I

really know nothing about what I am. I never lived in the Realm of Air. I've never met another...halfer?"

"That explains a lot. Well, I'll get you up to speed. First of all, I'm a half-marid, which is kind of the best thing to be. My life is like the *Little Mermaid,* all of the time."

"Really?"

"No. I'm from Houston, and I'm a chemist."

"Oh." I couldn't hide the faint disappointment in my voice.

"I mean, I go back from time to time. It's an amazing place. But I love living in Houston. Great food."

"This plane drains *all* your magic?" I looked back at her as I passed another door.

"Basically. And boy does it suck. Want a jet of water? I'll give you a sideways pee pizzle. Want a cloud of fog? I'll give you a puffer of steam."

"Yuck. I'm sorry."

"Cousin, take my advice—never visit the Realm of Earth, your opposite plane. Not planet Earth, but the *realm.* I don't know what would happen to you, but it wouldn't be good. You'd be weakened, for sure. Your powers...." She shrugged, then made plane-crash gesture with her hands.

"Would go kaput?"

"Well, you'll be feeling more like Lois Lane than Superwoman, that's for sure."

"Good to know. At least I can fight with a knife." I

reached for my khanjar but stopped short, feeling the ache of loss spread through my chest.

My khanjar was part of me. I needed to find it.

"And the worst part—you can't planes-walk in or out of a contrary realm. So, I couldn't leave here myself, even if I tried, which is just balls."

"But I could planes-walk out, if I didn't have these magicuffs on?"

"Nope."

"Why?"

"I'm going to show you." She put her head down. "Keep climbing."

Ten arduous minutes later, the stairwell terminated at a brass door. Amira undid the heavy locks and steel crossbar and swung it open.

A smoldering wind poured over me, instantly drying the sweat from my skin. I pushed through the door out onto the pinnacle of the citadel's solitary tower, defying the howling sky. The black stones baked through my slippers, and my eyes stung. "Fates. The heat out here is unbearable!"

Amira pressed her back against the wall. "I *told* you this is a horrid place. Look over the edge."

Wind whipped around me. Unlike in the Realm of Air, or even my own world, it did not replenish my spirit. But it *was* a relief from the hot, tomblike interior of the citadel. Even if it burned my lungs, at least I could breathe freely again.

I started forward, but Amira didn't follow. I turned to her. "Are you coming?"

"Hell no. I hate heights. Anyway, I'll keep a lookout."

"For what?"

"Oh, let's see, giant condors. Dragons. Fire drakes. You name it, it's up here, and we're standing on the tallest birdfeeder around." Amira pushed me forward but clung to the doorway with her other hand. "Go ahead. You need to see where you are. Then maybe you'll drop some of your crazy talk about escape."

I went to the edge of the tower and peered over the low wall. A molten lake loomed thousands of feet below, and I couldn't fly.

My stomach dropped, and my head spun. I squeezed my eyes closed and fought it back, then peered over the edge again.

The tower upon which I stood reached impossibly high, crafted of irregular basalt and dark stone. Its base expanded into a great black fortress rising from a lake of lava. All around us, the sides of a massive caldera rose.

"We're in the middle of a freaking volcano?" I bellowed above the roaring wind.

"I told you that! Did you think I was kidding? We're not walking out unless you're a fire dancer."

Plumes of gas rose from beyond the edge of the caldera, emanating from vents in the side of the volcano. Even up here, the air smelled acrid and rank.

"This place is a hellscape of death," I whispered.

"Do you see that shimmering light above and around the volcano?" Amira hollered over the wind.

A barren desert surrounded the volcano. The air on the horizon wavered, dancing in the heat. I squinted in the relentless light. Where desert met stone, there was a faint glitter, like the sun refracting off the surface of a lake. "I think so?"

I had a sinking feeling that I knew what that was.

"This citadel and the entire volcano around it are sheathed in a dome of anti-teleportation magic. No one can ether-walk or planes-walk in or out. You want to get home? You'll have to bust out of your anti-magic shackles, break out of the citadel, cross the burning lava, scale the sides of the caldera, get through the fields of razor-sharp stones, avoid poison gas, and survive the sky monsters until you reach the edge of the desert."

I scanned the scorched wasteland and nodded decisively. "Sounds like a plan."

Amira blinked. "You're insane. But I think I like it."

A dark shadow whipped across the stones. I looked up, spotting a black reptilian creature with flaming wings. It dove down out of the blazing sky and screeched, lashing the air with a barbed tail.

"Run!" Amira and I shouted at the same time.

We darted inside, swinging the door closed behind us. She latched the cross bar and locks right before something heavy slammed against it. Claws screeched across brass, and the door shook.

"Fire drake!" Amira raced down the stairs. I followed. The creature probably couldn't get through the door, but it definitely couldn't fit down the stairwell.

"Big birdfeeder," Amira huffed, shaking her head.

"I see what you mean."

We reached the bottom and I turned to her. "I'm getting the heck out of here."

She frowned, then nodded decisively. "It's completely insane, but I'm in. I never stood a chance on my own, but together we might just have a shot."

"We *definitely* have a shot. But first, we have to free Damian."

"First, we have to see to our duties, or we'll end up in the forges next to him."

That was the last thing we needed.

I spent the rest of the day shadowing Amira, biding my time until we were no longer needed and I could come up with a plan. We hauled vats of stew to the mess, scrubbed pans and performed nightly duties throughout the black stone fortress. The work left me sweat-soaked, with weak legs and an aching back.

As the day closed, exhaustion pulled me toward bed.

Just as I sat down, Amira poked her head through the doorway. "Come see the suns set."

"Suns?" Every inch of me felt raw, but I stood and followed her to the stairwell.

"There are four. One set hours ago. A second is almost gone, and the third is just crossing the horizon."

She pulled me to the stairs, and I staggered out onto the open balcony, clinging to her arm.

For all my aches and pain, it was worth a look.

The balcony was positioned low on the obsidian tower, below even the rim of the caldera. The raging lake of lava beneath us cast an orange glow upward. A spark of light flashed along the horizon as the sun slipped behind the rim of the volcano.

Far to the right, another enormous sun had set halfway, withdrawing its harsh red light from the world.

Amira gestured to the sky above. The obsidian spike of the tower pointed like a raised lance at the realm's fourth sun, a small reddish-brown orb. "That is the night sun. It is never truly dark here. It's always watching us, like the relentless eyes of the efreet."

My skin crawled. I was trapped by a sleepless overlord on an alien world without night.

Would we *really* be able to escape?

22

Damian

"Walk, angel." The guard leading me down the corridor yanked the chain secured to the shackles on my wrist.

I closed my eyes, focusing my mind on shutting out the pain. Closing my wounds with anger.

The more I let the darkness inside me take over, the easier it was to bear.

But I couldn't lose myself. Not yet. Not until I got Neve out of here.

I'd sensed her in the forges.

Alive.

Even with her magicuffs on, I had felt her, like a wire stretched taught between us.

I grudgingly obeyed as the two guards escorted me

down the corridor. There should have been four guards, but Neve's visit to the forges had incited riots that were preoccupying most of the efreet's forces.

It had taken every ounce of restraint not to smash the guards' heads in when the fights had broken out. The time hadn't been right.

"Faster." The guard jabbed me in the ribs—the same ones they'd cracked earlier. With the magicuffs on my ankles, I couldn't heal.

I gritted my teeth against the pain and stepped up to the dungeon's entrance. Two heavily armed sentries guarded the gate. Unlike those escorting me, they had scales for skin.

"Where are the others?" One of them barked.

"Busy," the guard said, shoving me forward. "Bloody idiots thought they could rebel. Not to worry though, we're teaching 'em a lesson they won't soon forget."

The sentry spat on me as we passed. I gritted my teeth. He'd pay for that.

The reek of sweat and blood and piss burned my lungs as we walked through the dark passage.

The guard in front of me stopped at the door to my cell. While he fumbled with his keys, I stepped forward, causing the chain he held to slack just enough for me to grab a hold of it.

The door snicked open, and he tugged on the chain. "Come on, *Fallen*."

They sensed what I was and didn't like it. Were afraid of it.

Good.

I stepped into the cell, pulling the chain hard and fast. The guard's eyes bulged as he lost his footing and stumbled toward me. I caught his chest with my arm and swung the chain around his neck, pulling it taut with my cuffs. He struggled as the metal links crushed his windpipe.

The second guard bellowed as he barreled into me, knocking me off balance.

My fractured bones screamed at the impact, but I elbowed him and unwrapped the chain from the unconscious guard's neck, allowing his body to collapse to the floor.

The guard maneuvered around the room with practiced, dancelike movements, taunting me. But I was practiced in the ring, and I knew this dance. Lived for it. He lunged, and I met his blow with a jab to the ribs and spun, my back to the door.

Sweat poured off his face, and his chest heaved. He launched forward, but I sidestepped, slamming my shackled fists into his head with a crack. His body went limp and fell to the floor, blood seeping into the cracks in the stone.

Reaching down, I grabbed the familiar brass key from the first guard's pocket. Holding it with my teeth, I unlocked the shackles on my wrists, letting them drop to my feet.

Now if only I could get these magicuffs off.

Slowly, I reached down to grab the dagger from the unconscious guard, and something slammed into my back. Agonizing pain shot through my broken ribs, and I leapt to my feet.

Three more guards.

One thrust a long sparking pole at me. I deflected it instinctively and searing magic coursed through my body. My muscles quaked and I collapsed as fog filled my mind.

"Damian." Neve's voice echoed through the darkness.

I opened my eyes, squinting in the bright light. Shadows danced across the obsidian walls of the chamber.

"There you are," she said, her lips brushing against my ear. The jasmine scent of her magic wrapped around me, overwhelming my senses.

This was a dream.

I sensed it but didn't care. I let the dream surround me, unwilling to relinquish the scent of Neve's magic.

My eyes adjusted as Neve pressed her hand to my chest. Her flesh warm and soft...so *real*.

"Neve." Electricity shot through me, and I reached

for her. My arms stopped short, the cuffs pulling tightly as they rang out with a metallic clang.

My vision cleared, and I looked up. The bare room was lit by burning braziers. My hands were bound above my head to a chain secured to a bronze ring on the ceiling.

"What's going on?" My heartbeat pounded in my ears.

"Shhh." She smiled, a lance to my heart.

I needed her. To hold her. Feel her. "Neve—"

Her fingers covered my mouth while she traced her other hand down my side. Her touch sent shivers across my skin, and my muscles tightened. The pain from earlier was gone, replaced with desire.

This couldn't be real. But after the endless suffering I'd endured these past days, ecstasy's embrace was too easy.

Eyes locked on mine, Neve slowly unbuttoned her blouse. My heartbeat ratcheted up at the sight of the sliver of pale skin.

"I've wanted this for so long," she murmured.

I breathed in deeply as she lowered her head and kissed my neck, licking until she reached my shoulder. She bit down, just hard enough. A low groan escaped me, heat cascading through my body, coiling tight, flaring between my thighs.

Gods be damned.

Neve raised her head, meeting my gaze with a sultry smile. "Do you want me to stop?"

"No," I said, my voice rough.

"Good."

She stood on her toes, and her lips found mine, warm and tasting of citrus. I moaned, the rough metal cutting into my wrists as I pulled on the chain—but it didn't budge. Need rose inside me, ravenous. I wasn't sure how much of this I could take.

Neve traced her fingers down my chest, moving them across my stomach, leaving waves of hot and cold in their wake. She paused above the waistband of my pants. Desire punched me in the gut, and I ached for her touch.

What I wouldn't give to be able to touch her right now. To taste her.

A metallic crash jolted me to my senses.

I scanned the empty room.

Neve was gone.

"Nevaeh!" Deep down I knew she hadn't been there at all.

A dream. A vision.

My muscles clenched as a familiar chuckle filled the space.

The efreet.

Sulfur burned my tongue, and the air rippled with heat. The pain of my broken bones and burnt flesh returned, almost too much to bear.

"You bastard," I said.

The efreet stepped into view, blazing like an inferno. Agony wracked my body as my skin blistered.

My vision flickered between consciousness, and his voice echoed through the darkness.

"You can't escape me, Damian. Not even in your dreams."

23

Neve

After watching the setting suns, I returned to my chamber, too exhausted to think.

Despite my doubt and fear of ever escaping this hellhole, I fell asleep as soon as my head hit the pillow.

Rest, however, did not come.

The relentless hot air and exhaustion of the day fueled a deluge of strange dreams.

I fled across the burning sands that surrounded the magical city of Helwan—though the city now sat atop a massive volcano instead of the dried floodplain.

A horde of ghuls flowed through the city's gate, scrambling over rocks with unnatural speed and reflexes. Their faces shifted, revealing inhuman mouths with serrated teeth, and their fingers erupted into twisted claws that would not stop growing.

I stumbled over a hill of dirt that looked at first like a rhino, and then like the back of a scorpion. It shifted, and I fell to my knees. The ghuls descended, grasping my arms, their curling claws cutting into my flesh as they pulled me down into the desert. Sand flowed into my mouth, silencing my screams.

Then the sand became water. My head was submerged in the cistern, and I had dropped my flashlight below. It kept flicking on and off, illuminating bestial crocodiles as they swam toward me—disappearing into darkness and reappearing closer with each flash of light.

I screamed, but water poured into my mouth, and the jaws of a crocodile loomed in my vision. Just as they snapped down, a hand pulled me from the water.

The hand of a ghul. I knelt in submission before the caliph of Helwan who was adorned with a glittering ornate coat crafted from Helwani cloth. The caliph's headdress hid his face in shadow, and he radiated an aura of smoking magic.

He ripped a dagger from its sheath—my khanjar. "You have trespassed in my city and stolen that which is most precious to me. For that, I condemn you to death."

The caliph plunged the khanjar into my chest, and I choked as blood flowed from my lips. I collapsed onto the obsidian floor, and my magic rose from me like white incense. The caliph bent forward, wrapped the tendrils of magic around his hand and devoured them, ripping the life and power from my corpse.

"Your power is mine." He chuckled, my magic illuminating his face.

Damian.

His face was Damian's.

My soul screamed as it departed my body.

Damian laughed and rose on a vortex of air. His cloak turned to white, covered in the radiant lines of my tattoo.

My body jerked upright, and I woke, choking. My sweat-soaked bedsheets clung to my clammy skin.

Just a dream. It had just been a dream.

I scrambled out of my sleeping alcove and into the room. The low breathing of half a dozen other servants filled the air, and the stifling heat hung heavy in the room.

I ran to the bathroom and splashed water on my face, but it offered little relief.

I stepped into the hall and took the spiral stairs two at a time. My lungs heaved after a few flights, so I forced open a side door and stumbled out onto a balcony—the same one where I'd watched the setting suns with Amira.

The sky was dim, and that blazing brown sun—the eye of the efreet—still radiated overhead.

The tears came, and my body quaked as I clutched my opal pendant.

"Rhiannon." I sobbed. "What do I do?"

There was no response, of course.

"Can I trust Damian?"

Silence.

I shook my head. Another dream echoed in my mind—one that had come while I'd slept aboard the *Jewel of Tayir* during our airship journey across the Realm of Air. In that nightmare, Damian had ripped my power from me, just like the caliph in tonight's dream. The memory sent shivers across my skin.

Nightmares. That was all they were. I needed to get my shit together. Damian was a thief, but he wouldn't—*couldn't*—steal my power.

So what was I afraid of?

I scratched my tattoo and thought of the djinn, his rage overflowing until he became a cyclone, ripping apart the world around him. I thought of what I had done to the guys in the bar.

I crossed my arms over my chest, squeezing tightly. Did some part of me want that power taken away?

My breast heaved with a deep sigh. "I wish I wasn't alone right now."

As soon as the words escaped my lips, a comet streaked across the sky. Once, I would have taken that as some kind of sign. Not anymore. Not in this place.

Then the comet turned and shot straight down at me.

I dodged out of the way as a sparking ball of light crashed into the balcony and rolled, sputtering, across the black stonework. A little glowing dragon uncoiled itself and looked up at me expectantly with its huge green eyes.

The creature was strange. Immaterial. Like it was made of pure light rather than flesh and blood. And only about a foot tall. It was too cute to be dangerous.

I hoped.

I cocked my head. "Hi there, little friend. What are you doing here?"

The creature wiped its brow with a tiny little claw and scampered closer. *You called me.*

I frowned. Was I imagining that he was speaking to me? The words rang in my mind, but his mouth didn't move.

"What are you?"

He met my eyes. *I'm a fire sprite.*

"Is that some kind of dragon?"

I'm a being of pure magic. I can look like a lot of things. With a burst of light, the creature flashed into a hummingbird and then a hedgehog. He wiggled his ears and flashed back into a dragon. *But when you can be a dragon, why be anything else?*

"Fair enough." I smiled. He *was* magnificent. If tiny.

"Do you have a name?"

The creature illuminated with a thousand flashing colors. *Not in your tongue. We speak in light. And thoughts.*

"Well, I need to call you something. How about Spark?"

That's got a nice ring to it.

"Spark. I'm Neve."

I know. I've watched over you since you were a child, though you haven't always been able to see me. Spark transformed into a bobbing light.

Recognition dawned. "You were the light that led us through the tunnels below Helwan."

That's right!

"You helped us fight off the ice devils on the airship and warmed me when I was freezing."

And don't forget I illuminated the djinn's dungeons when you hung in cages and the caverns in Cappadocia.

My mind raced. I had a guardian spirit.

"Where did you come from?

I come from this plane—the plane of fire and flame. When you were a child, you did not know how to planeswalk—you crossed many planes and pulled me with you. I have watched over you ever since.

I closed my eyes and recalled long nights in the archives—lights somehow always illuminated the books I needed. When I walked home alone through the streets of Magic Side—somehow, the streetlights never faded, and I never had to step in places of darkness.

Part of me had assumed it was simply magic.

And it *was.* Just not the kind I'd assumed.

And he felt so... *familiar.*

"You've never spoken before."

It is hard outside the Realm of Fire. I am so much stronger here. Spark landed in my palm and elongated into a ribbon of light. He grew legs and a head and transformed back into a long crawling dragon that wound its way along my arm.

"I've certainly never seen you do *that* before."

Transformation is easy here. Outside of this world, I have to draw on your magic to appear. The stronger you get, the longer I can linger. We're bonded.

He placed a tiny glowing claw on top of my outstretched hand. *I shine because of you.*

Spark's magic flowed through me, and my heart ached with joy. Somehow, a part of me had known someone was watching over me—a deeply hidden fragment of my mind—a part entangled with the sky and the winds and the planes. In quiet moments, had that part of my mind watched Spark in return? A flickering lightbulb or a wavering candle? A drifting star?

The flames coalesced as Spark turned into the image of Rhiannon. *Your bonds with her are also very strong.*

He switched into that of a man—Damian. *And him, even though you have only known him a short time.*

A lump formed in my throat.

My soul knew I could trust Spark in ways I could trust no other person. And that raised questions.

Spark transformed back to his dragon form, and I leaned on the parapet, gazing out over the glowing caldera. "Do you trust Damian?"

The tiny creature scowled and paced back and forth. *I have no bonds with him. I do not know.*

"I had a dream—that Damian would steal my power. Do you think he would do that?"

Dreams are dreams. He shrugged. *Who knows what they mean?*

"I'm afraid that maybe a part of my soul knows something I don't—that Damian is dangerous."

The dragon tapped the tips of his claws together, considering. *Maybe it is possible—I do not understand your kind. But this man protects you. That is what I have seen.*

Damian had risked his life for mine. Had fought to protect me. And I needed to trust someone in this infernal world.

Could it be him?

The little dragon flitted into the air on luminescent wings. *I don't think we have time to worry about dreams. The efreet is real. If he finds out about our bond, he'll eat me and torture you. We need to get out of here. And I think we'll need Damian to do it.*

I nodded. "Can you find Damian and speak to him?"

Yes.

"Tell him that I'm okay, and that I'll find us a way out of here. Tell him to be ready."

On it. With that, Spark vanished with a pop.

My hand jerked out, trying to catch him before he disappeared. The sudden loss brought an emptiness to my chest.

Was he real? Or was he a figment of my desperate imagination?

I returned to my bed, my mind churning.

I would get us out of this hell hole.

24

Neve

It was well into the afternoon, and the suns crept closer to the caldera's rim. I finished my duties early and spent the rest of the day holed up with Amira in her tiny room, plotting our escape from this cursed place.

My chest ached. Spark had found Damian last night and relayed my message. But according to Spark, *Damian was in bad shape*. I didn't know what that meant, but the thought of it made my stomach knot.

I had to get him out soon.

Amira stared hard at the schematic plan of the palace we had drawn, then stood, tension radiating from her. "For the record, I think this is a bad idea."

"It's our only idea."

"Fair enough, and I'm willing to risk it. But I want it on record that you're the crazy one." Amira paced the room, her hands clutched together. "We'll need to get Damian out first. He'll be brought to the dungeon soon, which is good because he'll be less heavily guarded there than at the forges."

"Spark said he counted at least two guards keeping watch, so we'll have to either disarm or distract them." My fingers itched for my khanjar. "Any chance we can get knives from the kitchen?"

She shook her head. "The kitchen guards watch those closely. We'd have to take them out somehow, and there would be a ton of witnesses."

I bit my lip. "Well, I have the toadstool dust. We could paralyze a few guards and take their weapons. But I don't know how many uses there are in the bottle. Any better ideas? I don't think biscuits will cut it this time."

Amira paused midpace, and a crazed smile spread across her face. "You just gave me a great idea."

She crossed to the beauty table along the back wall and opened a pearl-inlaid trousseau. Bottles clinked as she reached her hand inside and pulled out a tiny glass vial. Wide-eyed and beaming, she held it in her palm and glided toward me. "We'll drug them."

"Drug them?" I narrowed my eyes at the bottle, making out a clear liquid inside. "What is that?"

"Concentrated fire poppy juice. I stole a little from a vial hidden in the captain's quarters. It's super potent. A tiny dose will send you into deliciously wild fever dreams. Anything more than four or five drops can be fatal. Care for a taste?"

I raised my brows in shock.

"I figured I could use it if I ever needed to escape. Either from the tower or from the tedium." She winked.

I gently took the vial from Amira's hand, inspecting the contents.

"I'll bake some biscuits and top them with a gooey poppy juice glaze," she said. "We'll give them to the guards, and they'll fall into a dreamy coma. Then you'll take the keys and break your friend out."

"Once we have Damian, we'll go to the forges. He should be able to break off our magicuffs there."

"Hold up. The forges? Nope. That's a bad idea. Don't you remember our last foray down there?" Amira plucked the vial of poppy juice from my hand and pocketed it.

"Can we distract them? How many poppy juice-laced biscuits can you make?"

"Not that many." Amira slumped onto a chaise lounge and bit her lower lip. "*Maybe* we can distract them or lure them out with something else?"

"Could we smoke them out? I saw big pits of lava. Could we throw something in?"

"Holy potatoes, Neve, you're on a roll. I can make smoke bombs! Right under everyone's noses!"

"How?"

"I'm a chemist, dang it all! And I've got an industrial kitchen at my disposal. All I need is potassium nitrate, used for curing meat—and sugar, used for making things delicious, as well as a little baking soda to regulate the reaction. It's all here!" Her eyes had gone completely mad.

I took a deep breath. "Really? That's all you need?"

"As easy as pancakes."

I blinked. This might actually work. "You're brilliant, Amira!"

She tossed her hair like a model and crossed her eyes. "I know."

We spent the next hour laying out our escape plan and making sure it was watertight. We'd have one shot. If we botched it, we'd be dead, and judging from what Amira and Spark had told me of the efreet, it would be neither swift nor painless.

Neve

Several hours later, Spark and I waited outside the kitchens for Amira. The homey smell of fresh baking wafted under the doors, along with something awful that I assumed was residual from the smoke bombs.

Tapping my fingers on the hot stone wall, I walked through the plans in my head for the hundredth time.

Spark hovered beside me, taking the form of a tiny dragon. *You're going to wear your fingerprints off if you keep doing that. And it's making me nervous.*

"Sorry." I stopped tapping, but excitement bubbled in my veins, drowning out the fear. It was time to get out of here. Vile memories of Matthias and the djinn flooded my mind, but I pushed them aside.

The kitchen door swung open, and Amira stepped out carrying a tray of piping hot biscuits. Steam drifted off them, and they smelled divine.

"Here." Amira tossed me two unglazed biscuits and grinned. "I made a couple extras. Without the poppy syrup."

I caught them, shoving one into my pocket and biting into the other. How did this girl know me so well already?

Spark snatched a biscuit off the tray and gobbled it down in three gulps.

"Those are drugged!"

The dragon cocked its head quizzically, crumbs falling from its mouth. *I'm immune. I'm a being of pure magic. Poison does not affect me.*

I furrowed my brow. "But you need to eat?"

I feast on their essence. Which is warm and toasty.

He snaked out his neck to grab another, but Amira pulled the tray back. "No! We need these."

"Spark, can you lead us to the dungeon and alert us if you see anyone ahead?" I asked.

Mmhmm. Spark sped down the hall and disappeared.

"Do you have the smoke bombs?"

"Yep. In my satchel." Amira turned so I could access her bag. "Reach in and grab a few."

I snatched a couple of the dark, golf ball-sized pellets. "How do we light them?"

"No fuses. Just use one of the torches on the wall or throw them in lava. The whole thing will light up."

The little dragon returned a minute later. *This way. The coast is clear.*

We crept down the corridor behind him. Ten minutes and about a dozen turns later, we reached the hall leading toward the dungeon entrance. Flaming torches lit the dark space, and shadows danced across the walls. The humid air reeked of sweat.

Balancing the tray of biscuits in her left hand, Amira peered around the corner.

"Two guards at the front gate." She turned to me. "Stay here. Once they're drugged, I'll unlock the gate for you."

I nodded. "Do your thing."

Amira adjusted her posture, back straight, head up, and rounded the corner with the tray balanced on her right palm like a waitress.

Leaning against the corner, I listened to the muffled

chatter that echoed down the corridor. Unable to make out what was unfolding, I stole a quick glance.

Amira stood, hand on her waist, slightly turned, popping her hip out like a model. Jaws hanging, the guards appeared completely and utterly enamored. She let out a sultry laugh and handed each of them a poppy juice-laced biscuit.

A grin broke across my lips. She was unstoppable.

I counted down the agonizing seconds. Damian was so close, and though I knew it was impossible, I could almost feel his magic washing over me, sweet relief from the sweltering tomblike air. I closed my eyes, imagining him wrapped in chains before the anvil. My heart ached.

A high-pitched whistle rang down the corridor, and I peeked out. Amira frantically waved me forward, her eyes bright.

Darting from the corner, I raced down the hall toward her. The two burly guards had slumped to the ground.

"That was fast." I crouched down and lifted the head of one of the guards by his hair. He had the face of a man, but his skin was scaly. He was still breathing. Barely.

I unhooked the knife from his belt and jammed it through the sash around my waist.

Amira kicked the other guard with her toe. "I added a little extra, just to be sure they worked fast. It means I couldn't make as many." She unlocked the door to the gate with a set of keys strung along a large iron ring. "It's all you from here. Go find your friend. I'll keep watch."

She pushed the heavy metal door open and tossed me the keys. I caught them. "We'll see you in five."

Spark was already inside waiting for me. He turned down a dank passageway lined with cells. Some were empty, others had sleeping occupants.

Spark stopped in front of an iron door with a metal grate window. Standing on the tips of my toes, I peeked inside the dark room. A man lay on a cot in the corner, one foot resting on his knee.

"Damian," I whispered.

The form sprang from the bed, and Damian's face appeared behind the grate a half second later. "Neve!"

I fumbled with the keys, wincing when they clanked loudly together. There were at least a dozen on the ring.

On the fourth try, the door unlocked with a clack, and I pulled it back, using my weight to force it open a foot. Heart pounding, I slipped inside the dark room.

Bare arms wrapped around me, drawing me close.

"Are you real? Or am I dreaming again?"

I gasped. "Damian, I'm rea—"

His hand pressed against the back of my scalp. Grasping my hair, he gently tugged my head back. I obeyed, and his mouth found mine, hot and wet. Ravenous.

My fingers dug into his damp shirt, and he groaned, pulling me close.

A shrill whistle rang through the blackness, towing us back to reality. I drew in a shuddery breath and pressed my palm against Damian's pounding chest.

"I thought I'd lost you." His voice, deep and low, rasped over my nerve endings. Desire burned through me, chased by fear. The grief in his words twisted my heart.

I couldn't explain my feelings. Perhaps it was our brush with death. The thought of losing him. But something inside me had softened toward him.

But there was no time for this.

"We have to go, Amira is waiting," I said, still breathless from our kiss. "Can you get these magicuffs off us in the forges?"

Damian's jaw tightened as if he wanted to say more, then he nodded. "Of course. There's no time to lose."

"Who's Amira?" he whispered as we hurried out into the hall.

She appeared at the sound of her name and gestured for us to follow. "Get a freaking move on, slow pokes."

"Amira's a friend. A brilliant baker, chemist, and architect of our escape. She knocked the guards out with poisoned biscuits," I said.

"I'm in your debt." Damian nodded to her and then knelt to retrieve a long blunt spear from one of the unconscious guards.

Amira gave Damian a quick scan from head to toe. "*Wow.* You must be Damian. Neve didn't tell me what a looker you were. Though I do suggest a shower. And some bandages for those wounds."

Now that we'd stepped into the torchlight, I saw Damian's state. The brass collar was gone, but a pair of magicuffs still bound his ankles. Fire-red gashes streaked his arms and back, and a singed path of skin ran from his neck down to his chest.

I gasped, wincing at the memory of the way I'd manhandled him seconds ago. I leaned close and whispered, "I'm sorry, I should have been more careful."

"Careful was not what I needed." He took my hand, his skin rough and calloused, and pulled me forward. "Let's go."

Damian

Neve's kiss lingered on my lips, her essence still coursing through my veins like a drug. Or witchcraft. What was this power she had over me? It had grown since Helwan and morphed into something else. Something dangerous.

I clenched my jaw, driving those thoughts from my mind. I focused on revenge instead. Against Matthias.

The efreet. And the djinn. Heat rose in my chest, and I twisted the spear in my hand.

I would kill the efreet, rip his throat out, and strangle Matthias with it.

Rage colored my vision as we jogged down the passageways—my feet navigating through muscle memory alone.

I had to get control. First escape, then revenge. Then everything else.

The air grew hotter as we neared the entrance to the forges, and my muscles tensed. "There should be four guards at the outer gate to the forges. The rest will be inside, watching over production. If we can take them out quietly, we might be able to slip in."

Frustration tore at me. I would grind all their hearts to dust if I could use my magic. It strained for freedom, a dark fury raging inside my chest.

Fucking magicuffs.

"Amira, wanna try your luck with them?" Neve's smooth voice doused my rage.

I needed to stay calm if I wanted to exact my revenge. Be in control. Once Neve was safe, I could unleash the monster.

"On it!" Amira chirped.

Fates be damned. How were these two so upbeat?

Amira pulled out a tray of baked goods and strutted around the corner.

I reached forward to grab Amira's arm before she

turned the corner and was spotted, but Neve's hand caught my wrist. "She's fine. A pro, actually. Just wait and see."

A minute passed, then Amira whipped back around the corner. "Okay, the good news is that two of them took the biscuits. The bad news is that the others didn't and are going to raise an alarm as soon as their friends pass out. Which should be any second."

I nodded to Neve. "You take the ones on the right, I'll go left."

I threw myself around the corner, Neve at my side. One guard slumped against the wall and started slowly sliding to the floor. A second had dropped his biscuit, eyes groggy.

The other two glared right at us.

I hurled my spear into the chest of one of the sentries just as he started to shout. Lightning crackled across his body and he collapsed instantly. Unconscious or dead, I was not sure.

Is that what the guards had used to knock me out?

Neve was on the other guard as quick as the wind. She blew a cloud of dust into his scale-covered face and dodged his hooked blade. His eyes widened as his muscles locked up, and he collapsed forward midstride. She spun around his tumbling body, pulled a dagger, and brought down the final drowsy sentry.

I kicked the stiff leg of the paralyzed sentry. "What did you do?"

Neve cleaned her blade and slipped it under a sash at her waist. "Toadstool dust. A paralytic. It was inside the necklace that Yasmina gave me back in Cairo."

I nodded as I grabbed a dagger from one of the other guards. "Hell of a gift."

"Cripes. You two are lethal..." Amira whispered as she came up behind us, hand on the wall, biscuit tray dangling limply in her hand.

Neve tossed her the necklace. "Here. You should use this if we get jumped. I'm afraid there's not much left."

"And we're fresh out of biscuits..." Amira said in a daze.

Satisfaction surged through me as I yanked my spear from the dead guard's chest. "Looks like we'll have to handle this the old way. Blood and steel."

Neve

A wave of heat slammed into me as we slipped into the forges. Black lava stalagmites speared up from the elevated walkway, and a red glow from the magma channels below tinted the cavern. Clanging hammers reverberated off the stone walls, and I counted a dozen bareskinned captives working the anvils before five lizardlike guards whose skin was covered in scales.

Damian ducked behind a large furnace that would obscure us from view and motioned for us to follow. I shot forward, running along the walkway, and Amira followed. One of the guards turned as I scurried behind cover. Had he seen?

"Uh-oh. Incoming!" Amira hissed behind me.

I turned just as a reptilian guard whipped around the corner. Damian lunged past us, thrust a dagger into its neck, and shoved it over the edge of the raised walkway. The pounding of hammers covered the sound of its death rattle, and the body disappeared into the viscous magma.

"He's good," Amira whispered, motioning at Damian.

I nodded and glanced at him. His movements betrayed pain and exhaustion. They'd tortured him, and my chest ached as I pondered what that had done to his soul.

It would be alright once we got out of here. It *had* to be.

Damian glanced around the corner and motioned for us to follow. We slipped into a small workroom with a wheel for sharpening blades. A narrow channel of molten lava flowed along the back, making the space suffocatingly hot.

Damian gestured to the entryway. "Watch out for company."

"How do we get the cuffs off?" I asked.

"We'll have to do mine the noisy way. Then I can unlock both of yours with my magic."

He grabbed a chisel and hammer from a workbench and knelt, positioning the chisel over the pin that joined his right magicuff. He brought the hammer down with precision, sending a sharp clang through the space. The pin didn't budge, and Damian grunted in frustration, bringing down the hammer in a succession of blows. He snarled. "I need to weaken the metal. Spark, do you just look like a dragon, or is there any chance you breath fire?"

In response, Spark blew a tiny fireball into the air.

"Can you shoot a jet of fire onto my cuff?"

The dragon scampered over and stared at the cuff. *Won't the flames and hot metal burn your skin?*

"Acceptable risk. If I can break it off, I'll be able to heal."

Let me try. Spark landed on Damian's magicuff. *This might hurt.*

Damian nodded and braced his calf with his hands.

Spark opened his mouth and shot a continuous jet of crimson flame at the cuff. Damian gritted his teeth as the metal shackle around his ankle heated up, but he didn't flinch. Spark's glowing red fire transformed into a brilliant white, and the black magicuff turned orange.

"Neve, now that the metal is hot, take the hammer and chisel, and break the cuff at the hinge," Damian growled, his voice masking the pain.

Panic surged through me. *Shit.* I'd never wielded a hammer before, let alone hit a target with one.

I grabbed the hammer lying beside Damian's foot. He groaned as the flesh around his ankle sizzled off.

I raised the tool above my head, focusing on the glowing metal band. *Please fates.* I brought the hammer down, swift and hard, three times. The clang of metal sounded, and with a final blow, the magicuff crumpled to the floor, broken in two.

"Now this one." Damian shifted his hands to the other cuff.

Spark flew to Damian's left leg and began the process again. Sweat poured off Damian's forehead, but he bore the pain in silence. Once the magicuff turned molten orange, I aimed and cracked it with the hammer. It took four tries, but the cuff finally came loose.

As it did, Damian's familiar magic washed over me— and something new. Sweet and spicy, like burning sandalwood. Heat danced up my thighs, pooling low in my belly.

Damian leaned back and sighed.

"Uh, Neve?" Amira said. "Guard incoming. Ten seconds, maybe less."

Her words towed me back to reality. "Toadstool him."

She grinned. "You got it."

Cheeks blazing, I turned back to Damian. The charred skin around his ankles had begun to heal, and the burns and gashes on his arms and neck slowly receded. With the magicuffs off, his magic had returned.

"Thanks," Damian said. "You too, Spark."

Spark buzzed around the room and flickered.

Damian rose to his feet and turned to the side. "Now these."

His wings appeared, brilliant and bound in chains.

Something twisted in my chest. They had been ravaged and mutilated, the feathers pulled away. They were healing, but the sight was ghastly. Anger bubbled inside me.

The efreet will pay for this.

Spark blasted the padlock on the chains, and it broke free, easier than the magicuffs. I unwound the heavy chain that bound Damian's wings, dropping it to the floor.

"What the—" A voice hissed behind us.

I glanced at the figure in the door. The reptilian guard froze and buckled forward, eyes wide open in a blind stare. Amira caught him and dragged him to the corner. "I think they heard the noise and are getting suspicious."

"I can have you two free quickly. I have a way with locks." Damian wove runes in the air, and iridescent lightning struck the cuffs over and over until they shattered.

"Thank fates." I rubbed my ankles. "That was easy."

"I fashioned them myself. I wove the spells so I could

break them once I got my magic back." Damian hurled the cuffs into the stream of lava with distaste. "I am sorry that I had to create such a foul thing."

So *that* was why my magicuffs were lighter and less barbaric than Amira's—Damian had forged them for me.

"Unfortunately, Amira's will be more difficult," Damian said.

She grimaced at me. "You're on door duty."

I stood sentry while Damian worked on Amira's magicuffs. I summoned a ball of wind to my hand, ready to blast anyone that came close. My magic flowed through me like a soothing river. I shuddered with joy to have it back again.

No one will ever chain me again.

Five agonizing minutes ticked by. I bit my lip at the muffled sounds emanating from Amira, between the pounding of the hammer and crackle of Damian's magic. I didn't dare look back until her cuffs clattered to the ground. Her magic, released from its bonds, hit me like a gentle ocean wave, cool and refreshing. It smelled of fresh oranges and tasted like butter and sweet cream.

"Free at last!" Joy lit her voice.

Almost.

25

Damian

Relief poured through me.

And rage.

With my magicuffs off, my wounds healed, and I bristled with energy. After days of it being repressed, I let it flow freely. All but the dangerous part. I couldn't risk unleashing that around Neve. Not unless I had to.

The sentries in the forge had sensed something was amiss and were searching for their missing companions. It was time for chaos.

With a silent signal, we burst from the room, and Neve and Amira hurled smoke bombs into the streams of lava. Dark plumes of noxious gas billowed up as guards and prisoners alike began coughing on the fumes.

Neve called the wind around us, whipping the smoke into a choking cloud and pushing back the guards.

I wanted nothing more than to drink in the scent of her magic, which washed over me like a jasmine dream.

We hurried out the back of the forges and down the winding corridors of the fortress. I had no idea where we were, but Neve and Amira knew every turn.

Amira slowed and opened a heavy brass door along the side of the hall. She turned to us. "Ready to get out of this hellhole?"

You have no idea.

The door opened into a spiral staircase. Amira led us upward at a painstakingly slow pace. We passed several doors, but we didn't stop. At the fifteenth floor, Amira paused in front of the door, chest heaving, and cracked it open an inch.

"All clear." She pushed through the threshold into a room filled with couches and wall hangings. A sweltering breeze blew through the open balcony of the tower.

I shut the door behind me and sealed it with a magic lock.

Amira wrung her hands as she paced the room. "Now that we're up here, I'm having second thoughts."

"Amira hates heights," Neve said, grinning ever so slightly.

"Yes. And the monsters that fly *in* those heights. You haven't seen them yet, Damian. The things from nightmares. We'll be tasty morsels they can just pluck from the sky."

She isn't wrong about that, Spark added. *I do not wish to be eaten either.*

"Let them try." My skin itched for a fight, and I needed to vent my pent-up rage.

I crossed to the balcony and scanned the burning volcanic wasteland below. "Amira, can you fly?"

"Sadly, no. Half water genie."

"I'll need to carry you, then. We don't have far to go. Once we're out of the anti-teleportation dome, Neve can transport us home."

The golden dome extended at least a mile in all directions—much larger than the dome that shielded Helwan. It would be a long, unprotected flight and extremely dangerous if we were being hunted from above. The last thing I needed was a panicked passenger.

Neve gazed out over the balcony, calm and steady. She was cool, collected, and prepared—the complete opposite of Amira.

Neve pointed across the hellscape. "Let's head for that cinder cone at nine o'clock. That way, if we get separated, we'll have a landmark to meet up at."

I nodded. "Amira and I will meet you there."

Neve turned and took Amira's hands in hers. "Damian's the best flyer I know. We're gonna make it."

Amira swallowed hard, looking green. "I'd rather eat a tuna and marshmallow sandwich than do this. But we're fresh out of tuna, so let's go."

I scanned the sky. It was empty. "Amira and I will go first. Wait until the coast is clear before you follow."

"You mean, wait a few seconds to see if we're being hunted?" Amira said.

Like bait, Spark whimpered.

"We'll be fine. Just a precaution." I turned to Amira and gestured for her to take my hand. She stared at Spark, her face ashen, but she took it.

"Alright, be careful," Neve said. "I'll be right behind you."

I lifted Amira in my arms and unfolded my wings, turning my head so Neve could hear me. "Don't try to make nice with any dragons. The ones here might not be so friendly."

Neve had befriended a wind dragon in the Realm of Air. Something told me the creatures here would be less than welcoming.

Neve tossed her hair. "Hadn't crossed my mind. Now get out of here. I'm dying to get out of this hellish place and these sweaty clothes."

I couldn't agree more.

A hot gust of wind lifted Amira and me into the air,

and we dove over the balcony, gliding toward the ground. She stifled a wail of terror as the vast lava lake opened before us.

Stay low and out of sight.

It would be hard to fight with Amira in my arms.

I glanced up.

Neve stood on the railing of the balcony with Spark at her side, dancing in the wind. She leapt into the air, soaring several dozen feet before diving after us. Spark streaked behind her like a comet. I slowed to let them catch up. I wanted her in sight.

A bird-like screech rang through the air above, followed by another in the distance.

"Fire drakes," Amira shouted over the whipping wind, eyes pinned on the sky.

Neve shot by in a torrent of wind, and I picked up the pace.

My muscles twitched with anticipation. Where the hell were they?

A piercing screech strained my eardrums as a dark shape dropped like a meteor beside me.

Neve screamed, and panic tore at me as I searched the sky for her.

A hundred feet beneath us, she veered left, dodging the drake's fire breath, and then wheeled upward. Its black scales glinted in the sun as it followed, wings ablaze.

"Damian! Above!" Amira shouted.

A second drake whipped through the air above us. I folded my wings, and we dove straight down toward the boiling lava.

A gush of fire burst just inches beside us, and pain shot through my wing. Amira wriggled in my arms, making it nearly impossible to maneuver.

"Fates, woman, be still. I'm trying to fly." I shifted her so I could see. But a burst of force thrust me off course, and I had to adjust my arms to keep from losing her.

What in the gods' names is she doing?

I looked back. A stream of water blasted from her hands. The drake easily dodged.

"Damn it!" she shouted. "I don't have any juice in this realm!"

The drake veered to the side and then swung wide to attack again. It opened its mouth and released a jet of fire.

I spun out of the way, swerving hard right. Amira hurled a handful of smoke bombs into the flame, creating a choking cloud around the drake that blocked us from sight for just a second. I used the opening to loop behind it. I turned to Amira, who was looking over my shoulder. "Impressive. I hope you have a few more tricks up your sleeve."

She beamed back at me. "You betcha, handsome. I should have played for the Astros."

The drake burst through the cloud of smoke and quickly spotted us. It spun backward, and I dove out of the way, skimming uncomfortably close to the lava. It was working us down until we ran out of room to maneuver.

Screeches echoed from all sides of the caldera. Calls in response. We weren't going to make it if more of these monsters showed up. We needed cover.

Plumes of acrid gray smoke rose from the blackened rock at the edge of the crater. Poisonous. But it would have to do.

I spun in the air, scanning the sky.

Where the *hell* was Neve?

Neve

The drake's tail clipped my legs, sending a wave of agony through my lower half as I spun downward through the sky. Luckily, its poisonous barb had missed its target.

I recovered from the spin and shot a blast of wind at it.

Fates. That was too close. My luck had to be running out.

I pulled a hard turn and unleashed a burst of wind at the drake below. The beast screeched and cartwheeled downward, before pulling up in a wide arc above my head.

Finally, I spotted Damian and Amira. They dove down in the direction of the gas plumes as the drakes circled for another strike.

Damn. The cinder cone was only a quarter mile away. We were so close.

The drakes screeched as Damian's wings disappeared into the gray cloud that billowed from the ground. I took a breath and followed.

My eyes and skin burned. We couldn't stay in these toxic fumes for long.

My feet hit the hard lava, and a hand gripped my arm. "Neve."

The outlines of Damian and Amira appeared at my side.

"Can you make a path for us?" Damian coughed.

With the flick of my wrist, a gust of wind cleared the toxic cloud for a second, but more gas rose from the cracks at our feet.

Spark flitted in front of me. *Use your wind. Make a pocket of air.*

Hadn't I created a pocket of air over my face in the cistern? I didn't know how I'd done that, but I tried anyway. The gassy fumes blew away, but reappeared seconds later. Frustration welled in my chest, and my lungs burned.

Focus on making a bubble around you, Spark said.

I closed my eyes and imagined a bubble of fresh air expanding outward from me. Magic pooled inside my chest, and I raised my palms, releasing a gentle pulse of energy.

The burning on my skin abated as a pocket of fresh air swept out, blasting the acrid fog away. I breathed in, and Amira launched into a coughing fit.

"Nice job," Damian said. "Now let's get to the cinder cone."

The pocket of air followed us as we made our way over the smoking lava field. The heat from the surface cut through the soles of my shoes.

Screeches echoed above. More drakes were gathering.

With a gust of wind, the gas clouds around us blew away.

A drake hovered just above, flapping its wings to clear the fog. Its eyes narrowed, and it pulled its neck back for a strike.

Two black arrows whipped through the air. One lodged into the drake's neck and erupted in crackling electricity, while the other tore a hole in the creature's wing. The beast shrieked and wheeled out of sight.

More of the beasts circled above.

Damian held a black bow that he must have drawn from the ether. He slung the weapon over his shoulder then towed Amira forward. The gases closed in around us, shielding our bodies from above.

It wouldn't be long before they found us again.

We scrambled over the rocks as the ground began to slope up toward the edge of the caldera.

I dropped to my knees as a deep rumble shook the ground, echoing through the caldera.

"What the hell was that?" Amira said.

The quaking intensified, urging us to climb faster. Rocks tumbled down the slope, and the crashing of a landslide ricocheted across the crater.

"Time to fly." Damian took Amira and lifted her, turning his gaze to me. "Ready?"

Urgency and panic overwhelmed me. We were so close. "Let's go!"

Damian launched into the air with Amira in his arms. We burst up through the toxic clouds and were at the caldera's rim within seconds. The edge of the golden dome was but a hundred feet away.

"Seize them!" The efreet's voice shook the air around us, and the bottom of the caldera split open.

Terror iced my skin.

"Go!" Damian shouted over his shoulder.

We darted forward, closing the distance with the glistening edge of the anti-teleportation field.

Heat flared at my back, and I turned for a look.

Bad idea.

A river of lava shot over the caldera's rim. It writhed and surged into the air behind us, taking the form of a snake with gleaming black and red scales.

The lava serpent lashed out. I dove out of the way, suddenly separated from Damian and Amira. It slammed into the ground, exploding in chunks of lava that sprayed through the air.

Burns screamed across my skin. I darted upward as the monster reformed below.

Damian dove toward me, Amira in his arms.

The reformed serpent struck out, trying to intercept.

Amira unleashed a tiny stream of water at the monster. Its head exploded in a cloud of steam, and searing rock rained down around us.

"Get out of the field!" Damian yelled as the lava river reanimated, this time with two heads.

Screeches echoed above. We spiraled out of the way as a drake descended in a cloud of fire. Heat seared my skin.

They were trying to cut us off, separate us. Pick us off.

Screw this. Two can play at that game.

I sucked in my power until I was filled to bursting and released a wall of wind. The air around us shook with a sonic boom. The drakes wheeled out of control. One slammed into the ground, but the other recovered and arced overhead.

The river of lava surged after us, pinned behind the wind wall.

The efreet screamed in rage.

I couldn't see him, but his gaze burned into my back.

A blast of cool magic cascaded across my skin as I broke out through the dome and through the anti-teleportation field.

I spun around and reached for Damian. "Take my hand. We'll planes-walk!"

He grabbed me and pulled me to his chest. I wrapped my arm around him and took Amira's hand with the other.

"Hold on tight!" Closing my eyes, I focused on my apartment in Magic Side.

The ether sucked us in, pushing and pulling, threatening to tear us apart.

The efreet's voice trailed us. "You won't escape so easily!"

26

Damian

We arrived in Neve's apartment in a whirlwind of flame.

Amira immediately manifested jets of fine mist, extinguishing the small fires that leapt to life on the couch. "Where are we?"

"My apartment!" Neve spun in a circle, eyes wide. "Why is it on fire?"

"Because when you planes-walk, you bring some of the elemental power with you—particularly when you transport a big group of people. *Never* planes-walk indoors." Amira laughed.

Neve rubbed her temples. "Damn. Good to know."

Spark, as a ball of light, bobbed around the room.

I crossed to the window and looked through the slit in the curtains. The street was empty and quiet.

"Don't worry—I've got it under control." Amira surveyed the space. "Looks like you've been testing your wind powers in here or planes-walking with big groups of people."

Neve blushed.

I smiled and turned. There had been no planes-walking. She was just supremely untidy.

We silently surveyed the damp, smoldering, wreckage of her apartment.

Neve slumped onto the pile of clothes on her couch, looking exhausted. "We lived."

A massive smile stretched across Amira's face. "Holy fates, I am free!"

Neve stared at the ceiling. "We did it. Passed through the fire. But holy smokes that *was* close."

Free of immediate danger, my dark thoughts came rushing back. "Matthias. He's behind this. We must hunt him down."

Neve sat up, eyes locked on mine. "We need to tell the Order."

The Order. Hell. That would bring problems. "Fine. Let them know. But we must go after Matthias *now*."

"What about the efreet? Can he follow us here?" Neve asked.

Amira frowned. "I'm not s—"

A crack of lightning rattled the windows, and the

light in the apartment shifted from a cool afternoon blue to a vivid orange.

Not good.

I strode back to the window. The sky ripped open in a flaming scar, illuminating the street in bright firelight. The efreet crashed down through the cosmic rift, his feet quaking the ground.

His voice rocked the entire apartment. "Where are you, *fools*? I will burn the flesh from your bones!"

Neve grimaced. "That answers my question."

I grabbed her hand and pulled her to the floor, out of sight and away from the window's trajectory.

"I know you're here! Come out, or I'll have to start guessing." The efreet's voice shook the walls, knocking a painting off the wall.

Amira crawled up beside us. "Guessing?"

Neve's face turned ashen. "I led him right here, right to my neighborhood. He's going to attack different apartments until he finds us."

The efreet bellowed. "Fine. Stay hidden, cowards. It does not matter how I kill you."

An explosion rocked the street, unleashing a cacophony of blaring car horns. I ripped back the curtain. Bright yellow flames and dark smoke billowed out of an apartment two buildings over. Bricks and glass rained down on the sidewalk.

"Amira, get out! We'll lead him away!" Neve

unleashed a gust of wind that blew out the window, then leapt through into the air.

Shit.

I launched through the shattered window, released my wings, and soared after Neve.

"Keep him distracted, away from the houses!" Neve's voice carried on the wind.

An arc of fire whipped past me. I pulled in my wings and dove, then spiraled upward out of the efreet's line of sight.

Cold surged through my veins as I drew on my ice magic.

I whipped my hand and sent three bolts of ice at the efreet's skull. They evaporated in a puff of steam before they reached him.

"I will burn you alive." He laughed and unleashed a jet of lava at me.

I folded my wings and dodged out of the way. The lava rained down on the cars below, incinerating metal and plastic and sending up plumes of noxious gas.

Screaming citizens poured from the houses into the streets, taking cover behind cars and trees.

"Run, worms!" The efreet bellowed, his voice a thunderous inferno.

Before he could incinerate them, Neve swooped down, hurling a concussive blast of wind that tossed a Volkswagen into his back. The efreet bellowed, throwing an arc of flaming cinders back at her.

She dodged, barely avoiding the deadly blow. Fear for her twisted my heart.

I had to keep him away from Neve.

At all costs.

Neve

I dove behind a car as hot ash cascaded across the sidewalk.

Too close.

Above, Damian pulled out his black blade, dove, and slashed the efreet in the face—a blow to enrage—not to kill. "Come get me, you bastard. Let's finish this."

The efreet looked up at him and grinned. "I think not, little moth."

He pivoted and chucked a fireball into my apartment. Fire poured out of the shattered windows, and my stomach pitched. Bricks and the tattered remnants of my life's belongings rained down from the sky.

"Monster!" I unleashed a gust of wind at the efreet, sending him tumbling into the line of parked cars.

He bent down, heaved an old SUV over his head, then launched it in my direction. It detonated in a ball of flame as I flew for cover, searing shrapnel ripping across my skin.

Fates he was fast.

A fire hydrant behind him exploded, releasing a geyser thirty feet into the air.

"What the..."

Amira strode out into the middle of the pavement and twisted her hands. The geyser bent ninety degrees and slammed into the efreet with a blast of steam that shattered windows on both sides of the street.

Her water magic was back in full force. Nice timing.

The efreet staggered back, howling with rage. The geyser collapsed, formed into a snake, and slithered along the street. Amira snapped her hands, and the water serpent lunged forward.

The efreet threw up a wall of lava, and the water snake detonated as they collided.

"Amira!" I flew across the street and hauled her away from the falling magma. We toppled to the pavement on the other side of the street. My knees and palms stung as they scraped the asphalt. Head to toe, I was ravaged with cuts and burns. Amira looked about the same.

She grabbed my hand. "We've got to get out of here. We are *losing*. I'll take us to the Realm of Water. The efreet can't follow us there."

"No! We can't leave! There are hundreds of innocent people here. He'll destroy the city." I grabbed Amira and flew skyward.

"Then what the hell are we going to do?" she asked.

"I have no freaking idea." My mind raced. "Can we

force him into the Realm of Water? Won't his power be dampened there?"

Her eyebrows rose. "It would. If we create a portal to the Realm of Water, you can use your wind power to drive the efreet through. He'll be weak enough that we can maybe kill him there." She grinned widely. "This is the perfect payback."

Damian

Neve flew skyward with Amira. The efreet's gaze followed them, giving me the opening I had been waiting for. I pulled my spear from the ether and dove downward.

Near the ground, a light post twisted and slammed into my back, cracking my ribs. I dropped like a rock, landing on the glass that littered the street. Wheezing, I rolled to the side as my ribs knit.

Like a steel serpent, the light post hammered its head into the ground inches from my head.

Instinct drove me left, and I rolled, avoiding it.

What the hell kind of magic was this?

I took off into the air as an iron fence started thrashing like a crazed animal and shattered itself into pieces. The fragments launched into the sky after me, an army of rusty black spears.

Then the smell of smoke and hot iron hit me like a rogue wave.

Matthias. Iron mage.

I wheeled in the sky, searching for him.

There. A dark shadow loomed on the rooftop across the street.

I summoned my bow and fired a salvo of arrows. He dashed across the roof as bursts of crackling magic erupted behind him.

"Call off your efreet, Matthias!"

"You have no idea what you are meddling with, Damian. I am trying to create a better world. Once, we both were."

Visions of my past surged up. A war amongst the skies. Matthias at my side, our blades unified against our foes—the heavens themselves.

An explosion ricocheted down the street. Neve would have to hold off the efreet. I couldn't risk taking my eyes off Matthias. I pulled a black spear from the ether and hurled it at him. Matthias deflected it midair with a wave of his hand.

I slammed down onto the roof beside him and drew my blade, swinging for his neck. He flicked it away.

Matthias shook his head. "Damian. I helped you forge those blades. I am the master of iron. I am master of *them*."

My sword turned back on me, driving toward my neck. I dismissed it into the ether before it cut.

Mathias ripped its twin from the sky and swung.

I called upon the ice magic I had stolen from the ice devils in the Realm of Air, launching a wall of ice into the air, deflecting the blow.

Matthias lowered his blade, amazement crossing his face. "*Ice* magic. How did you get that, I wonder? Giving in to the cravings again, are you?" He grinned. "I knew you would. No wonder you are so fascinated with the girl."

His words clawed at my chest, and I unleashed a storm of icicles from my palms.

He leapt backward off the roof and unfolded a set of leathery black wings. Horns erupted from his skull.

Matthias. Iron mage. Demon. Once my friend. Now my nemesis.

I launched after him into the sky. The earth shuddered below me, and the winds began to roar. I released a plume of hail too broad for him to escape. "Your betrayal will be the end of you."

Matthias pulled a black shield from the ether, repelling the blast—a shield that I had forged for him decades ago. He lowered it and chuckled. "Damian. I have never met someone so good at deception. You deceive even yourself. *You* are the one that lies. Who has *always* lived a lie."

He hurled a spear at me, a reflection of my own.

Rage coursed through me. "You will pay for what you've done."

I reached out with my fist, crushing him with the dark power of my fallen angel magic. He struggled but mastered the pain and reached out his own hand. My heart hardened in my chest, waves of agony and dark magic cascading across my body.

I would be the stronger one, my rage deeper, more powerful.

Darkness crept into the corners of my eyes.

I must destroy him.

27

Neve

Where the heck was Damian?

Amira and I dropped back down to the street behind the efreet. All around us, the street was littered with broken glass and shattered cars.

I turned to Amira. "How the heck do we make a portal to the Realm of Water?"

"We do it together." She grabbed my hands. "You're going to be the anchor to Magic Side. I will planes-walk to the Realm of Water. As soon as you feel us start to disappear, I want you to try planes-walking right back here. Do *not* let go of my hands."

"Have you done this before?"

"Nope. I only know about it in theory. As long as we

don't get ripped apart by the cosmos, we'll be fine."

Well, crap.

"Okay, fantastic." I squeezed her hands. "I trust you. But for the record, *you're* now the crazy one."

Amira smiled. "Great! Let's not die."

And then she planes-walked.

The cosmos spiraled around me, dissolving my body, and we whirled through the stars. The darkness became viscous liquid that flowed around me. Cold seeped into my veins.

The Realm of Water. Time to planes-walk back.

I blocked out the primordial sea and focused on my ravaged street, forcing myself to planes-walk home.

The world flickered around me as a surge of power threatened to rip Amira and me apart. I dug my fingers into her wrists and screamed.

The sky split, and an unearthly reverberation jolted through us.

I opened my eyes. A massive circular portal undulated in the air before me, its edges blazing as they tore a hole in reality. I still held Amira's hands. She floated on the other side looking back at me, surrounded by a world of pure blue water.

Amira shouted, but her words came through delayed, distorted, and distant—like echoes beneath the waves. "Pull the efreet in, Neve—I'll hold the portal open as long as I can!"

I called the wind, wrenched a mailbox free of its concrete pad, and hurled it at the efreet's head.

It exploded on target, bursting into a snowfall of flaming letters.

That got his attention.

He hurled a ball of fire at me but I dodged it, zooming into the sky. I flew with all my might, darting in and out between the buildings, hoping he wouldn't realize where I was headed.

He dove after me, a flaming comet streaking across the sky.

I veered sharply and plunged straight through the open portal. Pain quaked through my body as I slammed full speed into the unending ocean that was the Realm of Water. I floated in a world of pure blue, Amira now at my side. My lungs burned, and I fought down the urge to suck in air—drowning was not on the menu.

Where was the efreet?

He hadn't followed me through.

A strange noise reverberated through the water around me—*laughter*. I wheeled around. The efreet stood on the other side of the portal, bellowing. I could barely make out his words. "Clever girl. But not clever enough."

"What do we do?" Amira asked.

I had no way to respond without inhaling a lungful of frigid water, so I zipped back through the portal to

Magic Side, gasping as I broke the surface of water into fresh air.

The efreet was waiting. A wall of fire engulfed me, searing my drenched skin, and I screamed in agony.

I called the wind and wrapped a whirling vortex around the efreet, like a lasso, and pulled.

He planted his feet into the ground below and cackled, utterly immobile, his eyes filled with cruel delight.

I raged, summoning the deep reserves of my power. The wind became my hands, and I pulled with all my strength. His feet dug into the street, melting deep gouges in the asphalt.

I screamed in fury, giving it everything I had.

The wind just wasn't strong enough.

But *I* was.

I felt something seething deep within me—the power of being something more. Commanding the wind was not enough. I had to *become* the wind.

As the air howled around me, I closed my eyes and sought the eye of the storm within. My mind cleared, and I caught a glimpse of what I could be. What my blood *meant* me to be.

A raging hurricane.

I called the name of the storm. It was my own name. My true name. It had been, all along.

Blinding white light cascaded through my tattoos, and with a flash, I became a whirling maelstrom. I screamed as my body morphed into a savage hurricane.

The remaining window glass shattered from the apartments lining the street. I devoured trees, planters, even cars. Nothing escaped my wrath.

The efreet screamed in horror as I slammed down on him with all my might, ripping jets of flame and chunks of ember from his body, dragging him toward the vortex.

He faded, as if about to planes-walk, but I pummeled him relentlessly until he lost both his concentration and footing. He flailed, spinning in the cyclone, out of control, and I devoured him.

Together, we surged through the vortex into a realm of pure blue.

Damian

A flurry of wind hurled me through the air, ripping the feathers from my wings. I crashed into a tree, and my left shoulder shattered, pain electrifying my body. I gritted my teeth as I slammed full force into something cold, something hard, something *fluid*.

I was submerged. Surrounded by icy water. *Drowning.*

I retracted my burnt and battered wings and spun about, searching for some form of orientation in the endless blue. But there was no sky. No sense of up or down.

What the gods was happening?

Light appeared from below. A blazing and churning fire, thrashing in the water.

I swam toward it, narrowing my eyes to focus.

It was the *efreet*—caught in a whirlpool. The ocean boiled around him, and black plumes of smoke drifted up through the water.

My lungs ached, and I searched for Neve.

Something soft and cold brushed against me, and I spun.

Neve slipped up beside me, tattoos alight, glowing like some creature of the deep. She clutched the bottom of my shirt and crawled across me, pulling my body to hers.

She pressed her lips to mine. They were warm, even in these dark depths—like sunlight cutting through a shadow. Electricity ran across my skin, and then she breathed. Life-giving air filled my lungs, and I gasped.

She pulled back, a bubble of air like a mask covering her faint smile. I reached up to my face, finding a bubble there as well.

"Glad you decided to join us. We have an efreet to kill." Her voice shook with exhaustion. Magic must have made it possible for us to talk because this couldn't be possible otherwise.

Gashes and burns covered her body, and her skin

was pale with hypothermia. She turned and dove toward the efreet in a churning stream of bubbles. Blood trailed behind her as she jetted toward the efreet.

She was relentless. And gravely wounded.

The efreet opened his arms, coaxing her forward. To death.

A torrent of hate drowned all thoughts but one.

Revenge.

Neve

I surged through the water on a jet of air.

It was time to end this.

My heart pounded.

Visions of my home, belching forth flames, filled my eyes. Fury flowed like blistering poison through my veins. I couldn't let the efreet escape.

My body shuddered with cold, my magic all but exhausted.

It didn't matter though. I would destroy him. No matter the cost.

Amira dodged out of the way as a boiling blast of water surged toward her. The efreet was weakened.

He fixed me with a wicked grin and laughed. "You should not have crossed me, half breed. I will boil you alive. Devour the flesh of your friends and leave nothing but ash."

He launched a pulsating ball of lava at me. It swelled as it approached, gases building within until it detonated, sending shockwaves through my body. Ringing echoed in my skull, and spots danced before my eyes, but I dove downward into the frenzy.

Exhausted beyond belief, I summoned my magic one last time, forming the water into a violent vortex. I unleashed it on him, ripping the embers from his body. His claws raked through the swirling water, latching onto me and digging into my flesh.

Darkness overcame me, but I shoved it away.

Killing the efreet might kill me, but my friends would be free.

I gritted my teeth.

Wind and fire, we would die together.

Damian

Too slow.

I was too slow.

Neve slammed into the chest of the efreet, a roiling underwater tornado driving him backward. Driving him out of my grasp.

My muscles strained as I swam as hard as I could, but she was too fast.

She was killing him. And herself.

Blood, fire, and wind boiled in the water around them.

"Help her!" Amira grabbed my arm, and we shot forward on a jet of water driven by her magic. As we moved, the icy ocean shot daggers into my chest.

The vortex around Neve had weakened, her magic almost spent.

"Faster!" I summoned my black spear from the ether.

We swung high and descended in a thundering dive, a torpedo homing in on its target.

The efreet had seared his name into my flesh and left Neve's body burnt and tattered. He had laid waste to home after home, family after family, trying to draw us out.

Well, here I am.

Death. Devastation. An angel of vengeance.

Neve's eyes locked onto us, and she released the efreet.

I rammed my spear into his throat and released every ounce of magic I had. A torrent of cold shot down my arms, pulling the lifeforce from my body. My spear became a lance of ice, driving down though his neck into his heart.

Neve, eyes flickering at the verge of unconsciousness, nodded, and her vortex surged one last time. I released my dark energy, and between us, we ripped the efreet in two, the force hurling me back from the cavernous wound where his neck once was.

His magic boiled away in plumes of yellow light, tantalizing in their beauty, like hypnotic reflections on the waves. The craving surged within my body, a dragon that demanded freedom. I struggled against it, but dark thoughts rooted in my heart.

Matthias was still out there with his genies. Amassing an army. He knew what Neve was becoming. He would bind her, too. Force her into servitude.

I looked at her body floating in the water, barely conscious. A ravenous beast rose within me: *Protect.* The need clawed at me, devouring my rational thought. I had but one purpose, one goal.

I would not let Matthias bind her.

I would protect her.

Matthias might be the master of iron, but I would become the master of fire. I would rend him down into molten metal and scatter him across the Earth. He would never touch Neve.

I dismissed my spear into the ether, watching the efreet. Rage tore the words from my throat. "I vowed that I would free Neve. And I have."

I swam down and placed my foot on the remnants of his smoldering chest. "I vowed that I would turn your heart to ash. And I have."

"I vowed that I would rip the magic from your corpse." I gripped the iridescent yellow plumes of magic that streamed from his body, dissipating into the ether. "I will."

The dragon within me roared as I tore the efreet's magic free. It spiraled around my arms and poured into my body, searing my veins. Ecstasy enveloped me like a drug. The efreet's fire burned within me, and the water began to boil as I let my new aura shine through.

A new strength streamed from my body. With this power, I could protect. With this fire, I could defend. The dragon had feasted.

This time it would be enough.

Neve

The shockwave of the explosion had slammed into my chest, hurling me backward through the cold water.

I gasped at the pain in my ribs and shuddered as my heart struggled to pump blood through my frozen veins.

But relief came, too. We'd defeated the efreet.

Damian floated motionless in the water, gazing down at the remains of our rival. His expression was hollow, distant—that of a man staring at ghosts.

Was he hurt?

He drifted downward to the shattered corpse. Reaching down with his hands, he wrenched the glowing streams of magic from the efreet's body. Ribbons of light flowed around him, and his aura shifted as it took on a brilliant yellow hue.

My heart clenched in my chest. Horror petrified the blood in my veins. Damian had just stolen the efreet's magic.

It all suddenly made sense. The lies. His hidden signature. The ice magic that he shouldn't have.

FireSoul.

My nightmares came flooding back—my subconscious had desperately tried to break through. To warn me.

"Neve." Damian's voice sent daggers through my heart. Flickering firelight poured from his eyes.

Terror coursed through my veins.

Damian opened his mouth but was silenced as the sea erupted in a churning wall of water behind him. He turned, surprise etched upon his face.

A colossal arm erupted from the bubbling wall, followed by the body of a giant who was half man, half swirling vortex of water. His eyes blazed, and light radiated from a crown of pearl and coral.

My mind collapsed inward in terror.

The marid king.

He turned his gaze on Damian, and his voice cascaded through the water, each syllable a shockwave.

"I see you for what you are, *FireSoul*. Your kind is banished from my kingdom. Begone!"

His hand shot out and slammed into Damian, who vanished in a streak of light.

The marid king turned his gaze to me. "You, however, have returned my daughter to me. You are welcome in this realm."

I opened my mouth, but it was frozen shut.

Everything was numb.

Flesh and soul, there was nothing left to feel.

28

Neve

Warmth cascaded over me.

My eyes fluttered, and I awoke surrounded by white pearlescent light.

Where was I?

The air vibrated with an unearthly music, sonorous and slow, like whales singing. I sucked in a deep breath as a thick, warm aroma of freshly baked goods wafted over me.

My stomach grumbled, and I rolled to my side, searching for the source of the smell. A plate of scones sat on the side table.

White light. Baked goods. Unearthly music. I must be dead.

My stomach aching and famished beyond reason, I grabbed a scone and bit in.

Definitely heaven.

I sat up, and muted pain poured down my back, legs, and shoulders. Everything protested.

Nope. Definitely still alive.

I brushed my hands across my body.

Seaweed?

It was warm and wet, and wrapped around me like a blanket.

I did some new calculations. White interior. A plate of delicacies. Soothing whale song. Sore muscles and a seaweed wrap.

A spa?

That would've been nice—to simply be waking from a series of bad dreams after a vigorous massage. Life would be so much simpler.

The truth twisted my heart. The nightmare was real. Damian. The efreet. Matthias. *All* of it.

I pushed the nightmare from my mind.

The iridescent white walls glistened like opal or pearl shell. Light came from small, bioluminescent creatures floating near the ceiling. Alien and beautiful.

I rose, taking another scone. It crumbled between my fingers. *Just baked.*

Amira, for certain.

A tall mirror of flowing mercury stood in the corner.

I studied my reflection. Singed hair. Small cuts healing on my cheek.

Considering what happened, I wasn't bad off, though my stylist wasn't going to be pleased. I parted the wrap and gasped. My tattoo had grown again. It spiraled up my right arm and over my right shoulder, cascaded down my chest and along my side, all the way past my right hip.

I pursed my lips. Honestly, it was kind of awesome—but it carried far too many connotations to think about right now.

I forced my eyes away from the tattoo to the rest of my body. Not too bad. Dozens of small pink cuts covered my skin but were already far along in the healing process. I traced my fingers across the surface of my burned flesh, where shiny patches of new skin glinted in the light. They were smooth, almost not there. Almost.

This wasn't natural. Either I'd been convalescing for a long time or someone with strong magic had healed me.

The room spiraled off in a clockwise progression. Fates. Was I inside a giant nautilus or a seashell? I snatched a scone for the road and followed the curve.

Just around the corner, Amira reclined in a shell-like chaise lounge, a thick romance novel bobbing in her hand.

"You're awake!" She dropped her book, pulled her

plush robe around her, and jumped up to embrace me. "Good news, we didn't die! Just as planned."

My heart leapt. I squeezed her tight and stepped back. "Thank goodness you're okay—I lost where you were in the battle."

"I'm right as rain." She bowed. "Welcome to my palace."

"Your palace?"

"Well, no. Not my palace. It's technically my father's. But I live here. Occasionally. Pretty rarely, actually. More like visit. Holidays. Once again, you have to understand, there's no cable TV."

"You're a princess?"

"Yeah. Did I not tell you?"

I waggled the scone in my hand. "I thought you couldn't bake here either?"

"Oh, I know. I know. The texture on the scones just isn't right."

"Don't say that about my scone—it's the best thing I've ever eaten." I shoved a piece in my mouth for emphasis.

"Ha! You would say that about two-day-old French bread after what you've been through."

Maybe. But it tasted utterly amazing.

I slapped my hand to my necklace. Still there, somehow. I rubbed it for good luck. "How long was I out."

"Only about a day."

A day. So little time had passed, yet so much could

have happened in a day. I traced my fingers across the new skin on my left arm. "And my burns?"

"The healing power of kelp. Well, that, and a ton of magic. Speaking of kelp, let's get you out of that and into something cozy."

She popped the lid off a squat woven reed basket and produced a large, sea-foam green fuzzy bathrobe. "I dress like a princess when I am here, which means I wear whatever the hell I want, wherever I want. These are woven from a seaweed fiber blend. It's amazing on the skin."

I slipped into the robe. It was the softest thing I'd ever felt. "This *is* amazing."

"It's yours. You can't get this goodness back home."

"Amira. Thanks for everything. Again."

"Don't mention it. Without you, I'd still be in that gods forsaken citadel."

I squeezed the robe tightly. It was probably the only piece of clothing I owned. My home had gone up in flames. I had lost everything. Clothes. Books. Memories.

Damian.

My shoulders slumped. Couldn't I just linger in a world of scones and fuzzy bathrobes?

No. There were too many questions.

I grabbed Amira's hand. "What happened to Damian?"

A kaleidoscope of emotion emanated from her eyes. Fear. Anger. Pity. They probably mirrored my own. "My father expelled him from the Realm of Water. The banishment spell would have sent him back to Earth, probably to Magic Side if that's the first place he thought of."

Tension eased from my shoulders, and my muscles unwound. He wasn't dead.

She bit her lip. "He was a FireSoul?"

I had no words, so I nodded.

"Did you know?"

I shook my head and shrugged. "I hardly know what that really means."

"My father says that FireSouls share the soul of a dragon, and that they will steal your magic—after they kill you, of course."

I recalled the ghul drinking in my magic—the horrible sensation of being consumed. Was Damian like that monster?

I shuddered. "Damian helped me escape. He's always protected me..."

Was that enough? Even if his intentions were good, could Damian protect me from himself? He was one of the Fallen *and* a FireSoul. Not one but *two* deadly species.

Amira placed her hand softly on my shoulder. "He may have been using you, Neve. He might have been waiting until you grew strong."

Horror opened a hole in my chest. Had that been his

plan all along? Wait until I had come into my power and then steal it?

My nightmares echoed in my mind. I closed my eyes, and all I saw was Damian floating before me in the vast ocean, sheathed in yellow light—the fire he'd stolen from the efreet. What was the expression in his eyes? Pain? Fury? Delight? Was he still a man or a ravenous monster?

"I don't know what to think, Amira. I just don't know."

She took me by the hand and pulled me into the hall. "Let me show you my city. It's time to forget and celebrate."

Bathrobes and slippers on, we traipsed along a pearlescent corridor until we reached a vast window that overlooked a cerulean world. Unable to restrain my curiosity, I traced the glass with the tips of my fingers.

Not glass. *Air.*

Limitless ocean stretched above, but a garden of coral surrounded us. Iridescent fish cascaded across the window in front of me. I had never seen such beauty.

Amira glanced at me. "Just think, a couple of days ago we were staring out across the caldera of a toxic volcano. But we escaped the efreet's palace. We stopped him from destroying your city. We killed him, putting an end to his torture and tyranny. We won."

Purple fans of coral wavered in the currents as light from somewhere reflected across beds of seagrass. But even in the presence of so much wonder, I couldn't escape doubt.

I shook my head. "Matthias is still out there."

"Who exactly is Matthias, anyway?"

"An iron mage, the efreet's master, and an old friend of Damian's. He was behind our capture. And more. He's collecting genies and is probably the one responsible for the efreet's army."

Amira frowned and shrugged her shoulders. "Look on the positive side. We killed the efreet—so technically Matthias has one less genie than he would have had. We've evened the score."

A shadow passed overhead as a massive eel slithered its way over the dome and down into the beds of coral. My mind churned. "The genie we found in Helwan, I think it was a marid and native to the Realm of Water. Do you think we're safe here? Matthias could send it to hunt us down."

Amira snorted. "Any marid foolish enough to get itself bound won't hold a candle to the strength of my father. He's king for a reason. Don't worry, we're safe."

Safe.

It was strange thought.

I was safe. But what about Rhiannon? My city? Damian...?

A tsunami of questions washed over me.

Where was Spark? I needed him now.

I recalled the fiery battle with the efreet in my neighborhood. I had become a cyclone, wreaking desolation just as surely as he had. Even now, the memory of it sent a thrill pulsing through my veins, a desire to transform, to consume, to rage.

Would I ever be able to control my powers—or was I destined to become a seething monster like the djinn, like the efreet?

Like Damian?

Archmage DeLoren had warned me. It was too much to handle on my own. I hadn't listened, and I'd laid bare a path of destruction through Magic Side. There was no question—I had to tell the Order—about Matthias, about the genies, about Damian. But what about myself?

I closed my eyes and took a deep breath.

I had no answers.

But I was a detective now, damn it.

Time to get some.

We hope you enjoyed reading *Dark Storm*! Book 3, *Cursed Angel* will be here in April 2021: http://hyperurl.co/cursedangel.

Would you like to learn how Damian discovered the original lamp... and what he wished for? Sign up for our newsletter to get access to the exclusive prequel adventure here: http://hyperurl.co/trailofthedjinn. (You can unsubscribe at any time.)

And if you'd like to chat more about the books, interact with fellow readers, and get the scoop on what's up next, join the Veronica Douglas Facebook group here:

https://www.facebook.com/groups/veronicadouglas

THANK YOU!

Thanks for joining us on this adventure! It means a lot to all of us! If you've got an extra minute, we'd appreciate it if you would leave us a review on Amazon (http://mybook.to/Dark-Storm).

Reviews make a *huge* impact. They help us become better writers and keep us going through the difficult pages!

Coming April 2021, pre-order here:
http://hyperurl.co/cursedangel

We're almost out of time.

Magic Side is under attack and the prison has been cursed. If I can't break the spell, my city will be overrun. The problem is, my magic is out of control, and I can't fight this battle alone.

There's only one person to turn to—Damian Malek.

But my strongest ally might also be my greatest threat. I've discovered what Damian is, and it's far worse than just being a fallen angel. I don't trust him, and it's too dangerous to be around him. My very soul, and my magic, are at risk.

But I have no choice.

Only Damian knows the truth of what is really going on, and he'll only share it with me. We've got to bargain with vampires and demons, battle mythical monsters, and expose the lost secrets of a ruined city before time runs out.

Will he help me save the city I love, or is it a trap to take everything I hold dear?

An action-packed urban fantasy, Cursed Angel *features a rebel heroine, a dark angel hero, and slow burn romance. Prepare yourself for edge-of-your-seat adventure amongst ancient ruins and mythical places.*

If you enjoyed the archaeology, history, and daring in Linsey Hall's original Dragon's Gift books, this adventure is for you!

Pre-Order: http://hyperurl.co/cursedangel

ACKNOWLEDGMENTS

VERONICA DOUGLAS

Thank you to everyone who has been so supportive, especially Linsey and Ben—we love you guys!

Thank you to Jena O'Connor and Lexi George for your patience and amazing editing. We'd be nowhere without you.

Thank you to the amazing readers on our advanced review team! Eleonora, Susie, Rachel, Penny, and Aisha —you all are lifesavers!

And finally, a huge shoutout to Orina Kafe for the gorgeous cover art.

ACKNOWLEDGMENTS
LINSEY HALL

Thank you so much to Veronica and Doug, it's still so much fun to write with you guys!

And as usual, thank you to Ben. There would be no books without you.

Thank you to Jena O'Connor and Lexi George for your amazing editing. And to Orina Kafe for the beautiful cover.

AUTHOR'S NOTE

Thank you for reading *Dark Storm*—we hope you enjoyed it! Much of our inspiration for this book came from our work and travels in Egypt.

Magic Side is our little slice of Chicago. It's located on an island in Lake Michigan and is only visible to people with magic in their veins. We'll be exploring Magic Side in more depth in the third book, *Cursed Angel*, as well as Linsey Hall's Guild City series!

Now, for some facts. The mythology of this series, and *Dark Storm* in particular, is heavily influenced by tales from *The One Thousand and One Nights*—often referred to as *Arabian Nights*. As Neve points out, it's not a single book, but a collection of stories from around the globe and from across the centuries. The various editions share a similar (very disturbing) framing story, in which a cruel king takes a new wife each day, and murders her at dawn. Our heroine, Scheherazade, devises a clever plan and bravely agrees to marry the king. Each night, she tells the king a new story, more amazing than the last. She always ends on a cliffhanger and won't share the ending unless the king lets her live another night.

Chicago is home to the oldest known excerpt from the *Arabian Nights*, on display in the Oriental Institute Museum's collection of Islamic materials. Written in Arabic in Iraq sometime before 879 AD, the fragment contains the title page and a portion of one tale. Curiously, the piece made its way to Egypt sometime during antiquity and survived only because it was re-used as a piece of scrap paper. If you're ever in Chicago, stop on over to the Oriental Institute Museum to check it out, along with the other extraordinary finds from the Islamic world.

Our *Tale of the Water Carrier and Three Magicians* was inspired by the stories that were added to the Egyptian version of *One Thousand and One Nights* during the 13th century. It was the first thing that we wrote for this book, and it mimics the style of the ancient stories (although it is a complete fabrication). It was too long to print in the book, but we'll send it out in our newsletter soon, along with some additional historical background. You can sign up at veronicadouglas.com

Since much of our work and travels have taken place in Egypt, we decided to bring our characters to Cairo to solve the riddle and track down the genie. The magical city of Helwan is based on a historical capital that was founded in 689-90 AD just south of modern Cairo. One of Egypt's early Islamic rulers, Caliph 'Abd al-'Aziz, founded Helwan after the plague struck Cairo, which was at the time known as Fustat. Though modern Helwan is at present a giant suburb of Cairo, the medieval traces of 'Abd al-'Aziz's capital have been covered by the modern city and desert sands.

And finally, a few words about our world. *Dark Storm* is set in the Dragon's Gift universe created by Linsey Hall. We're huge fans of her writing and are super excited that we were able to weave Magic Side into her world. We started writing this series while Linsey was working on Shadow Guild: The Rebel, so Neve and Damian first appear in the adventures of Grey and Carrow. They'll be popping up again in Linsey's new series, Shadow Guild: Wolf Queen, and you can definitely expect more exciting crossovers in the future!

That's all for now but stay tuned for *Cursed Angel*, book three of Neve's series coming out in April. Thank you for reading and sign up for our newsletter for sneak peaks, extra scenes, and super exclusive content!

ABOUT VERONICA DOUGLAS

Veronica Douglas is a duo of professional archaeologists that love writing and digging together. Veronica specializes in the archaeology of the early Islamic world, while Douglas studies ancient ships and Egypt. After spending an inordinate amount of time doing painstaking research for academia, they suddenly discovered a passion for letting their imaginations go wild! A cocktail of magic, romance, and ancient mystery (shaken, not stirred), their books are inspired, in part, by their life in Chicago and their archaeological adventures from around the globe.

ABOUT LINSEY HALL

Before becoming a writer, Linsey Hall was a nautical archaeologist who studied shipwrecks from Hawaii and the Yukon to the UK and the Mediterranean. She credits fantasy and historical romances with her love of history and her career as an archaeologist. After a decade of tromping around the globe in search of old bits of stuff that people left lying about, she settled down and started penning her own romance novels. Her series draw upon her love of history and the paranormal elements that she can't help but include.

COPYRIGHT

www.veronicadouglas.com

www.linseyhall.com

Printed in Great Britain
by Amazon